Worse Than Death

Worse Than Death

Barbara J. Ferrenz

Five Star • Waterville, Maine

First Edition
First Printing: May 2003

Published in 2003 in conjunction with Tekno Books and Ed Gorman.   MYS

Set in 11 pt. Plantin.   1463648

Printed in the United States on permanent paper.

Library of Congress Cataloging-in-Publication Data

Ferrenz, Barbara J.
   Worse than death / Barbara J. Ferrenz. 1st ed.
   Published: Waterville, Me. : Five Star, 2003.
      p. cm.
   ISBN 0-7862-5395-9 (hc : alk. paper)
   1. Horror tales—Authorship—Fiction. 2. Women novelists—Fiction. 3. New York (N.Y.)—Fiction. 4. Vampires—Fiction. 5. Mystery fiction. I. Title.
PS3606.E75W67 2003
813'.54—21   2003044881

For my mother, Sara

Chapter 1

Mary Kate lifted a spoonful of Cheerios to her mouth, dribbling milk onto the keyboard. She quickly pulled up her shirttail and wiped it off.

"We're leaving now!" Chuck called up the stairs.

"Yeah, yeah, I'll be right there." She began to read over the last paragraph on the computer screen.

> *The darkness enshrouded them. Ursula could barely see the sheen of blood on his lip, yet she knew it was there. The union was complete. All ties to her life and family and everything she had ever known had been severed. She and Dimitri were one, neither living nor dead. They were eternal.*

"That's what you said fifteen minutes ago!"

Has it been that long? She slipped her feet into the scuffs under her desk and ran downstairs.

"Have fun at Grandma's. If you're not awake when I get home Sunday night, then I'll see you bright and early Monday." She kissed each of her boys on the cheek. "Bye-bye, sweeties."

Thirteen-year-old David rolled his eyes dramatically. "I had things I wanted to do this weekend, Mom."

"Next weekend, Buckaroo. Anything you want. You, too, Ben. Promise." Ben looked thoughtful, giving her his evil spawn grin, exposing the gap where he'd lost his front baby teeth. "Almost anything," Mary Kate added, laughing.

"We've got to go." Chuck looked past her as if meeting her

eyes was more than his temper could bear. "We're going to be stuck in traffic as it is."

Mary Kate spoke to the boys, but hoped Chuck was taking it in. "Listen, guys, this should be the last convention for a couple of months, anyway. And the promotional stuff should be tapering off soon, too. I'll try to keep the book signings near home if I can. After that . . ."

"You'll be working on another book, and we'll still never see you," David finished.

"It's my work, honey."

Chuck ushered the boys to the door. "Let's go, guys. Grandma will worry if we're late."

Mary Kate watched her family pile into the Volvo, then back out onto Linden Lane. She wished it wasn't like this every time. Lots of mothers work. *Why should I feel guilty? Because I enjoy it so much?*

A paw stepped softly on her scuff, and she looked down to see Lestat curling around her leg, purring.

"Oh, darn, Lestat. I forgot all about you. I don't suppose you have someone to spend the weekend with. No? Okay, I'll take care of it." Picking up the tablet of phone numbers on the counter, she went down the list of neighbors who had pitched in for her before. Most weren't answering, and the others were too busy to run in and open a tin for one little cat. There was only one option left, not including taking the wretched beast with her on the flight to Atlanta.

"Hi. Mrs. Olsen?"

"Yes?"

"This is Mary Kate Flaherty across the street. Uh, I hate to impose again, but I'm in a tight spot here, and if you could help, I'd really appreciate it. You see, I have to go out of town for the weekend, and could you come in and feed my cat?"

Silence.

"I wouldn't bother you, except that I have to leave in about two hours, and I, uh, sort of forgot about Lestat in the shuffle."

"Your work, I suppose." The distaste in her tone insinuated that the work involved standing on a street corner flagging down men named John.

"I'll be back Sunday evening. The key's under the flower pot by the back door."

Another silence. Mary Kate was about to ask if she was still there, when Mrs. Olsen said, "I'll send my husband over." Click.

Mary Kate hung up the receiver. "Tell him to watch out for the casket in the basement."

Room 416 of the Corinthian Hotel was as attractive and comfortable as one could expect. Bright and clean, the artwork on the walls really quite good, it was still too quiet and impersonal. Mary Kate flopped down on the bed and punched the remote to the television. The phone rang.

"Hello," she said.

"Theodora! We saw you come in!"

"Hi, Michael. Who's here?"

"Everybody, babe. And we're all dying to see you."

"Great! Give me a few minutes, okay? I've got a panel at midnight."

"We'll see you in the bar."

It was time to become Theodora. Theodora Zed, Queen of the Vampires.

Mary Kate toed off her loafers and dropped her blue jeans on the floor. She pulled the bulky knit sweater over her head, tossing it onto the bed. The sensible, cotton underwear had to go, too. She had to be Theodora right down to her skin.

First, she put on the black lace, bikini panties and

9

matching push-up bra, then the garter belt and black stockings. She glanced in the mirror, turning from side to side, and could see where the five pounds she put on from eating too much McDonald's with the boys went. Digging through the open suitcase, she decided on the new, little leather number for the first night. Most of the conferees stayed relatively sober on Friday and were most likely to notice and remember how she was dressed.

She wiggled into the dress, feeling the compaction of the extra poundage as she zipped it up. "Not bad for thirty-six and two kids." She could begin to see the transformation taking effect as she looked at herself sheathed in black leather. The neckline was low, the hemline high. Silver buckles closed the gaps in the long, tight sleeves. She stepped into treacherously tall spiked heels.

Grabbing her cosmetics case, she sat at the well-lit vanity. Her face had few exotic lines, but it was amazing what make-up could do. She gave herself pale skin with a slightly feverish blush. Her eyes were deepened with liners and dark shadows. She lengthened her eyelashes and arched her eyebrows. Her lips became blood red with a full, sultry pout. A warm, electrified current ran up her spine to the base of her skull. She felt the release of the part of her personality ordinarily bound by sensible cotton undies. She let the excitement wash over her as she completed her metamorphosis.

Her hair was plain brown, shoulder length and straight. She teased it up high, spritzed on some red highlights from a can, then pinned it up loosely from her neck. Clipping silver death's heads onto her earlobes, Mary Kate looked into the mirror and smiled. "Hi, Theodora."

The music in the bar suppressed the conversations at the tables to a low buzz, punctuated by an occasional burst of shrill, female laughter. The sign at the door proclaimed, "Welcome, BloodCon," in dripping, red letters. The lights were low, and Mary Kate found herself looking over a sea of gray heads.

"Theo! Over here!" An arm waved over the throng. She squeezed between the tables in that direction.

A chair had been crammed between the others around the table to make room for her. Michael Kazdin put his arm around her waist.

"It's good to see you again, Michael."

"Likewise, babe. Cute dress." He removed his arm and gestured for the waitress. "I missed you at NecroCon. We had a wild time."

"I'm sure you did," she said, knowing this meant that Michael had gotten stinking drunk and had taken a nubile, young fan or wannabe writer back to his room. He was still handsome at fifty-two, but Mary Kate noticed that the gray streaks in his hair had disappeared since the last time she had seen him. She looked around. "Is Phyllis with you?"

"No, not this trip," he said without looking at her. "Red wine?"

"Of course."

Michael ordered while Mary Kate greeted the others at the table. Some were old friends, like Conner Drake. He tipped his mug of beer to her and winked. She winked back and smiled, always glad to see him. He had stepped in and shown her the ropes of surviving conventions four years earlier, when her second novel made a surprise jump in sales. In order to keep the ball rolling, she had to learn how to promote and sell. Conner helped her keep it all in perspective.

Beside him, fellow vampire writer Alissa Dibiase was dressed almost as outrageously as Mary Kate in a red sequined sheath. "Theo, darling," she said, "you're getting to

11

be a cow. You should leave the sexy vampiress bit to me."
She smiled, but Mary Kate was never sure when she was
kidding.

"Better a cow than a bloodsucking leech," Michael said.
Alissa scrunched her pretty little nose and blew him a kiss.
Michael suddenly realized what he had said. "Not that you're
a cow, Theodora! You're gorgeous! That outfit was made for
you."

Mary Kate held up her hand. "I got the point, Michael. I
don't listen to Alissa anyway." Conner chuckled softly beside
her.

Mary Kate didn't recognize the young man in the heavy,
green turtleneck. Michael introduced him. "This is Randall
Valentine. You're going to be hearing about this young
fellow. I met him after a reading in Denver. He gave me his
manuscript, and damn, it knocked my socks off. I don't know
why, but I sent him straight to my agent. This boy might just
give me some serious competition."

Nobody believed he meant it. Michael had been one of the
few horror writers to remain popular in the mainstream for
over twenty years.

Mary Kate accepted the drink from the waitress and took a
sip. "Welcome to the club, Randall."

"So, you're the Queen of the Vampires. I've heard about
you." His voice reminded her of her son, David, at his
whiniest.

"Dreadful things, I hope." She smiled.

"I read your, uh, novel, *Death's Delight*, or most of it. I'm
curious; are you purposefully going for the soap opera, Harle-
quin romance, housewife demographic?"

Mary Kate clamped her teeth together. The others at the
table sucked in their breath. Young Randall didn't know her
well enough nor have the status to join in the bitchy sniping.

She knew if she called him what she was thinking it would show up in a fan magazine somewhere, so she said civilly, "An interesting thought, Randall." He smiled smugly.

Conner leaned towards her and whispered, "Nice recover, Mary Kate."

"Better than pulling that turtleneck up over his head." She looked at her watch. "I've got a panel at twelve. You coming?"

"Wouldn't miss it," he said. As she sipped from the long-stemmed glass of wine, she enjoyed his warm smile.

Chapter 2

"Life after death is a basic tenet of most of the world's religions and accepted by most cultures. It makes sense to me that an exploration of the concept of vampirism is a reasonable outgrowth." Mary Kate heard her voice over the microphone. It sounded thin and young. She felt conspicuous under the fluorescent lights of the conference room. She sat at the end of the long, folding table, next to the sign announcing the topic: What's Worse Than Death?

Three other writers of speculative fiction and one author of a nonfiction book about the afterlife shared the stage. All had copies of their own books standing on the tables in front of them.

There was a good audience for this time of night. Conner sat in the first row, drinking the beer he had brought with him from the bar. Although he seemed somber and just vaguely interested in the subject matter, Mary Kate felt as if he hadn't taken his eyes from her for a moment. Less reassuring was the presence of Randall Valentine, several seats down on the front row. He seemed to be very interested.

"Theodora, you can't turn every discussion into one about vampires just because you write about them." George Moss, renowned for his intelligent, yet gruesome, splatterpunk trilogy, *Ain't Just 'Possums Flattened on the Highway*, rested his head on his fist as he looked around the others to see her. "I mean, half the fun of death is getting there." He laughed and appeared to enjoy the laughter from the audience. Mary

Kate wondered how long he'd been saving up that last line for a good opening. This wasn't it.

"George, dear . . ." She smiled. ". . . vampires are one of the oldest archetypes symbolizing mankind's fears . . . and desires. I'm just saying that there's a parallel between religion's offer of eternal life and the vampire's offer of eternal death."

Ann Orenstein, author of *Nightsongs* and panel moderator, moved forward to speak into her microphone, bumping it with her nose. When the electronic noise and ensuing squeal died down, she said, "Excuse me. Folks, I think we're getting a little off-topic. As horror writers, we kill off many of our characters in many creative ways. The question we're asking here is: Is death what our characters should fear and try to avoid most?"

George made a show of keeping his nose away from his microphone. "That's what I was saying to Theodora, Ann. Death is the end of the road. What our characters fear is dying. Dying is painful and ugly. It's the awareness that you will become nothing, the loss of all humanity and dignity. Death reduces you to an animal, no different from those that make our tires go thump-thump when we drive over their corpses in the road." He twisted his ponytail around his finger, obviously savoring his own turn of phrase.

"Well put," Ann said. "Do you have anything to add, uh . . ." She checked her notes. ". . . Patrick?"

Mary Kate was curious about the opinion of the ex-priest, sociologist, Patrick Henley. She knew most of the novelists at one level or another, but the tall, gaunt man in the ill-fitting suit was an academic, an outsider. He had spent his life seriously studying what they made up for the purpose of entertainment.

He didn't seem to hear at first, then he drew in his thin

shoulders further and spoke into the mike, his eyes cast down at the table. Even with amplification, his voice wasn't much above a mumble. "As with any kind of research, one must start with a premise, preferably one validated with quantitative data, but in the absence of that, as in the case of cultural belief systems regarding the afterlife, one adopts a presumption based on the frequency of occurrence and the generality of acceptance."

The audience's attention was breaking apart. Seat wiggling and looking around caused waves of motion that made Mary Kate a little seasick. She didn't think Professor Henley even noticed, as he never looked out at the recipients of his impressive and largely incomprehensible words. These people had come here for a show. They wanted to hear the writers of the books they had spent good money on say shocking things that nice folk aren't allowed to say. The professor's lecture droned on.

"So having accepted the premise that one is an animal, the subsequent collection of data, quantitative or not, will always result in the final judgment that one is indeed an animal, before and after death. There are those . . ." His eyes cut quickly over to George. ". . . who belittle their own existence in the universe and choose to identify with the lower beasts. I prefer to work from the premise that humankind is an earthbound, spiritual creature before death, and afterward, freed of mortal constraints, comes to his or her true fruition, as a force for good or evil."

Mary Kate's mouth dropped open, and she leaned way forward to get a good look at George's face. It was worth it. He hadn't missed it, even though the pointed insult had been couched in a bed of two-dollar words. George's round face was red, thick veins bulging in his neck. Even his ponytail was bristling. The mumbling academic had as good as called

George a dog, and worse yet, he had done it in front of the fans.

Mary Kate did the unthinkable. She laughed.

Both panel and onlookers stared at her in silence. Only Conner smiled, though he tried to hide it behind his fist. Mary Kate blushed behind her make-up.

She was grateful when Ann Orenstein cleared her throat and drew the attention away as George sputtered over a response.

"We have about ten minutes left. Let's open the floor to questions."

Randall Valentine shot up out of his seat. "I have a question for Theodora Zed, Queen of the Vampires." His Adam's apple peeked in and out of his green turtleneck. "Horror has traditionally expressed the dark side of our existence. How do you justify writing novels in which death is romanticized?"

Mary Kate still hadn't recovered from her previous gaff, and the wine she had earlier was starting to make her sleepy. She stifled a yawn, then affixed a smile. *It's show time.* "You don't have to use the whole title, Randall. 'Your Highness' will do. Just kidding. Call me Theo."

"Okay . . . Theo," he said condescendingly.

She worked to keep her smile going. "I don't feel I romanticize death. I see it more as accepting the dark side of life, the loneliness and despair, and looking to the other side for fulfillment. The vampire lover can focus completely. He doesn't have to get up at six to go to work in the morning. He doesn't have to worry about job stability, property taxes, or mowing the lawn. You just have to get used to the idea that he's dead."

Some of the audience members tittered. Mary Kate had used this same speech in a fanzine interview a couple of months ago, and was glad she remembered it.

Looking out, she could see some familiar faces. Some were writers, most flirting on the edges of discovery, but the majority were the people who kept them in printer cartridges —the book reading and buying public. And what made this audience special was that their taste in reading ran to the macabre.

Given their predilection for gore and supernatural atrocities, they appeared unusually normal. The horror conventions attracted a young crowd, but a few longtime, diehard fans still came, even though they'd look more at home at an Amway convention. What really distinguished these attendees from those of a mystery or romance book convention were the small pockets of true aficionados who dressed for the occasion.

Mary Kate recognized most of them. Their whited faces and dyed black hair showed up at most of the cons and readings. She was popular with them because of her own bizarre appearance. She flashed a smile of greeting at the motley group in the back of the room. As she did, a figure in a long, black hooded cape came from behind them and pushed through the door to the corridor. Mary Kate didn't blame him. It had been a long evening, and she was ready to go herself.

"So, Theo," said the still standing Randall Valentine, who was quickly getting on her nerves. "I guess I didn't emphasize the word 'romanticize' enough. Isn't it true the main thrust, so to speak, of your books is getting your heroines laid, and that these are romance novels with neck-biting thrown in as a novelty?"

She looked to Conner for support. He was sitting on the edge of his folding chair, wearing an angry expression she hadn't seen on him before. His hand tightened around his empty beer mug. Turning back to the kid, she decided she had had enough of his foolishness. "What's your problem, Randall? Fifty thousand copies of my last novel sold out worldwide. Somebody likes them."

"That's my problem, Thee-o." He drew the name out maliciously. "While you're raking in the bucks writing pure crap, serious writers are ignored because we aren't appealing to the prurient interests of the lowest common denominator."

A chorus of boos erupted from the back of the room. A voice shouted out, "Hex him, Theodora!" She thought of a few choice things she could say, but before she could, Ann Orenstein bumped her nose on the microphone again.

"I think that's enough for tonight. Thank you, ladies and gentlemen, for coming. Let's have a hand for our panelists."

As a weak applause went around, Randall gave Mary Kate a triumphant glare and left the room with his head high, ignoring the heckling from the costumed fans near the door. Mary Kate dropped her head into her hands, exhausted. She felt someone rubbing her leather-clad back and looked up to see Conner. She smiled wearily.

"Come on, Vampire Queen," he said, "let me buy you a drink."

"You sure you want to be seen with me? I'm not a serious writer, you know."

His jaw hardened, the way she had seen it when young Mr. Valentine was trashing her. "The little, nobody punk. He had no right to talk to you that way. Somebody ought to tie a knot in that scrawny neck of his; that'd shut him up."

She had never seen him angry before. Mildly irritated, yes. Frustrated, yes. But never out and out angry. It was a little frightening. She had always seen him as a big, huggy bear, the Gentle Ben type. The hard focus of his eyes suggested a grizzly. A grizzly with a major mad on.

"Forget it, Conner. I have. We've weathered these young, unpublished geniuses before. It's like my son, David. He's thirteen now, and he knows everything, and I know nothing. As far as he's concerned, I've been living the last thirty-six years in a box, just waiting for him to come of age and enlighten me."

The jaw softened, and she felt relieved. Conner took her hand, and they stepped down from the stage. The room had emptied quickly, as the bar closed at two a.m. At the doorway, he stopped and put his hands on her shoulders.

"You're a special lady, Mary Kate. Don't ever underestimate yourself. Anyone who doesn't appreciate you for who you are is just . . . just stupid."

Standing and looking up into his face suddenly took on a flavor it never had before. She let his hands hold her up as she leaned forward, wondering about the harm of one little taste. Were his lips rich and spicy, or warm and comforting? They were certainly inviting, but she knew it was dangerous. As his head bent toward hers, she looked down at the pointy toes of her spiked shoes. One tiny morsel could lead to complete abandon.

He cleared his throat and stepped away. "Let's go get that drink."

The room was too warm. She spoke without looking at him. She was afraid to look at him. "No, Conner, I'm really tired. I think I'll turn in early. You go on ahead. I'm sure the gossip will be rich tonight, and I'll want a full report tomorrow."

He nodded, but looked preoccupied. After a moment, he said, "Well, good night, Mary Kate."

"Good night," she called after him. His hand lifted in a half-hearted wave as he ambled down the dim hallway. She considered running after him, and, for a brief moment, saw herself saying, "I changed my mind," as she took his arm.

They had, after all, had many drinks together over the last four years, as well as many late into the night conversations alone in hotel rooms. But he had never looked at her that way before, at least, not that she had noticed. And still more alarming, she knew she had never looked at him that way, either.

"It's been a long day," she said, taking off the four-inch heels, immediately feeling small and dumpy. Her hamstrings twanged from being stretched all evening. She hooked her fingers into the shoes and padded up the carpeted hall, trying to remember where her room was.

She pulled from her pocket the piece of paper on which she had written her room number, not trusting her memory. 416. She'd need an elevator. Earlier, there had been a crowd of people around her when she had gone from the bar to the conference room. If she'd passed an elevator, she never would have known it. Another hall intersected, all directions promising what seemed to be miles of floral carpet, awash with dim nightlights. The one to the left felt like a likely candidate, so she headed off that way. The room numbers were no help. The first floor only had conference rooms in this wing.

Past a number of doors marked "Utilities" or "Employees Only," the hall ended at an exit. Having had numerous experiences getting lost in large hotels, Mary Kate decided to go with what had worked for her before. She went out. She would go around to the front of the building and enter the lobby, where a friendly desk clerk could give her specific directions to her room. Her total lack of a sense of direction had always been embarrassing, but she had found techniques for coping with it.

Outside was unlighted, and Mary Kate watched with some

dismay as the last of the illumination shrunk with the closing of the door. Underneath her stockinged feet was a large concrete pad with huge metal boxes on either side of the doorway. Pipes and hoses snaked out of the boxes like techno-Medusas.

She guessed they were air-conditioning units. One kicked on with a loud, industrial hum, startling her. She squeaked, throwing up her arms as she ran up the sidewalk. Stopping to catch her breath, she laughed. *I should have gone with Conner,* she thought. *He always walks me to my room.* That thought would have been completely innocent yesterday, or even early this evening.

She walked along in the dark, not wanting to think about it, but unable to get out of her mind that spark of electricity set off by the meeting of their eyes. It was only when a pebble cut into the sole of her foot she realized she was carrying only one shoe. "The Medusa box," she said, knowing she must have dropped it when the air conditioner frightened her, but also knowing she wasn't going all the way back there. She backtracked a short way anyway, but didn't want to go too far. The parking lot was within sight, which meant the bright lobby doors weren't far beyond.

"I guess I'll have to be the barefoot Vampire Queen the rest of this weekend."

Finding a black shoe in the dark was a task she wasn't up to. Starting back, she saw a figure move near the parked cars in the lot. A distant street lamp threw out enough light for her to recognize the hooded cape from the panel audience. It moved toward her.

"Hi!" she called out. "I remember you from the panel."

The black figure stopped and seemed to be weaving on the lawn between the trees.

"Are you okay?" Mary Kate called. It didn't answer, but

stepped back, then forward, as if undecided which way to proceed. The silence tripped a switch in her head, bringing on the full realization of her situation. She was standing outside a dark building, nobody knew where she was, and a few yards away was a silent, disguised person behaving erratically, making no attempt to identify himself. This was not good. In fact, it was downright spooky.

"Well, I've got to go now." Her voice was high and quavering. She took a couple of steps backward, banging her heel on the edge of the sidewalk. The cape advanced toward her, the bottom of it brushing the grass, giving the impression that it was floating.

Mary Kate turned and ran, limping and hopping, the runs in her nylons bursting up her legs, not sure if she was imagining soft footfalls behind her. As she fell into the daylight brightness surrounding the glass double doors, she looked back. Every tree and shrub could have been concealing him. He could be right around the corner. She pushed through the door and hurried to the desk.

"What's the quickest way to Room 416?"

Chapter 3

"Yeah, uh-huh, okay. And Daddy said you couldn't have it, and Grandma said you could. I see." Mary Kate ducked her head to yawn so Ben couldn't hear as he related the most recent injustice based on sibling age discrimination. This complex case had something to do with the last slice of pizza in the box. She wasn't altogether sure because she still wasn't all the way awake, and Ben's missing teeth gave his speech a juicy texture that watered down most of his consonants. "Lift the receiver so I can hear you, sweetie. Now, was Daddy right? Did you still have an unfinished piece on your plate?" More evidence was coming into the light.

Someone knocked on the door, surprising because nine a.m. was very early at a con. "Hold on a minute, honey. Someone's here." She put the receiver down, and looked at the door. All she was wearing was a long tee shirt and white cotton panties. She grabbed her jeans off the floor, calling, "Just a minute!" as she wriggled into them.

Zipping and buttoning, she leaned toward the peephole and saw a man's face. He stepped back a little, and she could see he was wearing an Atlanta city police uniform. Running her fingers through her uncombed hair, she opened the door.

The young man looked at her tousled hair and sleep-squished face, then down at her braless chest. Mary Kate crossed her arms in front of her.

"Are you Mary Kate Flaherty, AKA Theodora Zed?" he asked.

"Well, yes, but Theodora Zed is my pen name, not an alias." She smiled pleasantly, but he didn't, so she stopped. "What can I do for you?"

He jerked his head to the side, and another officer came in, her black spiked heel hanging from his finger. The first one spoke again. "Is this your shoe?"

"Oh, good, you found . . ." Their expressions made it clear that finding her missing shoe wasn't the main point of their visit. "What's this about?"

"Then you admit that this is your shoe."

She looked at the metal name bar on his shirt. "Of course, Officer Hendrickson. I lost it outside last night. Has something happened?"

"What time were you outside last night?"

"It was after one. You're going to have to tell me what this is about."

The officers looked at one another. The one with the shoe nodded, then dropped the shoe into a zippered, plastic bag. Officer Hendrickson turned back to her. "One of the guests at the convention was, uh, injured last night. Your shoe was found near the, uh, near him. We've been questioning some people this morning, and a few of them said you knew him."

Mary Kate clutched her shirt near her heart. Most of her friends were here. "Who?"

"Randall Valentine."

The name meant nothing to her . . . at first. Then she remembered the rude, young upstart. "I'm so sorry. What happened to him?"

"That's what we're trying to find out, Miss Zed. Did you know him?"

"Flaherty, Mrs. No, not really. I just met him last night."

The officer wrote this down on a pad. "And you were outside the hotel after one o'clock this morning?" She nodded.

"And, was anyone with you?"

"No, I was on my way back to my room after a panel session." He looked puzzled, so she explained. "A presentation, you know, a group discussion."

"Why did you have to go outside to get back to your room? I understand that the conference rooms are in the hotel."

She rubbed her forehead and smiled weakly. "It's really kind of stupid. I hate to admit it, but I got lost. You know, with all the hallways and all. I mean, it's happened to me before, and I've found that the quickest way to get where I'm going is to leave the building and walk around to the front." She looked at their faces. They weren't about to say, Oh, yeah, I know exactly what you mean. "Then it was dark, and the air conditioning unit cut on, and it frightened me, and I must have dropped my shoe."

A tinny barking emitted from the phone on the nightstand. Mary Kate turned from it to the policemen. "I forgot, I was talking to my son when you came in. If you could excuse me a moment . . ." Hendrickson nodded.

"Ben?"

It wasn't Ben. "What the hell is going on there, Mary Kate? You leave the boy standing here holding the phone? What the hell are you thinking? This call's going to cost a fortune."

"Chuck," she said as calmly as she could, "the police are here. Someone's been hurt, and they're asking questions."

After telling Chuck that she'd call him back after she knew herself what the hell was going on, Mary Kate was relieved that the policemen only wanted to know, at this point, how long she was going to be in the city. She told them she'd be in Atlanta until Sunday. She called Chuck back and explained what little she knew.

He yelled for a few minutes about the damn weirdo writers, but what could he say when she might be needed for further questioning? "It's always something, isn't it, Mary Kate? Whatever's going on around there, get yourself out of it. Then get yourself home." He hung up.

Mary Kate raspberried the phone. She found the implications of being involved in a crime frightening, yet a bit exciting. She wished she knew more about what had happened. Had Randall Valentine been mugged? Had he had an accident? She didn't even know if he was in the hospital or back at the hotel. She decided to find out and make a good will visit. Maybe then he'd stop busting her chops.

She showered and dressed for a busy day. Tight jeans, a silk halter top, dangling earrings, and a fake tattoo of a bat on her shoulder were her daylight Theodora-wear. Her first appointment was a book signing at a local Waldenbooks in about an hour. She had time to locate coffee and some good gossip on last night's events.

As the hostess walked her to a table in the coffee shop, Mary Kate craned her neck to see who had already been seated. Locating Conner in the corner, she asked to have her coffee brought there. Walking over, she decided not to mention last night. If she pretended hard enough that the almost-kiss didn't happen, then it didn't happen.

"You'll never believe what happened this morning," she said as she sat.

"You woke up before ten?"

"Very funny. The police were in my room asking me a bunch of questions. It seems I'd lost my shoe near where that kid, Randall, was hurt."

"Your shoe? What was your shoe doing outside?"

"Then you've heard about this already?"

His forehead creased, and he put down his cup. "What

were you doing outside last night, Mary Kate? I thought you were going back to your room."

A waitress brought her coffee. Mary Kate waited until she left. "I did. I just went on a detour first. Tell me what happened last night. The cops wouldn't tell me anything."

Conner kept his eyes trained on his coffee cup. "I was getting some air, outside, when one of the maintenance people found . . . found the body."

The body. When you lose your name and become the body, it is a definite sign that you are dead. The next step in reasoning led her to the fact that Randall Valentine was now the body, so therefore Randall Valentine was dead.

Conner continued. "I was standing by the door when I saw this guy running toward me. He grabbed me and could barely talk. I tried to calm him down, but all he could say was that there was blood all over."

Following her line of thought, Mary Kate put her shoe and Randall Valentine together, which meant that the police had found her shoe near a dead body. Conner's voice had become background noise. The interrogation this morning took on a more serious meaning.

"I followed him back, and then I saw something on the sidewalk, like something had been spilled. I looked closer, and that's when I saw the body. I went back with the janitor to the lobby, and had the desk clerk call the police."

Mary Kate grabbed Conner's arm. "Randall Valentine is dead?"

He put his hand over hers. "Murdered. He'd been stabbed. What were you doing out there, Mary Kate?"

Her own coffee sat cooling on the table. She didn't think she could keep it down if she drank it. Her fingers dug deeper into his forearm as she remembered the cloaked figure by the parking lot. "There was somebody else out there," she said quietly.

"Who? Did you tell the police?"

"No, I didn't think of it. They didn't tell me what it was all about. And it might have nothing to do with it. I mean, I thought it was a drunk con vamp."

"Could you tell who it was?"

"No, he was wearing a long cape with a hood over his face. I'd seen him earlier at the panel, but he didn't say anything when I said hi. He was acting strange, so I got out of there. I'd hate having the police hassle the costumed fans. They already get blamed for everything that goes wrong at the conventions."

Conner pulled his arm away. "Damn it, Mary Kate. You could've been killed. Why don't you take the next flight home?"

This was the second time this morning she had been told to go home. It was two times too many. "You sound just like Chuck."

He looked as if he were about to say something more, then dug in his pocket for his wallet and tossed some bills on the check. "I've got to be somewhere in a few minutes," he muttered.

"I'll see you later, okay?"

He left without answering.

The line in the bookstore was down to three autograph seekers. Waldenbooks had sold out of Theodora Zed's novel, *A Lover's Blood*. She would be able to thank them and get out in time to meet Alissa for lunch, she thought as her stomach did a slow rumble. Her backside hurt from sitting too long in one place. The row after row of books seemed to absorb the air from the store, leaving her light-headed. Mary Kate lifted her weary smile into place one more time. She wrote "To" and asked, "And your name is . . . ?"

She looked up, then her smile faltered and broke down.

The face of the young man in front of her was painted bright red. His eyes were encircled in white with dark eyebrows arched devilishly. He threw the black hood back from his head, showing curly, brown hair to his shoulders. The cape flowed down to his boots. "Todd," he said in a youthful voice. "But could you write it out to Doctor Death? That's what my friends call me."

He's just a boy, she thought, *sixteen or seventeen.* Recovering, she said, "Sure, Doc." She signed the book and handed it to him. "Have you been at BloodCon?"

The white teeth of his smile were bizarre in his tomato red face. "Yeah! You remember me?"

"I think so. Were you out by the parking lot last night? Around one or one-thirty?"

Doctor Death looked disappointed. "No, not me. I got talked into a game of Vampire Killers with some people I didn't know in one of the rooms. We played all night, but none of them were experienced players. Bummer."

"Yeah, bummer." She watched him leave, his cape swirling around his legs. He was just a gamer, a kid who liked to play role-playing games, throwing dice and matching skills with like-minded people. Their cerebral games were harmless. But he had given her a fright. And reminded her that there was a murderer somewhere at-large at the con.

There hadn't been time to go back to the hotel and change clothes. Mary Kate stood inside the grand mahogany doors of La Palais Restaurant, looking for Alissa. She groaned as the black-suited *maitre'd* approached.

"May I help you, madam?"

She tried flattening her hair with her hand to no avail. "I'm meeting a friend for lunch."

"His name?"

"Her. Her name is Alissa Dibiase. My name is Theo . . . Mary Kate Flaherty." As the *maitre'd* turned brusquely to enter the dining room, Mary Kate decided it would be bad form to call him back to tell him she really wasn't a prostitute.

Alissa smiled wickedly as she sat at the table in her strikingly sophisticated, off-white suit. Her long black hair was pulled back demurely in a gold clasp. Her make-up was downright matronly. Mary Kate pulled out a chair across from her and sat down. "I would've looked that good if I'd had time to change."

"No doubt about it," Alissa said, still smiling.

They ordered lobster salad on croissants and a half carafe of Chardonnay. After discussing Mary Kate's successful book signing that morning, the conversation turned to the murder of Randall Valentine.

"How well did you know him?" Alissa asked.

"Not at all. You were there when I met him."

Alissa patted her lips with the linen napkin and put it back in her lap. Mary Kate had never seen this refined side of her. She had always been her main competition in the vampire lines, the author of *Veins of Fire* and *A Taste of Blood*. At the cons, there had been a friendly contest to see who could be most extravagant. Outside of the Theodora get-up, Mary Kate knew she was just a suburban housewife with pile of dirty laundry waiting for her at home.

"Everybody is saying that you and Valentine had a feud going," Alissa said, "and that it got nasty at the panel last night."

"That's not true! I mean, yes, he was very rude, and I was getting a little ticked off, but there's no feud. I don't know why he came after me. I guess he was jealous because my books are successful. I don't know. A feud? No. I'll never get used to the way writers spread rumors. It must be part of the creative urge."

Alissa nodded. "It's true. We're very bad about that. Does this mean I can't ask you about the other rumor? That your shoe was found near the body?"

Mary Kate sighed. "That really happened. But only because my shoe was outside and so was he." Before Alissa could ask the next question, Mary Kate answered it. "No, I won't explain why my shoe was outside. I'll just tell you that it was innocent. No use feeding the rumor mill more than I have."

"Fair enough," Alissa said. "Knowing you as I do, it probably was innocent." She twirled her wine glass between two fingers, watching the pale gold liquid swirl. "Have you seen Conner today?"

The way Alissa had asked sounded too intentionally offhand. "Yes, this morning. He was still upset about finding, you know, the body."

"He was upset before he found it." Alissa looked up quickly, as if gauging Mary Kate's reaction, then back down at the tablecloth. "My guess would have been that he was upset because you weren't there."

Mary Kate was puzzled. She looked at Alissa until their eyes met. "I don't know why you would think that."

"You don't? I've been assuming . . . I could be wrong, so I'll ask. Is there . . . something . . . between you and Conner?"

The thought had never crossed Mary Kate's mind. Until last night. She stumbled around for a response. "No, of course not. Conner and I are friends, good friends. It's nothing like . . . I'm married, you know, for fifteen years now."

Alissa was smiling. "Theodora, dear Theodora, I didn't mean to accuse you of anything. I was mistaken. For the last few years, you two have been practically fused at the hip at these conventions. So, one might think . . . Anyway, I'm glad I asked. In fact, that's one of the reasons I wanted us to have lunch together. I'm interested in Conner. Very interested. I wanted to clear it with you before I did anything about it. So, what is it, Theo? Red light or green light?"

Mary Kate remembered what it felt like looking into his face the night before. Was it true? Would they have kissed if she hadn't torn her gaze away? Uncomfortable with her own unenthusiastic response, she said, "Sure, go for it. Green light. I have no problem." Alissa was intelligent, graceful, beautiful, and young. She could be a good partner for Conner. Mary Kate thought these things, but still couldn't help feeling as if she were giving away something precious.

Shopping for spiked heels was next on her agenda. Stores were nearby, and after three failed attempts, she was able to find two-and-a-half-inch spikes. The Queen of the Vampires would be shod, but shorter.

She entered the main lobby of the Corinthian just before two o'clock. Her afternoon still included an interview with Bloodsucker Magazine at two-thirty, a reading at four, and a panel at five.

Ordinarily, her energy at cons fed on itself, and she grew more vivacious with every activity. Saturday night was a circus sideshow she had always looked forward to. As she trudged toward the elevator to refresh herself in her room before taking off again, she wished she could take a nap. There was a pallor cast over all of BloodCon this year. It was the color of reality. And the reality was death.

"Ms. Flaherty!"

Mary Kate turned to see a young woman in a navy blazer at the main desk motioning for her. She walked over.

"Ms. Flaherty, there's a message for you."

"Thank you." She opened the sealed envelope and unfolded the single sheet of white paper. She read the typed message. There was no signature.

IS IT REAL YET?

Chapter 4

After ten p.m., BloodCon at the Corinthian Hotel of Atlanta cranked into high gear. The bar was packed beyond fire code regulations, and a second bar had been set up in the expansive lobby. Public events were scheduled for every available space. Private parties broke out in the suites and rooms. Raucous instrumentals from the rock band in the ballroom filtered into the hallways each time the doors were opened.

Groups of revelers in the lobby ranged from a middle-aged, blue-jeaned crowd loudly singing bawdy songs to a small cluster talking quietly in cocktail garb to a single, young vampiress wandering between them looking lost. A collection of young adults around college age were politely discouraged by the staff from building a human pyramid by the front door.

Down the hall and around the corner, The Freeman Publishing Company was sponsoring a party in honor of their best-selling author, Theodora Zed. The party had started at eight o'clock, the food and drinks ran out by nine. Only the fans remained. The muscles in Mary Kate's face spasmed. She didn't believe she could stop smiling if she tried. The young, overweight woman in the long dress beside her continued speaking earnestly in a mellifluous Georgia accent.

"And when that happened, I knew I had a story to write. My grandmother had come back from the grave to tell me. I jumped out of bed and wrote it all down, but then, the next morning, when I read what I had written, it was all gibberish."

Mary Kate kept on smiling. "My, how interesting," she said and wished her luck, considering herself lucky that the young lady hadn't asked her to read something she'd written. Several people had already come forward to ask her to read their stories, novels, and screenplays. One middle-aged lady actually had a wonderful idea concerning stone as a metaphor for sin, but all were told to write to her through her editor, Donna Brooks.

Her face stuck in a dopey grin, Mary Kate waved her arm to get Donna's attention across the room. She had to go the bathroom bad and wanted to know if this shindig could be called officially over. Donna seemed to be deeply engrossed in a conversation with a short, balding man by the empty buffet table. Mary Kate signed a few more books and handed out souvenir bookmarks touting her latest release. Noting that the room was clearing, she headed over to where her editor was tucking her purse under her arm as in preparation to leave. Mary Kate caught up with her. "Where are you going?"

"To the ladies'. I'm not abandoning you."

"Me, too. If I don't go soon, we're going to find out real quick what massive amounts of pee does to Spandex."

Breaking into a run as soon as she passed through the rest room door, Mary Kate entered a stall and began rolling down her black, strapless cat suit. "Who was that guy you were talking to?" she called over to Donna in the next stall.

"The bald guy? He's a Midwest buyer representing most of the bigger chains out there. They've already made a sizable purchase of your books, but I think I've convinced him that it wasn't nearly enough." She flushed. "He also told me a little about how some of the others are selling."

Mary Kate flushed, then wrestled to get back on the outfit that was about as comfortable as a wet suit. Meeting Donna at the sinks, she cringed as she saw her reflection in the mirror under the fluorescents. She had gone too heavy on the pale face powder, and the Carnival Red lipstick was smudged. She looked like Bette Davis in *Whatever Happened To Baby Jane?* "Give me a Kleenex. I look terrible."

Donna dug in her purse. "You're supposed to, darling. You're Queen of the Vampires." As she pulled out a roll of tissues, a fluttering of business cards fell to the floor.

Mary Kate helped her pick them up. Her eyes stopped on the name across the front of the card in her left hand. She looked at Donna. "It's Randall Valentine's."

Donna took the cards and put them away. "I spoke with him yesterday," she said. "He was a very intelligent, intense, young man. If he wrote half as well as I've heard, I think we could have had a major talent on our hands."

"Really? Oh, what a loss." After all, he was one, like herself, who spun elaborate webs, thread by thread, often neglecting personal needs to accomplish the task. But, unlike her, he might have had something important to say to the world. Conner had said Valentine had been stabbed. She imagined the terror and pain at the moment of the boy's death, how he might have looked into his killer's eyes. She quickly pushed the thought aside. It was too ugly. Too real.

Donna pressed a tissue into her hand. "Fix your face, Mary Kate. I asked Randall to send me his manuscript. He was very cynical about it. Two other editors at Freeman had already rejected it. He's been trying to sell his novel for five years now. He told me he was going to be signing on with Walter Truesdale."

"Michael Kazdin's agent?" Mary Kate knew that Truesdale rarely took on new clients, having an impressive stable of successful writers already in his able hands.

Talking through puckered lips while she touched up her

own lipstick, Donna said, "It surprised me, too. Truesdale is much better known for stealing established writers, than for giving a break to a new kid. Rumor is his main cash cow's gone dry."

"Michael?"

"You didn't hear it from me, but that buyer told me that Michael's last two books were major dust collectors. He's ordering a few for the bookstores who specifically ask for them, but other than that, Michael's off the 'A' list."

The elevator opened onto the noise from the private party in the penthouse suite. The doors were propped open at each end of the hall where the overflow of guests gathered. The cat suit was giving Mary Kate a wedgie, and she worried about the strapless top slipping. If it hadn't cost so much, she would have chucked it into the trash. She took a deep breath and walked as gracefully as she could into the crush of bodies at the door.

"Hi! How are you? So nice to see you again!" she said over and over as she searched for Conner. She wove in and out, keeping an eye out for the tallest head. A familiar voice growled in her ear. "You're such a bitch, Theodora."

She turned to see George Moss smiling as he sipped from an iced drink. "And you're shorter, too," he added. She was now nose-to-nose with him, where before she always had the pleasure of looking down on him from her four-inch spikes.

"I haven't been feeding enough lately," she said. "And why am I a bitch?"

His broad, round face reminded her of the Cheshire cat. He twirled his ponytail around a finger of his free hand. "Nobody else laughed last night. You know that, don't you? That defrocked priest wasn't talking about me, per se. I asked him. He bored me to death for a half hour with a lecture from

Sociology 101. And it's all your fault."

She grabbed the ponytail from around his finger and gave it a tug. "I love you, George. There, does that make everything all right?"

"I'd rather have your body."

"It would look terrible on you, dear. What have you been up to all weekend?"

"The big excitement, of course, Theo, has been the murder. We're all suspects. Nobody knows more about sticking knives in people's backs than writers. Have you heard the latest joke?"

"No-o," she said tentatively.

"What's the difference between Randall Valentine and Swiss cheese?"

"George, I don't want to hear this."

His grin spread from ear to ear. "The Swiss cheese doesn't wear tacky turtleneck sweaters!"

"Get away from me, George. You're sicker than I thought you were." She moved on to the sound of his wheezy laughter. *Is this what we're coming to? Murder as entertainment?*

"Is it real?" whispered a woman's voice by her ear. Mary Kate turned suddenly, encountering a thin, drawn face. The young woman touched her earring. "Is that a real ruby?"

"Uh, no. Glass."

The woman smiled and disappeared into the throng. Mary Kate pressed her hand to her heart and felt it pounding rapidly through the Spandex. She had forgotten about the note. IS IT REAL YET? She had assumed one of her friends left it, expecting her to know what it meant. At the time, she had considered the note a minor annoyance, but its simple message must have made more of an impression than she had thought. "I need a drink," she said.

"Red wine, as usual, Theodora?" Michael Kazdin led her

the last few steps to the bar. "It looks like everybody's here."

"Almost everybody," Mary Kate added. The violence with which he blanched made her want to take back her words. He had known Randall Valentine personally. *How could I be so insensitive?* The murder must have strongly affected him. He appeared to have aged overnight. Dark bags hung under his eyes, which drooped at the ends from the weight. "I'm sorry," she said. "It was a terrible tragedy."

"Yes," he said distractedly. "If you'll excuse me . . ." He handed her the wine glass. "There's a buffet on the far wall. Please, help yourself." And he was gone.

As distressing as it was to see him that way, Mary Kate was touched by his restrained emotion. She sipped from the glass, wishing she weren't there. The bursts of laughter and the macabre costumes all seemed to be in very poor taste, given the circumstances.

From across the room, she saw a gray figure coming toward her, parting the partygoers like a shark cutting through the ocean. His steel gray hair matched his eyes, as well as his expensive suit. She knew who he was, but couldn't imagine that he knew her. He stopped directly in front of her, putting out his hand and flashing perfect, white teeth. "Theodora Zed. We finally meet."

"My pleasure, Mr. Truesdale."

"Call me Walter. And should I call you Theodora or Mary?"

"Theo is fine. Are you enjoying yourself?"

"They are." He pointed his perfect nose in the direction of a couple curled around one another on a divan by the window. As they were both dressed in black, it was hard to tell where one left off and the other began. Walter chuckled. "Her husband is in a back room with someone else. His wife is at home, plotting a divorce. I know everyone, you see. And

I know what they're doing."

"My, how interesting." Mary Kate was not impressed, but her curiosity was piqued. Why was he bothering to show off to her? And what did he think he knew about her?

"Michael throws quite a bash, doesn't he?" Walter continued. "Just like the old days. His divorce settlement was devastating, you know."

"Michael and Phyllis broke up? I didn't know."

"Bad timing. Speaking of timing, your own career has leveled off in a good place, hasn't it, Theo?"

"I'm very happy with the way it's been going."

"I read *Death's Delight*. Very marketable." He scrunched his eyes as he smiled, as if they were sharing a secret. Mary Kate began to feel uncomfortable with this conversation.

"It's doing well," she said.

"But could it be better?" His scrunchy smile was making her nervous, and she looked around. Michael was a few feet away, looking back at her intently.

Walter followed her gaze and saw Michael. "Here, take my card," he said. "We'll talk again later."

She took the card, and stood holding it, not having a purse to stuff the wretched thing into. She felt like a traitor, even though she knew she had done nothing to encourage this. She was perfectly happy with her current agent, but Michael didn't know that. He only knew that his career had hit the rocks, and his agent was trolling for new business. Mary Kate dropped the card on a table, and started walking in the direction she believed would take her to the exit.

As she gently extricated herself from one group of acquaintances, then another, she concluded that the suite had no end, but was an eternity of party.

Breaking into a clearing, she found herself at the point farthest from the door, where the tall windows overlooked the sparkling Atlanta skyline. Sitting on one of the divans in front of the windows was Conner, his face buried in Alissa Dibiase's neck. Alissa smiled. "Hi, Theo!" She grabbed Conner's thick, brown hair at the back of his head. "Conner, darling, Theo is here."

His initial expression was one of being caught, then he broke into a big, drunken grin. "Theo! Come over and sit with us! I'll have a pretty lady on each side."

Alissa hasn't wasted any time, Mary Kate thought. She was in no mood to play out this situation. "I don't think so, Conner."

"Suit yourself," he said, squeezing Alissa's shoulders with one of his big arms.

"Could you point me in the direction of the door?"

Conner's arm dropped away. "You're not leaving, are you?"

"Yes, I am."

"By yourself? No, Mary Kate. I'll walk you to your room." He failed at his first try to lug himself to his feet. The second time was touch-and-go, but he managed to stay upright.

"I think you were better off sitting," Mary Kate said. "I don't need an escort."

He turned to Alissa. "I'll be back in five minutes."

"Con-ner!" she whined. She frowned at Mary Kate as he took her arm.

They went down the elevator in silence. Mary Kate thought he looked a little green. Getting off at the fourth floor, she said, "Looks like you and Alissa hit it off."

"She's nice," he said noncommittally. They walked side-by-side on the floral carpet. "What did you do all day?"

"Signings, panels, you know." There were other things she wanted to tell him about, but now, it didn't feel right. She looked up at him and felt their friendship slipping away.

42

"What's wrong?" he asked.

She shrugged. "Things are changing. I feel it."

He wiped one big paw over his mouth, then slipped his fingers through his hair. "If you mean about me and Alissa, what did you expect? I'm a man, Mary Kate. And I'm getting older. I can't wait forever."

"What?"

"I'm going to end up an old writer, sitting by himself at home and making a fool of himself with the groupies at the conventions."

She stopped and took his arm. "What are you talking about?"

He looked at her with what had to be the most stupid, open-mouthed gawk she had ever seen. He tipped his head toward the ceiling. "Damn," he whispered.

"Conner?"

He dropped his head and shook it like a woolly bear. "I just told you, didn't I? I've been drinking too much tonight. I'm sorry."

"What did you tell me?"

He looked into her eyes, and she looked back into his watery, red-ringed eyes. "For a long time, Mary Kate . . ." he began. "Hell, I'll just say it. I'm . . ."

They turned toward steps coming rapidly toward them. Officer Hendrickson turned the corner and approached with several more uniformed officers behind him. "Mrs. Flaherty, come with me, please." As he came closer, he asked, "Who's that with you?"

Conner stepped forward as if to shield her with his body. "Conner Drake."

"The guy who found the body? Both of you, come with me." They were immediately surrounded by the police and escorted to Mary Kate's room.

Chapter 5

"Over here, Mrs. Flaherty, Mr. Drake." Hendrickson took Mary Kate's arm and led her to a man standing by the window on the other side of her bed. Conner followed. "This is Detective Pumphrey. He wants to ask you some questions."

"I have a question or two," Mary Kate said.

"Mary Kate," Conner whispered with a hint of warning. She shot him an irritated glance. There were cops in her room, which she had paid for, and they were walking on her underwear. She thought a few questions were in order. She turned back to the detective and saw what might have been contributing to Conner's reticence. Detective Pumphrey was a big man, and, from the way he was chewing the heck out of the poor, defenseless toothpick in his mouth, he was a mean man. His face, shadowed by the brim of a nineteen-forties fedora, was wide and brown. His eyes, browner still, didn't move.

White teeth thrashed frantically at the stub of wood.

Mary Kate toned down her approach. "Why are you in my room?"

Pumphrey cleared his throat and deftly moved the toothpick to the side of his mouth with the tip of a pink tongue. "Search warrant."

Mary Kate jumped from the sound, a cross between a bull frog love song and a rusty hinge. Pumphrey stared at her. She realized that his line of sight was falling on her cleavage at the top of her cat suit. She tugged it up a little higher, and that seemed to be enough to start the interrogation.

"Mrs. Flaherty," Pumphrey croaked, "do you own a knife?"

"Am I a suspect? Are you arresting me?" Looking around and seeing she was getting no response, she answered his question, as ridiculous as it seemed. "A knife? Well, of course, I do. I have a whole set of them in my kitchen."

"In Annapolis, Maryland?"

"Actually, it's Edgewater. We don't live in the city."

"Hrrumph." The toothpick shifted back to the forefront.

Assuming that that was all they wanted to know, Mary Kate felt it was her turn. "I can only guess that this has something to do with the death of Randall Valentine." The deceased man's name rolled off her tongue with ease. It was funny how someone she had never heard of forty-eight hours ago had become such a major player in her life. "I'd like to see this search warrant."

Pumphrey glared at her a moment longer, then slowly rolled his eyes to the left, where they landed on Hendrickson. Hendrickson immediately straightened up and pulled a folded paper out of his back pocket. He handed it to Mary Kate. "We tried to locate you to sign a consent-to-search form. Since new evidence came in, and most of our witnesses are leaving the city tomorrow, we went ahead and obtained a warrant."

It was an unimpressive document, a printed computer form with signatures and dates scrawled at the bottom. She saw her name, pseudonym, home address, and phone number. She looked down to the section, Probable Cause.

A shoe, which Mary Kate Flaherty (referred to as Subject) identifies as her own, was found 16 feet, 4 inches from the victim. Subject admits being outside of the hotel at the approxi-

mate time of the crime. The desk clerk reports seeing Subject enter the lobby in a distressed and disheveled state at or around one-thirty a.m. Several witnesses (see affidavits) report over-hearing an argument between Subject and the victim shortly before the crime took place. Wounds on the victim's body are similar to those described in Subject's books.

"Wounds on the victim's body?" she repeated aloud.

"Vampire bite," Pumphrey barked.

Mary Kate could only gape, her mouth dropping open wider by the second. She felt hands on her shoulders and turned to see Conner. He wore that wild, new angry look.

"Is this some kind of a joke?" His fingers squeezed deeply into her bare skin. "I saw the blood and slashes on his clothing, and now you say he was bitten by a vampire?"

Pumphrey's eyes widened, the toothpick disappeared behind his lips, then protruded from a far corner. "Mrs. Flaherty, do you know about vampires?"

She shrunk back against Conner's chest. "Uh, uh, yes."

"What do vampire bites look like?" Pumphrey was almost smiling.

"This is unreal. What do vampire bites look like? Uh, two little holes in the neck?"

"Correct!" Pumphrey shouted, shooting the toothpick stub across the room. He promptly took another out of his jacket pocket and loaded it between his teeth.

"I didn't see . . ." Conner began.

Hendrickson interrupted him. "He was wearing a turtle-neck sweater. We didn't see it either. The Medical Examiner called this afternoon . . ."

"Hrrumph." Pumphrey's cheeks puffed out, his eyes narrowed.

Hendrickson stepped back and lowered his head, muttering, "I thought, since it was already in the newspapers . . ."

Mary Kate caught a glimpse of Theodora in the dresser mirror and groaned. "You don't think I'm a vampire, do you?"

"The question is," Pumphrey croaked, "do you think you're a vampire?"

"I'm a writer! I dress like this to sell books!"

"About vampires." Pumphrey seemed to be enjoying the exchange.

Mary Kate shrugged Conner's hands off her shoulders and stuck her chin up to Pumphrey's big face. "You'll find at least two dozen other writers here who write vampire stories. I didn't kill Randall Valentine. If I killed every person who said I wrote crap, then I'd have been on a coast-to-coast murder spree for months. If you want to find the killer, you should find out who the weirdo was by the parking lot last night, instead of coming in here with your ridiculous, trumped-up charges!" She wiped perspiration off her lip with the back of her hand.

Pumphrey smiled. "What did I tell you, Hendrickson?"

"What?" Mary Kate exclaimed, thoroughly confused.

Hendrickson also smiled. "You were right, sir."

"Tell us about the weirdo in the parking lot, Mrs. Flaherty," Pumphrey softly growled.

Mary Kate didn't like tricks, and she felt one had just been pulled on her. "No, wait a minute. What's going on here? Am I being arrested or what?"

Pumphrey rolled his eyes to Hendrickson, who explained. "No, Mrs. Flaherty, we haven't found any solid evidence that you were involved, but we had to make sure before you went back home. Detective Pumphrey thought we might have a chance at getting a lead if he, uh, questioned you."

"You mean bullied her," Conner said.

"No one's hurt, Mr. Drake," Pumphrey said. "And now, if Mrs. Flaherty would be so kind as to tell us what she saw."

"May I sit down first?" Mary Kate asked. Exhausted, she sat on the edge of the bed and told them about the mysterious, caped figure who might or might not have chased her back into the hotel. Pumphrey thanked her for the information and motioned the other officers to leave.

"Detective," she said as he moved toward the door, "how do you think Randall got the holes in his neck?"

"Read about it in the newspaper," he growled and left.

She fell back onto the bed and closed her eyes for a moment. When she opened them, Conner was standing over her. "I'm ready to go home," she said.

"I know." He walked to the door, then stopped with his hand on the knob.

"Even from the grave, that piss-ant is screwing with you. Good-bye, Mary Kate."

She watched him go, wondering if she really knew him at all.

Opening the Sunday morning edition of *The Atlanta Constitution* on the coffee shop table, Mary Kate read the front page headline.

NO LEADS ON VAMPIRE KILLER
Conventioneers Leave Today

In the land of conventions, time stands still, and so does the news. She had no idea the press coverage of the murder had been so extensive. The Vampire Killer. *The reporters in the newsrooms must be getting absolutely tingly over this one.* The headline dashed any notions she might have had about the detective just trying to throw her off-guard by talking about vampires last night. And it meant that the murder was directly related to the convention. The odds of a random street mugger leaving teeth marks in the neck of his victim were pretty slim.

She read on about how the police were trying to collect as much evidence as possible before their witnesses dispersed to the four winds. Many had left upon hearing that one of their own had been killed on the premises. Hotel and restaurant owners expressed concern about the effects on the tourist and convention trade. Mary Kate was grateful her name was not released.

The preliminary report from the Office of the Medical Examiner stated that cause of death was any one of three mortal stab wounds to the back and chest. The weapon could have been a large, single-bladed knife. In addition, as reported yesterday, two small wounds had been discovered on the neck of the victim. The shape of the punctures and the scratches between them indicated that the wounds had been inflicted by a common dinner fork with the two center tines broken off. The wounds apparently had been administered after death.

"Ugh." Mary Kate's vivid imagination served up a picture of the black-caped figure kneeling over the bloodied corpse, pulling back the turtleneck collar with one hand, then jabbing a fork into the flesh with the other. It was more gruesome than any of the vampire scenes she had ever written. *Is it real yet?* she thought. She was glad to be going home this afternoon, right after the BloodCon Awards ceremony.

A crowd had gathered near the coffee shop window facing the front of the hotel. As she folded the newspaper and finished her coffee, Mary Kate thought she heard voices from outside. Feeling comfortable in her Mrs. Flaherty traveling clothes—jeans and sweater—she joined the group looking out the window.

Pacing in a circle outside the lobby doors were six women, varying in age, dressed in their Sunday best. Each one held a hand-lettered sign on a stick. HERETICS GO HOME! ATLANTA DOESN'T NEED VAMPIRES! GOD FORGIVE YOU!

They chanted as they marched. "Horror writers, go home! We don't want your sickness here!" Standing in the sunlight, talking into a reporter's microphone was the ex-reverend, sociologist, Patrick Henley.

"I can't believe it," Mary Kate groaned.

A nice-looking, young mother with a squirming toddler in her arms stood beside her. "I saw Mr. Henley on the news last night," the woman said. "He said there are people here at the convention who write books about killing and perversions and stuff, and that it was just a matter of time before someone was hurt."

"Right here?" Mary Kate asked.

The woman nodded and gripped her baby tighter. "The hotel people told us that it was all in fun, you know, like Halloween. But someone was murdered here Friday night. I'm sure glad the convention will be over before we have to spend a night here."

"I don't blame you," Mary Kate said. She hurried out of the coffee shop before someone could recognize her. Writing escapist fiction wasn't the safe occupation it had been a few days ago.

"And the winner of this year's BloodCon Writer of the Year Award is . . . Michael Kazdin!"

Mary Kate applauded with the others from her seat in the back of the ballroom. Too many chairs had been set up for the few remaining conventioneers. They were scattered about the large room, giving the clapping a weak, perfunctory note.

This was the final award; Michael's was the final speech for this year's BloodCon. He ambled up to the podium, his head hanging down. He looked as if he hadn't bothered to shave or change his clothes from the night before. That wasn't like Michael. Appearances were very important to him.

He stood in front of the microphone, blinking his eyes, holding onto the oak podium as if that was all that was holding him up. They waited a few moments, then one of the presenters from the first row stood and began to move toward him. Most likely on his way to lead Michael away, the presenter stopped as Michael began to speak in a clear, but uncharacteristically solemn voice.

"I suppose I should thank you for making me Writer of the Year. It's a great honor and all that crap. Under ordinary circumstances, I would have played the game and acted as if this award had something to do with my writing. But we all know that I'm Writer of the Year because they were getting me in before my career went completely down the tubes." He stared off into a point directly over Mary Kate's head. He sniffled before going on. She couldn't see from this distance if he had tears in his eyes.

"As you all must know by now, there's a vampire killer on the loose, a killer of writers. That particular killer did his stabbing with a knife in the back. Others murder writers with whispers and innuendo and . . . betrayal, a knife as sharp and deadly, a wound that bleeds as profusely."

He clenched his fist, his voice becoming tight with barely restrained anger. "Friends . . . people you thought were friends, people you went out of your way to help . . . they climb over your corpse, kicking you in the face as their grasping hands reach for glory."

He looked around into the faces of the audience as if he had just discovered they were there. "To hell with it!" He pushed his palms against the podium, sending it crashing to the floor, the mike emitting a shrill whine. He stomped down the center aisle, shoving away those who tried to stop him, and threw open the back door. He was gone before Mary Kate could get out of her seat and look for him down the hall. Walter Truesdale pushed past her and followed him, a shark on the trail of fresh blood.

After getting lost in the labyrinthine Atlanta airport, enduring a stuffy, smelly flight with more than its share of turbulence, then getting lost in the Baltimore-Washington International Airport, Mary Kate had no resistance left to combat Chuck's surly mood.

"I thought your flight was coming in at ten," he said without turning away from the television.

She dropped her suitcase by the stairs. "It did. I couldn't find the luggage carousel."

"Did they move it since the last time you were there?"

It was a nasty little rhetorical question, the kind she had learned to ignore over the past few months in order to keep the peace. "Did the boys get to bed okay?"

He thumbed the remote, turning off the television. He walked past her, muttering, "I'm going to bed."

She leaned on the banister, looking up at his back. Her nerves were raw from the stress of the weekend. She didn't have the strength to suppress her feelings and let it ride the way she usually did. "So you're not talking to me now?"

He turned around slowly, looking at her with the now familiar disgust, as if she had overstepped the bounds of common decency by speaking to him. "Okay, I'll talk to you, Mary Kate. How was your weekend? Did you have fun with your drunken friends? Did you even remember you had a family?"

"Is that it? Is it the conventions? Fine. I won't go to them anymore."

"No, that's not it! You go off on your conventions, supposedly for your work, and I'm expected to take care of the boys. Okay, I can do that. Somebody has to. But you have one little thing to take care of before you go, and you don't even bother."

"What are you talking about?"

"The cat, damn it! You couldn't even remember to get somebody to feed the damn cat! It was half-starved by the time we came in this evening." He stomped up the stairs. A moment later, the bedroom door slammed.

"I did that," she said to the dark hallway. She remembered Mrs. Olsen's stinky attitude when she had called Friday. She had said she would send her husband over, didn't she?

Mary Kate felt the anger she wanted to blast Chuck with being misdirected to her neighbor. *The bitch!* She stopped herself in the kitchen, the phone receiver in her hand. *What am I doing?* She felt tears well up in her eyes, and her anger dissipated as the first one rolled down her cheek. Her home felt as lonely as the hotel room. She replaced the receiver into the cradle.

At the top of the stairs, she turned right, not to the bedroom she shared with her husband, but to her office. She sat in the chair in front of the computer. She turned it on and began to write.

Ursula awoke in Dimitri's arms. The day had passed as they slept, and now the darkness once again caressed them. She touched her neck and felt the crust of dried blood, where his teeth sinking into her flesh had given her both exquisite pain and pleasure. The wound felt like . . .

53

"Like a fork with the middle tines broken off," she whispered. She didn't have the stomach for writing a violent vampire love scene tonight. Her feeling of isolation increased. She was suddenly afraid that this outlet would be cut off from her, that she would no longer have the la-la land of fiction as a safe haven when the real world got too real.

She looked at the clock. It was almost one a.m. She leaned back in her chair and, sighing, looked at the papers strewn across her desk. There were things she could do to put off climbing into the cold bed with Chuck.

She reached for the stack of fan mail she hadn't had time to answer. It wasn't where she knew she had put it on the right hand corner of the desk. Moving the piles carefully—it was a complicated filing system that included coffee mugs, candy wrappers, and photos of her kids—she covered the full length of the six-foot-long desk. She stood and immediately saw the letters on the floor. Someone had knocked them off the edge.

Her last bastion of privacy had been violated. Chuck and the boys had always taken seriously her sign on the door, "Knock or Die," and never, as far as she knew, came into her office without her permission. She would have to remind them in the morning. Maybe just David and Ben. Right now, she couldn't think of a thing she could say to Chuck that wouldn't be taken the wrong way.

For the next two hours, she wrote short letters to the readers who had taken the time to let her know how much they enjoyed her books. She thanked them and sent them a bookmark carrying a message about her latest novel. Then, slipping off her clothes in the dark bedroom, she rolled onto her side of the bed, Chuck's back to her saying all that could be said about the state of their marriage.

Chapter 6

Mary Kate leaned on the mailbox, her arm draped around it like an embrace. Checking the mail was an important time of day. Contracts, advances, and royalty checks came in the mail, as well as the dreaded rejections. Every writer remembers the time in his or her career when that's all there was, and family and friends looked on with disbelief at the insanity of hopefulness and perseverance in the face of failure. Yet, there was always faith that this time it would sell, that the rejections sound less rejecting, the market is picking up.

"It's late," she said to Nancy Reiner, who was crossing the street with a mug of hot coffee in each hand.

"Here, take this, it's burning my hand," Nancy said. "Are you expecting something important?"

"It shouldn't be long before they're sending me the galleys for *Sweet Eternal Sleep*, but no, not really."

Nancy joined her in gazing up the street, waiting for the U.S. Postal truck to turn onto Linden Lane. Mary Kate sipped her coffee, enjoying the company they shared once or twice a week. She knew Nancy would be waiting for no more than the latest *Ladies Home Journal*, but that was okay. Nancy was one of the few mothers in the neighborhood who didn't treat her as if she had a contagious disease because she wrote erotic horror.

They talked about the successful book fair last week at the elementary school and how the azaleas were doing well this year. As Nancy told her about the stroganoff recipe she had tried last night, Mary Kate couldn't help but think that Nancy was the kind of wife Chuck really wanted. Looking great in the middle of a weekday, her house undoubtedly clean, her lawn tidy, her kids picture perfect, Nancy still managed to do volunteer work at the hospital and crochet afghans for gifts. One could guess that she never forgot to do laundry, served Dinty Moore canned stew for dinner no more than once in a lifetime, and never went without shaving her legs so long that she needed a lawn mower for catch-up.

"It's about time," Nancy said as the truck stopped at the first box. Two minutes later, Mary Kate took her mail from the driver and flipped through it.

"Oh, good, this issue has a review of *A Lover's Blood*," she said, holding up the lurid cover of *Cemetery Dance*, a demoniacal creature leering out from it.

"Ick." Nancy grimaced. "That reminds me. Were you at that convention in Atlanta where the man was killed by a vampire?"

It probably wouldn't do any good to explain that he wasn't killed by the tiny punctures in his neck, that the sudden fatal loss of blood was caused by the ripping of flesh and muscle and arteries by a weapon as mundane as a knife. "Yeah. Was it on the news?"

"Just a short report. I thought of you when I saw it, but I didn't know you'd gone. I almost called you, but Doug is Scoutmaster to Billy's troop and they had a meeting after dinner, and, well, there went the rest of the evening. Did you see anything?"

Mary Kate quickly debated how much she should say. The weekend's events had been bizarre, and there must be a limit on how weird a friend Nancy was willing to tolerate. "Not really. The police were questioning everybody, so I had to answer a few questions. It was very upsetting. I had just met the boy who was killed."

"Oh, how awful!"

Mary Kate nodded. "On a different note, speaking of last weekend, what's with Mrs. Olsen? She told me she'd feed my cat, and she didn't."

Clicking her tongue and shaking her head, Nancy sidled up a little closer and gestured toward the Olsen house with her mug. "I think they're having problems. Marital problems."

"Oh," Mary Kate said, wondering if that's what Nancy said about her to the other neighbors.

"Gregory hasn't been home in days, and Margaret doesn't speak or wave or anything when you see her."

That shows how much I pay attention, Mary Kate thought. She didn't even know the Olsens' first names. She had lived on Linden Lane for the last six years and couldn't recall an instance when she'd shared more than two words with Gregory Olsen. Now, Margaret, she'd spoken with her. About the Flahertys leaving the garbage cans out overnight. About the Flahertys not mowing their lawn. About the Flahertys' cat peeing in her bed of impatiens. Mrs. Olsen was one of those neighbors who felt it was her duty to keep the others in line, lest the whole community fell into decay and ruin. Then, something Nancy had said struck her. "Wait a minute. How long did you say Mr. Olsen had been gone?"

"Oh, gee, I don't know," Nancy said. "I really don't have time to keep track of their comings and goings. Linda, on the other side of them, told me." In response to Mary Kate's puzzled look, she said, "Linda Goodman, Joey and Nicole's mom."

"Oh, okay." This would be Joey's mom, who told her kid she would beat him raw if he stepped one foot into that pervert writer's house. Ben had asked her what a pervert was.

Mary Kate had told him it was somebody who passes judgment on something she hadn't read.

She decided it wouldn't be worth pursuing whether Mr. Olsen had actually been home when Mrs. Olsen said she would send him over to feed Lestat. Saying their good-byes, Mary Kate and Nancy retreated to their homes and very different lives.

In the broad light of day, Mary Kate had no problem writing the blood-drenched scenes her readers loved so well. David and Ben found her hovering over the keyboard when they came in from school. After knocking on the open door, Ben greeted her with a hug. David leaned against the doorframe, accurately mimicking his father's look of disgust.

"What's with you?" she said.

"It's starting up again." David came in and flopped into the easy chair in the corner. "Why do you have to write this crap?"

"Hey, watch the language, bud. And this crap bought those fancy basketball shoes you're wearing and paid for last summer's trip to Florida."

He lifted his feet onto the chair and fiddled with the laces. "The kids were bugging me. They said that my mother was the vampire that killed that guy."

She rolled her chair closer to him. "And you know this isn't true, right?"

Not looking at her, he mumbled, "Yeah."

"And you know that in junior high, if they didn't tease you about this, they'd find something else."

He lifted his head, his face full of adolescent anguish. "They pass around your books, Mom! They read the dirty parts out loud!"

"I'm sorry." She reached out to touch his hand. He pulled

away. "I don't write them for children. I can't stop them from getting hold of them." David put his hand over his face, hiding the building tears, and pushed past her as he ran from the room. She looked up at the framed paperback cover on the wall with a picture of herself in full get-up. Damn you, Theodora.

Spinning around in the chair, she saw Ben standing by the desk. He looked small and worried. "Come here, sweetie," she said. He climbed into her lap and squeezed his little arms around her neck.

"I love you, Mom," he said, "even though you write trashy books."

"Trashy?" It didn't sound like a seven-year-old's word.

"That's what Daddy said."

The mood around the dinner table was oppressive. Other than quick bursts of chatter from Ben breaking the silence, their concentration was focused on their plates. Mary Kate had spent the remainder of the afternoon preparing the meal that no one seemed to be enjoying. Peeling potatoes and pounding boneless chicken breasts had helped allay some of the guilt she had been feeling. The banana pudding with maraschino cherries on top, waiting in the refrigerator for the grand finale, made her feel most Mom-like.

It wasn't as if she never cooked for her family, but more and more, they had been making do with hot dogs and beans and carryout pizza. No more. Mary Kate planned to cook every night, and starting tomorrow, the house would be de-junked, the plants watered on a regular basis, and clean, fresh laundry delivered to every dresser drawer without delay. And somehow, somewhere, she would find the time to be a writer, too.

They're not happy, yet, she thought, *but they will be.*

By the time she presented the banana pudding, even Ben's compliments were halfhearted. After wolfing it down, the boys asked to be excused, then disappeared upstairs. Chuck wordlessly retreated to the living room and his favorite companion, the TV. Mary Kate sat alone in the kitchen piled high with dirty dishes, pots, and pans. She was tempted to put them in the sink to soak, then wash them in the morning, but she knew Nancy would never do that. She stayed in there until the whole kitchen was gleaming, even cleaner than before, stopping only to say good night to the boys. David had given her a kiss on the cheek, something he hadn't done in a long time. Knowing that it was his way of saying he was sorry for the way he had behaved, she still made a mental note to make banana pudding more often.

It was almost ten o'clock, and the rest of the family was asleep before she made it back up to her office. Her deadline for the current novel was still three months away, but she had promised short stories to three different magazines and had agreed to write a book review for another. After three a.m., exhausted and her eyes burning, she crawled into bed behind Chuck's back.

The phone rang, waking her up. Mary Kate glanced at the clock in the VCR and saw that it was nearly eleven-thirty. "Damn." She had seen the boys off on the bus at eight and promptly fell back to sleep in the living room. She had meant to rest her eyes for only a few minutes. *So much for Super Mom.* She answered the phone in the kitchen. "Hello."

"Hello, Theo. What are you doing on the twenty-second?"

"Hi, Alissa. I have no idea what I'm doing on the twenty-second. What did you have in mind?"

"A stroke of genius, darling. Everyone is talking vampires these days, since the Valentine kid was whacked. I'm talking

60

opportunity. I've planned for you and me to do a reading and mass signing at the Food For Thought café-bookstore right here in New York. And I can guarantee at least one television interview on a local news show. What do you say, Theo?"

It was a grand opportunity. Exposure in New York City. Television. Books would sell. Publishers would be impressed. It felt wrong taking advantage of the media's sick interest in Randall Valentine's death, but there had been a pre-existing interest in vampires. Recent movie and book sales proved that. Sales of her own and Alissa Dibiase's books. Which led to her next question. "Why are you asking me along? You're a vampire writer."

A moment's silence. "They asked for you, Theo. They said my market was too narrow to draw much of a crowd."

"That's not true. We pretty much share the same market, I always thought."

"I thought so, too. So, you'll come?"

They had asked for Theodora Zed. It was flattering. It was also a chance to break through to a wider audience beyond the dedicated fans of horror at the conventions. It was a rare dream-come-true for a genre writer. "Hold on while I check my schedule. It's upstairs."

Leaving the receiver on the counter, she ran up to her office and lifted the stack of fan letters she knew she had put on top of the short story draft that she had put on top of her calendar. Not finding it, she began searching in an ever-widening circle.

Frustrated, she picked up the office phone. "Alissa? I can't find my schedule right now. I think I'm okay on the twenty-second, so why don't you consider me in, and I'll get back to you if I find out otherwise."

"I have to let them know, Theodora."

"Okay, yeah, tell them yeah."

"Great. I'll give you the particulars when I get them." Alissa paused, then said playfully, "Oh, I heard that Michael went nuts at the awards Sunday."

"It was absolutely heartbreaking, Alissa. Did you leave early?"

She giggled. "Mm-hmm. I took a side trip to Connecticut."

"Connecticut?" Conner lived in Westport, Connecticut. "Oh, I see."

"Don't be jealous, darling." She laughed again.

"I'm not. I hope you had a nice visit. You and Conner make a cute couple."

"Not as cute as you would, I bet. No, forget I said that. I don't want to make you angry before the twenty-second." Click. "What's that? Did you hear that?"

"Yeah. I left the phone off the hook in the kitchen. It's probably the cat looking for his lunch. I've got to go, Alissa. Call me when you know more."

Mary Kate went downstairs to hang up. As she entered the kitchen, she was startled to see Chuck standing by the phone, the receiver already resting in the cradle. His face was emotionless, his expression unreadable. After her heart stopped racing from the surprise of seeing someone when she had thought she was alone, she said breathlessly, "You frightened me. You're early. Is something wrong?"

He didn't move, only looked at her as if he saw something about her he'd never noticed before. "I thought we could spend some time together," he said. "Alone."

Puzzled, she said, "I'd like that."

Then his face clouded over with anger, the anger he refused to explain. "Would you?"

"Yes, of course. I'll fix us lunch. You go change your clothes. Okay?"

She detected some softening in his face as he went upstairs, loosening his tie. As she took the cold cuts out of the refrigerator, she prepared herself for the soft shoe it was going to require to keep the afternoon from turning into a brawl. *This might be a good thing,* she thought. He had, after all, made the effort to come home early. Her expectations were low, but she still hoped they could start negotiations to end the long Cold War. She knew in her heart that the role of family diplomat was taking a toll, and that she couldn't keep it up forever.

Chapter 7

A calm settled over the Flaherty household as the unspoken truce held for the next two weeks. Mary Kate turned down writing assignments and appearances, and used the time to attend to more domestic chores, even going so far as to buy new kitchen curtains and flowers for the pot by the back door. She spent her evenings watching television with Chuck, and occasionally, they spoke—about the kids, about the weather, about the traffic. But never about her work, and never about their feelings.

Her appointment book was not found, but she was able to patch together most of her schedule through a phone call to her agent and by calling the places she could remember, verifying when and where she was supposed to be there. The boys swore they had not gone into her office, so she assumed her own slovenliness had finally caught up with her. She spent an afternoon cleaning her desk and filing the papers in a real file cabinet. She started a new calendar, including the signing in New York with Alissa on the twenty-second.

Three days before she was supposed to go, she remembered to tell Chuck at dinner.

"This Saturday?" He put down his fork. "We're taking my mother out to dinner on Saturday."

"Her birthday! Oh, jeez, I completely forgot." It had been in the calendar. The old calendar. "I'm sorry. You take the boys and go ahead."

His jaw hardened. "I guess I'll have to."

"If this weren't so important, I'd cancel, really. But Alissa is counting on . . ."

"I don't care, Mary Kate . . . or Theodora or whoever the hell you are this week. Do what you want."

The cease-fire had been broken. Hostilities were resumed.

Mary Kate backed the car out of the driveway and parked on the street. There was a trick to turning around, but she couldn't do it without taking out a corner of the lawn. Nancy waited by the mailbox. "I'm doing a reading in New York this weekend, and I need new shoes," Mary Kate explained, leaving out the detail that the Atlanta city police had kept her four-inch spike as crime scene evidence. Obviously, they hadn't ruled her out as a suspect altogether.

Nancy recommended a couple of stores in Annapolis, then suddenly tugged on Mary Kate's shirt sleeve. "Look over there," she whispered. "No, don't look like you're looking."

Peeking around as discreetly as she could, Mary Kate saw Margaret Olsen in a pink sweat suit, chugging up Linden Lane in the other direction. Although she seemed to have lost some weight since the last time Mary Kate had seen her, she was still hefty. The uncombed hair at the back of her head looked like a fuzzy ball of lint.

"She's taken up walking," Nancy whispered, even though Mrs. Olsen was over a half block away.

"That's good," Mary Kate said. "It shows she's still concerned about her health."

"She's been very busy since Gregory's been gone."

"Where'd he go?"

Nancy began talking out of the side of her mouth. Mary Kate assumed this was to discourage lip-reading spies. Nancy didn't gossip often, and it showed. "Nobody knows. Linda . . . you know Linda on the other side of the Olsens?"

Mary Kate nodded, even though she only knew Linda to see her. Mary Kate wasn't exactly the Belle of Linden Lane. Most of her neighbors seemed to believe she was the devil incarnate without ever having spoken with her.

Nancy continued. "She said Gregory probably had enough and left her. Supposedly, this has been coming for years."

"I didn't know," Mary Kate replied sympathetically, though she was thinking, *I don't really care.* Her experiences with Mrs. Olsen had been less than pleasant. She couldn't imagine anyone actually living with her.

"Well, living right next door, I've seen a few things." Nancy shook her head to emphasize that these were things she'd never do, which to Mary Kate meant crimes against nature like letting the wind blow the leaves away, instead of raking them. "Linda has lived next to the Olsens for twelve years, and she says that Margaret's problems started when her daughter died."

"Her daughter died?"

"It was a long time ago, ten years, maybe. I don't know much about it, only that Margaret hasn't been able to work since."

"That's so sad," Mary Kate said, meaning it this time. "I can't think of anything worse than losing a child."

"There she is," Nancy whispered, trying to hide her pointing finger. They could see through the yards to the next street over, where Mrs. Olsen turned the corner, a disappearing pink marshmallow. "She looks like she's on patrol for citizen association rule violations."

Mary Kate made a point of looking over at Nancy's magazine cover-quality, landscaped yard. "And you have so much to worry about."

Nancy's face fell, and she lifted one neatly groomed hand

to the corner of her mouth. "Everyone has something," she said as if to herself.

The automatic garage door creaked as it closed, leaving Mary Kate sitting in the gray dusk of the garage's interior. She gathered the packages from the passenger seat, and finding her hands full, picked up her purse by clenching the strap between her teeth. Kicking the car door closed, she stood with no hand free to open the door to the yard. "Damn," she said around the leather strap.

She looked for someplace to put the packages. The lawn mower, ladders, and household overflow piled around the walls made dark caves. The part of her mind that composed stories of terror sized up these dark spaces. Several of them were large enough to hold a caped figure armed with a knife and fork, gripping them in his fists as if preparing for a grisly meal. The snow shovel and gardening trowel became weapons of defense in her mind. The trapped gas fumes made her nauseated. She dropped the packages and opened the door. In the bright sunlight, something jumped in front of her.

Mary Kate screamed, frightening Lestat into frizzing up his fur and laying back his ears. They stared at one another a moment, then Mary Kate let out her breath and smiled. The cat was not as forgiving. He backed away from her, his tail poufed out three times its normal size. "Be that way," she said, turning to get the bags from the garage floor.

She carried them across the yard to the stoop at the backdoor, where she put them down to dig her key from her purse. Glancing down at the geranium she had planted recently in the flowerpot, she saw that it had been knocked over. The black potting soil was fanned out around it, red petals sprinkled through it like drops of blood. She scooped up the dirt and patted it back around the plant. Remembering the extra house key, she looked before she set the pot down. It was there. The cat must have been playing with the plant and toppled it. That would account for his freaky behavior upon seeing her. Lestat obviously had a guilty conscience.

Having the house to herself for another hour until the school bus arrived, Mary Kate put on a pot of coffee and headed upstairs to work on her presentation for the café-bookstore. Food For Thought was trendy and very New Yorkish. This was going to be her one shot at convincing the Anne Rice crowd that Theodora Zed's sexy, gory brand of vampire might be more fun.

As soon as she stepped through her office door, she saw it.

She had been keeping the desktop clear after the calendar's disappearance. When she had left this morning, only the computer, the telephone, three disk cases, and the photos of her kids sat out. Now, there was an envelope. White, business-size, no stamp, no address.

I could have left an envelope out, she thought, approaching the desk carefully, keeping a safe distance. She knew she hadn't. She had been doing a rewrite on a story this morning, not writing letters. No one had been home the last few hours. The sun from the window hit the white envelope, making its illogical presence glow. Mary Kate struggled to keep her imagination from creating more from this than was there. An envelope on a desk. Nothing mysterious about that.

There was a simple solution. Open it. *If it's empty, then I just left one out. I started to send something to somebody, got distracted, then forgot about it. Yeah, that's it.* Or, something in it would make her slap her head and say, Now I remember! A bill, a note, a check. She wasn't so organized that she was above such slips of memory.

Feeling more confident, she picked up the envelope.

Three black grains fell from the flap. She pinched them between her fingers and looked at them. Potting soil. Slowly, she opened the envelope and unfolded the single sheet of white paper.

IT ISN'T REAL YET, IS IT?

She dropped it as if teeth had appeared in the words and snapped at her. The note looked up at her from the floor as she backed away. Somebody had put this on her desk. Somebody had been in here while she was gone shopping. Somebody had knocked over the geranium on the back stoop. Somebody had been in Atlanta, and now, was here.

She ran through the house, checking each room until she was satisfied she was alone, stopping to breathe heavily beside the knife block on the kitchen counter. The kitchen knife, the traditional weapon of women hearing bumps and thumps in a dark house, now had a gruesome history for her, and she recoiled at the thought of picking one up. *I could never do it,* she thought. Not even to protect myself. Her hands shaking, she poured herself a cup of coffee and sat at the table. A little word with a big question grew in her mind until it almost floated in the air in front of her. *Who?*

Chapter 8

The taxi stopped in front of the brick building bearing the sign, Food For Thought, in blue neon. The driver's expression of intense boredom didn't budge as Mary Kate paid him. This was New York, after all, and the sight of a vampiress in Manhattan wasn't enough to raise an eyebrow over.

She had kept the Theodora hair and make-up as she dressed in the hotel room, and wore her new four-inch spikes, but her dress was an attempt at a sleeker, more sophisticated Theodora. Long and tight fitting through the hips, the black gown split at the knees into soft, irregular shreds above her ankles. The bodice was low-cut, the sleeves long and flowing. Her earrings were black cameos with red eyes. She wore a velvet choker around her neck and rings on every finger. As she walked up to the door, carrying her canvas bag with her notes and extra books, she hiccupped. *No, not now. Please.*

She went in and was shown to a back office by the clerk at the cash register.

"Theo! Darling! You look good enough to eat!" Alissa sat on the edge of a desk, wearing a knee-length, green silk dress topped with a beaded bolero jacket. She would have been *en vogue* in any uptown cocktail party.

"It's too much, isn't it?" Mary Kate dropped her bag in the corner, then hiccupped again.

"No! It's so Theodora! But those hiccups have got to go."

"I think I need a drink of water. I'll be back in a minute." Mary Kate left the office and passed the round tables surrounded by bookshelves. The four customers browsing through the stacks didn't notice her as she walked by, nor did the man and woman sipping coffee and reading at separate tables. *This is going to be a total bust.* The non-Anne Rice vampire ladies weren't exactly packing them in.

She could see a long table, shrouded in black crepe, set up in the back. Candles stood around the prominent display of Theodora Zed and Alissa Dibiase books. Above, black spiders and bats spangled thick, draping webs. She began to feel better about her costume. This dress was going to look great in that setting.

A waitress in white blouse and blue slacks came out of the double doors to the kitchen. Mary Kate asked her for some water. While she waited, a few more customers dribbled in, beginning to fill in the expanse of empty seats. *Come on, come on,* she thought. She had incurred the worst of Chuck's wrath to be here, and the least they could do was give her a dozen people for an audience.

Accepting the glass of water with a quiet thank you and a smile, she brought it to her lips and stopped. A tall, broad-shouldered figure filled the entrance from the sidewalk. As he stepped in, and the glare from the setting sun disappeared behind the closing door, she saw Conner's face turn toward her.

Her first thought was that he had become better looking since she had last seen him at BloodCon. The firm lines of his nose and jaw, the shaggy, brown hair falling over his brow had more appeal than she had noticed before. He walked toward her, and she felt her breath catch in her throat like a schoolgirl being approached by the captain of the football team. *I'm just glad to see him,* she thought. *As a friend.*

"Hi, Mary Kate," he said. His voice was low and warm.

She hiccupped loudly.

Conner smiled, then laughed, looked at her, then laughed again. As she feebly explained how her nervousness must have brought on the hiccups, he laughed harder, wrapping his arms around her. "I've missed you," he said.

"Me, too." She hugged him back, feeling both cherished and safe. Stepping back, she said, "I didn't know you were coming down for this."

"Alissa didn't tell you?"

"No. I would've planned to stay longer. I'm catching a flight home at five in the morning." She realized what she had just said. If Alissa had told her, she would have stayed longer. Alissa didn't want her around more than was necessary. And Conner knew this.

"Hello, Conner." Alissa slunk up beside him, slipping her arms around his waist. She turned her face up to him to be kissed. He hesitated, then pecked her lips and glanced down at his shoes. "Conner's here for the weekend to give us moral support," she said to Mary Kate. "Michael was going to come, too, but he had to cancel. His apartment is just a few blocks from mine on Fifty-Seventh. He put in a good word for us here, you know."

"No, I didn't know," Mary Kate said. *He must have forgiven me for talking to his agent in Atlanta.* "How is Michael?"

Alissa looked puzzled. "Didn't you see him last week?" She went on as Mary Kate shook her head, equally puzzled. "He had a couple of appearances planned in Washington bookstores, so he was going to give you a call to get together for lunch or something. Or so he told me."

The manager of Food For Thought, a bookish-looking gentleman in brown tweed, motioned to them that it was almost time. Mary Kate looked around and was pleasantly surprised to see that most of the tables had filled with customers as they had been talking in the corner of the dining area.

"I'm first," Alissa said, then added dryly, "your opening act, Theodora."

"I better go review my notes, then. You're going to raise their expectations." Mary Kate excused herself and went back to the office. She walked directly to the corner where she had dropped her canvas bag, but that particular patch of floor was empty. The hiccups coming faster, she checked behind the desk, on the other side of the file cabinet, even in the wastebasket. The notes contained factual information about vampire mythology through the ages, as well as vampires in literature, she had researched for the presentation. She could remember some of it, but would be a lot more comfortable if she had her notes.

Through the door, she could hear Alissa's introduction. Not wanting to miss any of her colleague's reading, she gave up and slipped into the back of the main room. Conner sat alone at a table near the staged area. Alissa stepped out from the shadows to the side, smiling congenially. As she sat amidst the black crepe and spider webs, Mary Kate thought she looked like a princess abandoned in a dark dungeon.

While listening, Mary Kate alternately held her breath and drank water, trying to smother the bothersome hiccups. Alissa was charming and sexy, as always. She spent little time talking, but went right into reading an ethereal, nightmarish scene from her last novel. The audience was transfixed.

". . . and he watched as the stars above the horizon melted into an ochre sky, the corpses of his victims lying about him in cold repose. Running his tongue over his teeth, he tasted the sweetness of their blood, the saltiness of their blood, rivaling the saltiness of his tears. He had fed, and once again, he was alone. Morning threatened. It was time to run."

Alissa lifted her chin and looked over the silent audience. She was beautiful and dangerous.

As if awakening from a dream, first one person then another began to clap, until the room rang with their applause. Alissa graced them with one of her lovely smiles. *She's good,* Mary Kate thought. *Better than I had thought.* She clapped louder than anyone, adding an unladylike whistle to the kudos.

As the manager introduced Theodora Zed in glowing terms, Mary Kate felt as if she were going to look like a clown in comparison. *What the heck. Let's have fun with it.* Alissa sat next to Conner. She stared ahead, shredding a paper napkin with her long, red nails.

Mary Kate lowered her head and crossed her arms, so that the billowy, black sleeves obscured her face. Allowing a moment for dramatic effect, she stepped slowly forward, toward the candlelight glowing dully through the fabric. She stopped near center stage, hoping their silence didn't indicate a lack of interest. A suspenseful beat later, she raised her head, threw out her arms, and cried, "Listen to them! The children of the night! What music they make!"

To her surprise and delight, the audience broke out into applause. Bram Stoker's *Dracula* was, as always, a hit. Going from memory, she talked about how Dracula grew from the legends of Vlad the Impaler in Romania, then spoke of other literary vamps, legends, and medical theories on the origins of the myths. By the time she had finished reading her excerpt from *A Lover's Blood*, the adrenaline was whizzing through her. She felt great, as if she really were a successful writer.

All of Alissa Dibiase's and Theodora Zed's novels sold out at the signing. As the two women sat at the table, greeting each customer and writing a personal note in their books for over an hour, Conner stood at a distance, smiling like a proud uncle. As the crowd began to thin, Mary Kate was able to do some people watching. No con vamps here. These were the urban, upper middle class, heavy on the older age range, readers of nonfiction and novels with good reviews in the *Times*. *I can't believe they're here,* she thought.

As an artsy-looking couple stepped away, she glimpsed what she thought was a familiar face. A tall woman in a wide brimmed hat and black dress dipped behind the biography shelf. A hard flintiness in her eye gave the impression that she didn't approve of the ghoulish masquerade in the back of the room. Mary Kate hadn't seen enough to place a name with the snatch of profile, so she laughed off the improbability of running into someone she knew so far from home.

Alissa checked her watch. "We have to finish up here. The television interview is in an hour."

Mary Kate smiled. "I'm ready for it."

"You were wonderful, Theo. I'm amazed that my books sold as well as they did."

"We were both wonderful, Alissa. Let's go kick some more New York butt."

The interview was short, only three minutes answering questions with the entertainment reporter on a local evening news show, but Mary Kate found it very exciting. The hiccups and missing canvas bag had become a distant memory. She was now, in her mind, the toast of the city. Though she barely had time to mention the title of her novel, she was experiencing the living dream of the mid-list, paperback writer.

Afterward, they went out to dinner at Vince and Eddie's Restaurant. Conner had left them at Food For Thought with plans to meet at Alissa's apartment for drinks at nine. Mary Kate was still so exhilarated by the day's successes that Alissa's glum demeanor disappointed her. "Smile, Alissa. This is a celebration. Today, we are the *grande dames* of death."

The answering smile was forced and fleeting. "You forget, Theo, I live here. Before the Queen of the Vampires made her Gotham debut, I was hardly noticed."

Mary Kate bit back the hollow words of protest she almost spoke automatically. It was true. Even she had no idea what a talented writer Alissa was. She had assumed Alissa wrote the same mindless fluff she did. Mary Kate knew her own work was simple entertainment; "accessible," the editors called it. Steamy sex scenes and blood-drenched murders were what her readers expected, and that's what they got, over and over, with little variation. The Theodora persona at the cons and signings had been an effective selling technique. *But, can I write?* Her mood sunk down until the two of them looked like mourners trying to eat at a wake.

When it looked as if they had picked at the food enough, Mary Kate said, "Maybe drinks aren't a good idea tonight. I've got to catch a flight before dawn. I should try to get a little sleep."

"Don't be silly, Theo. Conner would never forgive me if I didn't bring you back. He wasn't going to come to the reading until I told him you'd be here." She sighed, then smiled. The smile was not friendly. "I'm not a fool, my darling, innocent Mary Kate, but maybe you are. Conner may be sleeping with me, but he's thinking about you. I wanted him, so I got him. But don't believe for a minute I like being the consolation prize."

Again, her friendship with Conner was being muddied with something it was never meant to be. *Maybe I am a fool,* she thought. At the convention, she had believed their relationship had changed, but maybe the only change was that she had opened her eyes and had begun to see what was there all along. She spoke carefully. "Alissa, I'm not in competition with you. Whatever Conner might or might not think, I'm not involved. I think you're wrong, though. He's not the kind of man who has a relationship of convenience. I can't say there's no attraction between us, but I can say with all certainty that we both know nothing will come of it. He has the best there is with you. And, as you are my two best friends, I'm happy as hell."

Alissa brought her napkin to her eye and patted a tear. "I'm sorry. I shouldn't be picking on you, but I've been feeling like Avis to your Hertz lately. I still think he's in love with you, but perhaps, it's one of those pure and chaste loves like in a fairy tale, never to be sullied with carnal desire." She laughed sadly. "At least I've got the man capable of such feelings." She reached across the table and placed her hand over Mary Kate's. "Come back to my apartment and have a few drinks with your best friends. I promise to behave and keep any lingering jealousy to myself."

There was no way to say no. It might be weeks or months before she saw them again. Any and all bad feelings had to be vanquished tonight. "Yeah. How could I turn down an offer like that? Can I meet you back at your place? I want to change and wash my face."

"Nine o'clock, Theo, darling. Remember, we're the vampire ladies. Conner doesn't have a chance against the two of us."

Mary Kate laughed as she paid her bill. Crossing the restaurant to the door, she saw the back of a broad-brimmed, woman's hat at a corner table. *Small world,* she thought, remembering the lady with the big hat at the bookstore. Even in a city of seven million, the odds of seeing two different hats that ugly in one day were pretty astronomical. She hailed a cab out front. There was time to call her kids, as well as remove the ton of make-up from her face and get the red gook out of her hair.

The evening promised to be awkward after the frank conversation she had with Alissa, but she couldn't say to herself she was upset about Alissa's evaluation of Conner's feelings. She'd say it to Alissa, and she'd say it to Conner. But she knew better.

Chapter 9

Mary Kate hung up the phone. Still at Grandma's.

For the last few days, Chuck had gone as cold as Siberia after she'd blown it with his mother's birthday. When she had tried to explain about the missing calendar and how that might have been related to the mysterious note on her desk, he wouldn't listen. Friday evening, he had muttered something about ". . . other women understanding men." He had said it through clenched teeth, so she felt it was in her own best interest to let it pass. *I'll make nice when I get home. How mad could he be anyway?*

Some of her excitement about the events of the day returned as she looked at her own face, not Theodora's, in the hotel room mirror. Whatever Alissa had said aside, she was still looking forward to hearing Conner say how proud he was of her. What he thought mattered. Her accomplishments meant so much more when shared with someone she cared for.

The taxi driver aggressively manipulated through Broadway traffic, turning onto West Sixty-Sixth Street at Central Park West. Mary Kate had her doubts about her destination as he stopped at the walkway of an old, distinguished building, reeking of big bucks. He snarled when she asked him if he was sure this was the correct address.

She passed through the wrought iron gate and walked up the steps to the double doors, having a silly flashback to *The*

Wizard of Oz, where Dorothy and company ring the bell to the Emerald City, only to be shown the Bell Out Of Order, Please Knock sign. Not seeing a sign of any sort, she opened the door. A uniformed doorman rushed from his station to meet her.

"Good evening, ma'am. May I help you?" The gold braid on his hat and the epaulets on his shoulders were definitely of Oz quality. He frowned, but offered no explanation, as Mary Kate's eyes dropped down to the wet knees of his trousers. She hadn't had much experience with doormen, but assumed someone dressed less formally scrubbed the floors.

"Alissa Dibiase is expecting me," she said.

"Yes, apartment 2C." He checked the leatherette book in his left hand. "Your name?"

"Mary Kate Flaherty."

"Of course, Ms. Flaherty. Let me show you to the elevator."

Stepping off on the second floor, she was faced with a hall reminiscent of the many hotel corridors she'd been lost in. The light fixtures looked as if they'd been installed in the nineteen-twenties, throwing useless cones of illumination beneath each one. She walked from dark to light to dark, squinting to see the brass letters affixed to each door. With only one door for each wall, she guessed that the apartments were enormous. "Alissa must be loaded," she whispered in amazement. And, for darn sure, that money didn't come from writing paperback horror. *I could make more checking groceries at the SuperFresh.*

At the next dark corner, she came to apartment C and pressed the doorbell. As the musical chimes rang inside, she saw a bead of light along the edge of the door. Laying her hand against it, she felt it inch open.

"Hello?" Mary Kate called. The doorman could have

called up to let Alissa know she was on her way. Alissa might have been busy and left the door open for her. *Then, why isn't she answering?* She stuck her head in. "Alissa!"

A faded oriental rug lay on the marble floor of the foyer. Pen and ink line drawings of architectural ruins hung on the textured walls. Mary Kate stepped through the open French doors to the living room. Almost everything was white—the fourteen-foot high walls, the Berber rugs, the two facing sofas. The absence of color in the black-on-white artwork and the glass tables made the dots of red seem all the more incongruent.

"Alissa!" Her voice echoed through the tall, empty spaces, the cold whiteness bouncing the sound back to her, minus the emotion. She was drawn to the red, fearing what it might mean, but subconsciously relishing its color and warmth.

Moving across the thick, wool rug, she recognized the red before she reached it. Alissa's fingernail polish. Closer, she could see the still hand beyond the edge of the sofa. The red-tipped fingers dug into the deep pile.

The sudden fear drew the oxygen from her brain. Still hand on the floor. Alissa's hand. Her thoughts sluggishly clicked together. *Alissa!* She might need help. *I need to help her.* Yet the hand was so still. "Alissa?"

Mary Kate stepped closer.

A smell filled the air around the white sofa. A raw, wild, terrifying smell, a smell that shouldn't be in such a civilized place. Her instincts tugged on her, urging her to flee. She stifled a small thin cry in her throat, forcing herself to use her mind, rather than her gut, for guidance. *Fell and hit her head. Heart attack. Must help her. Get help.* A crystal lamp was overturned on the floor. *Danger!* her mind shrieked. Slowly, she circled around the sofa.

Red. Red on white. The blood filled the space between the

sofas and made bright, wet patterns on the fabric of the one that had hidden Alissa's body.

The carpet soaked up much of the blood, puddling in the intricate design. The top of the coffee table was broken. Spots and smears floated on the shards of glass. Mary Kate defensively threw her arms up to her face, but couldn't pull her eyes away from the red.

Little animal sounds of terror seeped from her as she realized she had to look away from the carnage on the lifeless furniture and down at what horrified her most. Her eyes dropped to Alissa, sprawled on the floor, the red having overtaken her.

The sleeves of her blouse were blue, her pants legs were blue denim, but her torso shimmered in grotesque contrast. The sodden cloth of her clothing was shredded, coated skin showing through the gaps. Dark, purple wounds gaped in her chest. Her head, twisted at an unnatural angle, was splashed and smudged, her black hair matted. Her eyes stared ahead in an empty gaze. Her mouth hung slack, sideways and ugly.

Alissa was not there. Only the beautiful body, now battered and brutalized, remained. But someone else had been there. A large, red shoe print marred the floor beside her head. He had stepped in Alissa's blood, then wiped it off on the rug. The repulsiveness of this offense made Mary Kate's diaphragm heave.

Alissa's neck stretched toward the floor, exposed. Mary Kate crouched down, feeling the screams pummeling her chest for release, but wanting to know, needing to know one last thing before she let her terror loose. The skin was covered in blood, but looking closer, she could see. Two tiny holes, darker than the surrounding red.

Moaning, she backed away, the stench of death in her nose and mouth, the silence of death stopping up her ears. She stumbled through the French doors to the foyer, then through the open door to the darkness of the hall. A tall figure stepped from the shadows. She screamed.

"Mary Kate! It's me! Conner!"

She screamed again, backing down the hall, her knees trembling, her heart beating wild and irregular.

He reached out to her. "Come here, Mary Kate. Come to me."

She turned and threw herself into the dark, light, dark of the hallway, pumping her knees. She couldn't feel her feet touching the floor.

Conner called after her. "Don't run from me, Mary Kate!"

His footsteps thumped on the carpet behind her. She looked over her shoulder and saw his face appear, then disappear, a monster in strobe lights. Her breath pulled raggedly through her lungs. A knife. *Was that a knife in his hand?* She turned the corner and saw another corridor just like the last one. They were all the same. Another corner, another hall. No way out.

"Mary Kate! Stop!"

He was getting closer. She was running slower. She screamed again, willing her legs to move, please God, move, faster, faster! Feeling as if she could faint from the pressure inside her head and chest, she ran into a door, and squinting at the brass plate, read the word, Stairs. She flung it open, crossed the landing, and fell down the first five steps. Ignoring the pain in her knees, she scrambled downward in the inadequate light, crying out, then clapping her hand over her face as the door above banged open once more.

The door at the bottom opened onto a hall with a linoleum floor smelling of disinfectant. A few yards up on the right, Mary Kate saw another door. Falling through it, she entered the lobby. The doorman looked up from his magazine on the counter.

"Help me!" Mary Kate screamed, then hearing the stairwell door slam, ran towards him. "Help me, dear God, please!"

"What? What?" the doorman stuttered, trying to pull her away from him.

She clung to his betassled coat, tears streaming from her eyes. "He's coming! Help me!"

Conner burst into the lobby, his face flushed, his hair fanned over his brow. The doorman stepped back. Mary Kate screamed.

Wiping his nose with his fist, Conner stood, catching his breath. "Mary Kate," he said between gasps, "why are you running from me? What's wrong?"

She hid behind the doorman. "Alissa, Alissa," was all she could say.

"I'm calling the cops," the doorman said.

Conner moved toward them, and she whimpered.

"What about Alissa? Is she hurt? Talk to me, Mary Kate. Should I go check on her?"

The doorman shook a trembling finger at him. "You stay right there, buddy, until the cops get here. Don't you move."

Conner pressed the button for the elevator. Mary Kate burst into wracking sobs, the doorman patting her shoulder until the police arrived.

A blue uniformed officer stood beside Mary Kate as she sat in the doorman station chair, watching the detectives talk to Conner on the other side of the lobby. What seemed like scores of criminal investigation professionals had disappeared into the elevator, on their way up to apartment 2C. One of them had come down and collected Conner's shoes in a plastic bag. Mary Kate was physically tired and emotionally wrung out, but whenever she closed her eyes, she saw red.

By the time the first of the police officers had come through the front double doors, she had managed to get her crying under control. Though she wouldn't go near Conner or speak to him, he had ceased to look dangerous. He seemed hurt and helpless and confused as he stood alone across the room from her. She began to feel as if she had been mistaken about him. But the knife? *Did he have a knife?* She really wasn't sure she had seen one. He was hiding outside the door. Or standing outside the door, wondering why it was open. Even these things didn't negate the most damning evidence she had. Conner had been in Atlanta. And now, he was here in New York.

"Mrs. Flaherty, I'd like to talk with you a few minutes." In his brown suit and round glasses, the man could have been an accountant, but he took her back to Atlanta for a momentary flash. Cold, predatory eyes. A hunter. A homicide detective. He was trying to appear sympathetic to her grief and trauma, but his eyes betrayed him. He would say or do anything to catch the murderer. She was just a piece of the puzzle. "I'm Detective Malone. I realize you're still upset, but I'd like for you to tell me what happened."

Conner watched her from the other side of the lobby. She wasn't ready to talk to him yet. The terror of his pursuit of her through the halls was still too fresh. She felt so alone.

"Mrs. Flaherty?"

"Oh. Yes. Alissa invited Conner and me up for drinks, and . . ."

"Together?"

"What? No, I came alone. I arrived about nine o'clock, and when I got there, the door was open. Open a crack. Then I went in and found . . ." *Red. Red and white.* "I found . . ." The sobs broke through, and though she could hear the detective speaking, the words were meaningless. Through the torrent of her tears, she heard her name spoken.

"Mary Kate?"

"Conner!" She reached out to him, and he wrapped his arms around her. She buried her face in his chest and cried.

"I didn't mean to scare you," he said. "I'm sorry. I'm so sorry." He held her, stroking her hair, until the crying slowed to soft snuffles.

"Mrs. Flaherty," Detective Malone said, "I'd like the two of you to come to the precinct and give a formal statement." He turned as the double doors burst open, and a uniformed officer came in holding the elbow of a thin, teenaged boy.

"This young fella might've seen something at the time the doorman was away from the lobby," the officer said. The boy rolled his eyes and smirked, as if being dragged about by the police was his cross to bear in life. "He says he seen the kids throwing mud out back, and the doorman coming out to yell at 'em."

Malone walked up to the boy. "What did you see?"

"Like he said, man."

"What else?"

"Nothin' much. I left and went back up on Sixty-Sixth, you know, and I seen this guy."

"You saw that the doorman was behind the building away from his post, and you went around front, just to watch the front door for him like a good citizen, right?"

"Somethin' like that, man."

Malone shook his head and gave the cop a sideways grin. "Tell me about the guy."

The boy brightened up. The spotlight was off him. "Sure, man. It was an old mother. Fat guy with gray hair. An artist."

"Why do you say he was an artist?"

"He's all dressed in black, man, wearing one of them,

what-do-you-call-em, turtlenecks, and a hat, artist's hat, uh, uh . . ."

"Beret?"

"Yeah, that's it! And he watching out back, too, then he comes around and goes up the stairs and sort of peeks in. Then, he went in the lobby, and I didn't see him no more."

Malone looked over to Mary Kate. "Did you see anybody like that?"

"No. I don't remember seeing anybody."

"You?" he asked the doorman.

"No, just those kids throwing mud at the rear door. I was only gone a minute," he pleaded. "And I couldn't leave it like that. The tenants would be after my hide. But I only took a minute to hose it off."

"Sure, sure, bud. How were you to know you were letting a murderer in?"

Malone waved to the officers and other detectives. "Let's take the whole bunch down. See what we can get."

Four hours later, Mary Kate trudged, bleary-eyed, down the steps of the station house of the Midtown Precinct. Conner sat in a metal chair, his legs crossed, showing the dusty bottom of his sock. She smiled weakly. "How long have you been here?"

"Not long. Are you ready to go?"

She nodded. "And I never want to come back. This place stinks of cigars and burned coffee. What time is it?"

"Four-thirty. You're going to miss your flight."

"I've got a room at the Ramada. You?"

"No, I was going to stay with . . ." He looked down.

Her heart went out to him. "Let's go back to my hotel and get coffee. Drinkable coffee. I have to talk to you. I saw something."

Chapter 10

Night was losing sway to gray cotton morning as they arrived at the Ramada. The restaurant wouldn't open for breakfast for another two hours. Conner and Mary Kate went up to her room and ordered coffee from room service. Sitting on either side of the wood grain melamine table, they nursed their mugs in silence. Mary Kate gripped hers in her hands as if to warm them, though the room was dry, hot, and stuffy. The steam under her nose moistened the bottom of her face.

"You should sleep," Conner said softly.

"Can't. I don't want to close my eyes."

He nodded. He knew as well as she what's on the back of your eyelids after you've found a body.

Mary Kate blinked her eyes against a wave of loss and sadness. Alissa was now the body. "I have to tell you something," she said in almost a whisper. "I don't think the police know yet, but they will soon. It's the same, Conner. Same as Atlanta. I looked." She remembered the tiny, dark holes as deep, red eyes, glaring at her. "The Vampire Killer. He was here."

What little color was left in Conner's face after the stressful evening drained away. "The fork holes in the neck? I didn't see . . ."

"I looked close. They were small, but they were there. Detective Malone didn't ask me about them. Everything else imaginable, but not that. They must not know yet, but when they do, we're going to find ourselves connected to two identical murders."

Conner ran his hands over his face as if he were trying to mold what he had heard into something comprehensible.

She went on. "The artist must be the same person as the caped guy at the con. I told the police about a woman in a black hat who might have been following Alissa and me. She was at Food For Thought, then again at the restaurant where we had dinner. She was big, so it could have been a man disguised as a woman."

He dropped his hands. "Then you can identify this person?"

"No. I never saw her face."

"And you didn't tell the police about the murder in Atlanta?"

She shook her head. "Did you?"

He shook his head. They sat quietly with their thoughts a few minutes longer. It could have been her overwhelming tiredness, but Mary Kate felt as if she were tangled in a sticky, black spider's web. She had fallen into it unintentionally, and now, all there was left to do was sit back and wait for the spider to arrive for supper.

Conner banged his fist on the table, rattling the cups. Mary Kate jumped back in her seat with a start.

"Who the hell is doing this?" he shouted. "Who would want to kill Alissa?" Tears filled his eyes. "Why would anyone want to kill Alissa?"

Mary Kate began to stand and go to him, but he waved her away, wiping his tears on his sleeve.

"No. I'm okay."

She gave him a moment to collect himself before she spoke. "Maybe there's less coincidence to this than we could imagine."

"What do you mean?" He pulled a handkerchief from his

pocket and wiped his nose.

"Well, what do we know? Each involved a person dressed in black, probably the killer. Randall Valentine and Alissa are . . . were both writers. Horror writers. Okay, uh, you and I were both around at the time. Who else?"

"Michael," Conner said, his voice low. "Michael Kazdin. He lives near her. He was at BloodCon." He sat forward as if he was really onto something. "And didn't he go weird after the first murder? More than you would expect? Damn, Mary Kate, think about it. Michael's career has been on the skids lately, everybody knows that. And everybody knows Walter wasn't going to hang onto him as dead weight much longer. Maybe he cracked. Maybe . . ."

"Whoa, stop! Let's not jump to conclusions." Mary Kate held up her hands as a yellow shaft of morning light shot across the table from the window, a signal for the nightmares to creep back into their corners. The time for reality had come. Mary Kate knew they were in no shape to rationally evaluate anything after a sleepless night of fear and mayhem. "I don't know about you, but I'm too tired to think clearly. Let's see what else we know, okay?"

"You're right. I know you're right. But, it does fit, doesn't it? You did know that Alissa was dropping her agent and signing on with Walter Truesdale."

"No. No, she didn't tell me." *I knew nothing about Alissa,* she thought. *What do I really know about Conner?* His suspiciousness was contagious.

"She wasn't happy with the way her interests were being handled and thought she had a good chance at a mainstream audience. Walter thought so, too."

Alissa's reading had demonstrated her talent. She had that little bit more that separated her from the rest of the paperback hacks. That's what people had been saying about

Randall Valentine, too. What had Donna told her? "Conner, the Valentine boy was going with Truesdale. Donna Brooks told me in the ladies' room at the con."

Conner stared. "You're kidding." He must not have really believed a word he'd been saying about Michael. "You're kidding," he said again.

"It doesn't seem real, does it?" she said, then, pausing in the grip of revelation, smacked her hand against her forehead. A chill shuddered through her, a cold blast of recognition. "Oh, holy cow! Oh, no, this is too scary!"

She stood and paced across the floor, her arms wrapped around her chest.

Conner walked over to her, touching her elbow. "What, Mary Kate?"

"Notes," she said. "One in Atlanta, right after the murder. Another, two days ago at home. Somebody had gotten into my house and left a note on my desk."

"What kind of note?"

"I didn't pay much attention to the first one. I thought it was some kind of inside joke I'd missed. It said, 'Is it real yet?' The second one scared the bejesus out of me. It said, 'It's not real yet, is it?' "

"It's not real yet, is it," Conner repeated back to himself. "Does it mean anything to you?"

"No. Nothing. But he was in my house, Conner. In my house while I was gone." Another frightening thought struck her. "He knew when I'd be gone! Somebody's watching me! And killing other people!"

"For now," he said. "Mary Kate, I think you're in danger. Like you said, it can't all be coincidence. I think we should call Detective Malone and tell him about Atlanta and the notes."

She didn't want to go back to the police station. Hours

more of questions laced with suspicion and innuendo. Hours more of sitting in a hard chair, breathing rancid air, and remembering every little detail of what she most wanted to forget. There was going to be publicity. Once the connection had been made between the two murders, the headlines would almost write themselves. *Horror Writer Held For Questioning In Second Vampire Slaying.* It was going to happen eventually, so why speed up the process? "Can we wait? I'm so tired. If I could rest a bit first, then I could handle it, but I'm just not up to it yet. And I want to call home. They'll be getting up soon, and the kids might worry when they realize I'm not there."

Conner's face was pinched with indecision. She knew as well as he did that calling the police was the right thing to do. But he was drained and exhausted, too. She hoped he would see how badly she didn't want to do this now.

"Okay. Two hours, that's all, Mary Kate. I'm going to go out and try to find some shoes. You lock your door up tight. Don't let anybody in. Okay?"

"Nobody, but you."

He almost smiled.

After a shower and fresh clothes, Mary Kate felt ready to call home. Chuck would be angry, as usual. David and Ben, such good Hebrew names for little Irish Catholic boys, would be concerned. She dialed and listened to the tinny ring inside the receiver. Ring. Ring. Six, seven times. Ring. Thirteen, fourteen. *They're not home.* She hung up. Chuck did it again. For all his whining about how he has to take care of everything while she's away, he could be counted on to take off for his mother's house where all three would be treated as royal dignitaries. She raspberried the phone.

Sleepiness had been filling her head until she felt as if she were becoming transparent and would soon disappear altogether. She lay down on the bed, and her head pounded from surprise at being given what it had wanted for hours.

Within moments, she drifted away.

Randall Valentine, wearing his green turtleneck and a nasty sneer, emerged from a red fog. "So, you're the Queen of the Vampires," he said before sinking back. He drifted forward again, whispering, "Serious writers are ignored because we aren't appealing to the prurient interests of the lowest common denominator."

Alissa came out of the blood smoke next. Her smile was the one that Mary Kate could never quite figure out. "Is there . . . something . . . between you and Conner?" she asked. Her face disappeared a moment, then returned. "He had a couple of appearances planned in Washington bookstores, so he was going to give you a call to get together for lunch or something. Or so he told me." Engulfed once again, Alissa's voice echoed in the red. "Remember, we're the vampire ladies. Conner doesn't have a chance against the two of us."

Smokey, black clouds drew in from all around, replacing the red with night. A cool breeze blew against Mary Kate's cheek. A distant light caught her eye. She stood on the sidewalk outside of the Corinthian Hotel, a few yards from the parking lot. A tall, hooded figure slowly floated toward her.

She knew without seeing that a knife was hidden by the sleeves of the black cape. His movements were unnaturally slow, and she wanted to run, wanted to run now, but she couldn't. She was frozen, watching him, knowing who was there, not wanting to know. *No! Stop! Get away!* She screamed in her head, but was unable to utter a sound. *It's real! It's real! Okay? Stop!* The specter hovered above the ground within an arm's reach. He lifted his left hand

and threw off the hood.

Conner stood before her, the cape gone, a black turtleneck and jeans in its place. He wore a ridiculous wool beret over his fuzzy, gray hair. In one hand, he held a serrated carving knife, in the other, a two-pronged dinner fork. He smiled, and she could see white, razor-sharp canines arching over his lower teeth. Mary Kate screamed and screamed in her head, and was barely able to hear the voice beside her.

"Theo, darling."

Mary Kate wrenched her eyes away from the Conner-beast and turned. Alissa, wearing a long, black dress and a wide-brimmed hat, stood beside her. She was as beautiful as always as she daubed at the blood smears on her face with a black lace handkerchief.

"Theo, he had some appearances in Washington book-stores, so he was going to meet you for lunch or something. Or so he told me."

"Who? Conner?"

"No, silly." It was good hearing her laughter again. "Michael."

"Michael," Mary Kate said to herself. Conner and Alissa had disappeared. She sat in her office in front of the computer. She heard a soft meow and turned to see Lestat sitting at the door. "You must be hungry," she said.

The cat spoke angrily. "The least you could do was feed the damn cat!"

Mary Kate awoke with a cry dying on her lips, her heart racing. She sat up suddenly, taking in her surroundings, trying to remember where she was and why. The room at the Ramada was flooded with sunlight. *New York City. Alissa is dead. I remember.*

She got out of bed and walked over to the table to see if

there was any coffee left in the carafe. Empty. Pacing back across the room, she looked down. "Oh, no."

A plain, white, business-size envelope lay on the floor just inside the door. No stamp. No address.

She looked at the door. Her macabre pen pal had stood inches away on the other side. Her fear compressed and exploded into anger. "How dare you?" she shouted at the door. The phantom might be standing there listening, but she wasn't quite brave enough to check for sure.

Picking up the envelope by the edges with the tips of her fingers, she smiled grimly. "Evidence." If there was a finger-print to be found, she wasn't going to be the one to smudge it. Carefully, she lifted out the folded sheet of paper.

IS IT REAL YET?

"Yes, damn it. It's real."

Chapter 11

The door erupted into loud rapping. Mary Kate stumbled backwards, the letter fluttering from her fingertips onto the floor. Her imagination fed her a film clip from *The Shining*—Jack Nicholson leering through the axed-out hole, announcing, "Here's Johnny!"

"Who is it?" she called out tremulously. *Is that what Alissa said before she opened the door to . . . who? A friend?*

"It's me! Conner!" came through, muffled.

She stepped quietly to the peephole. Yes, it was Conner. No, he wasn't wearing a beret. He had run a comb through his thick, brown hair, but his chin was scruffy with dark whiskers. *I should let him in,* she thought, her hand moving toward the latch.

Her hand stopped. He could be the one. She didn't really know him that well. Two or three conventions a year. A phone call, now and again. He had been terribly angry with Valentine for giving her a hard time at BloodCon. And Alissa had believed she was just a poor substitute for the person Conner really wanted. Was murder the only way he could resist her charms? Mary Kate peeped at him again. *He looks so sweet and concerned.* The motivation for murder was pretty flimsy.

"Mary Kate, are you okay?"

"Yes!"

"Are you going to let me in?"

"I don't know!"

He turned and looked down the hall, rubbing his chin. Mary Kate's fingers danced over the lock, wanting to open the door for him, but resisting in deference to an interior voice of warning. Randall Valentine might have been bush-whacked, but all Alissa had to do was open a door. Mary Kate's memory of the outcome was as fresh as the blood she had seen on Alissa's face.

"Mary Kate!" he called. "I'll meet you at the police station! Do you know how to get there?"

"Yeah! Midtown North!"

"Good girl! I'm leaving now!" Through the tiny, grimy hole, she could see him smile. "You're one smart lady, Mary Kate Flaherty!" He moved out of the peephole's range.

She smiled. *He just wants me safe.*

The smile faded. *Or, he's waiting for me to come out.* Figuring the worse that could happen was that she'd look stupid, she called down to the front desk. "Hi, this is Mary Kate Flaherty in Room 337. I'm leaving my room now to come down to the lobby. If I don't show up in the next five minutes, could you send someone up to check on me?"

Conner was waiting in the interrogation room with Homicide Detective Malone and another, Detective Ambrose. Mary Kate passed on a cup of the scorched motor oil that served as coffee.

"Okay, Mr. Drake," Malone said, "she's here now. What do you have to tell us?"

Conner ran his hands through his hair, pulled on his earlobe, and rubbed his chin. Mary Kate couldn't stand the suspense, so she blurted out, "Have you heard of the Vampire Killer of Atlanta?"

Both detectives' eyes popped wide, but Ambrose recovered first, leaning his elbow on the table. "Yeah. So what?"

"He's here. We know. We were there."

Like a good collaboration, Mary Kate and Conner told the police the story, one picking up when the other's narrative flagged, filling in essential details, keeping it taut and exciting, but always consistent. The differences in their writing styles showed as Conner tried to maintain a low-key build-up of suspense, while Mary Kate preferred broad melodrama. Questions from the detectives interrupted the flow, but both handled it like pros. The only problem remaining after two hours was that the story had no ending.

Malone looked tired. He had sent Ambrose to the morgue to check Alissa's body for puncture wounds on the neck. "So, you think this guy Kazdin did it?"

Conner said, "Yes," as Mary Kate said, "No."

Conner pressed his lips together and rubbed his whiskery chin. "Mary Kate, everything points to Michael. You just told us he was in Washington and had an opportunity to leave that letter at your house. That cinches it for me."

"No, it's too flimsy," she said. "Almost as flimsy as . . ." *The case against Conner?* "Why would he kill Valentine and Alissa? Because they were going with Walter Truesdale? Why not knock off some of Truesdale's more successful clients? If he really wanted to eliminate the competition, why not Stephen King or Dean Koontz?"

"King and Koontz didn't betray him," Malone said.

"Revenge," Conner whispered. Mary Kate didn't like the look in his eyes.

Conner and Mary Kate agreed to stay in the city for another day. Malone would be bringing in Michael Kazdin for an interview, and the Atlanta Police Department was sending one of its investigators to New York to compare notes. The NYPD kept the IS IT REAL YET? note and envelope, though the chance of lifting fingerprints from it was slim. A police car dropped them off at the Ramada in the middle of a sunny, Sunday afternoon. Conner was able to get a room for the night.

"See you for dinner?" he asked outside her door. She had been looking into his face all day, trying to find a trace of the malice it would require to mutilate two human beings so horrifically. Does anyone really look like a killer?

"I've been lucky, Conner," she said. "I'm thirty-six years old, and I've never had any violence in my life. No one's ever hit me or even threatened to. I've never been mugged or had my purse stolen. I've never even been yelled at very much. The problems I've had are all comparatively blasé."

He reached out and touched her hair. "That's good. That's the way it should be."

"Yes, I know. But why do I write about violence and death? Is there some kind of balance that needs to be maintained? Are we basically blood-thirsty creatures, seeking mayhem vicariously when we've been blessed with a peaceful life?"

His hand dropped onto her shoulder. "No, Mary Kate. I don't believe that at all. You're intelligent and creative. That's all. And who says all violence is physical? A person's heart can be ripped out with a word."

She spoke softly. "Has your life been peaceful, Conner?" She wanted to know him better, more than a con-buddy. He had a whole past of which she knew nothing, a childhood, a youth, of which he'd never spoken.

His eyes shifted down the hall as if he were watching a memory unfold there. His thumb rubbed her shoulder blade, an unconscious motion. He blinked, then looked down at his newly-acquired shoes. "Not always." Clearing his throat, he stepped way. He wouldn't tell her about it now, but a door had been opened.

"Is eight good for dinner?" she asked.

He nodded, then walked away, waving his arm. *He's a lonely man,* she thought, and felt very lonely herself.

Another call home was fruitless. *Grandma must be laying it on thick to keep them this long.* As she put down the receiver, the phone rang under her hand. She picked it up, hoping it was Chuck. "Hello."

"Is this Theodora Zed?"

"Uh, yeah."

"This is Kristin from Food For Thought. We found something we think belongs to you. Did you lose a canvas tote full of books and papers?"

"Yes! Where was it?"

"I'm sorry, Miss Zed. I don't know how this happened, but it was stuffed in a trash can in the alley outside the kitchen door."

"Trash can?" Who would put something like that in the garbage? One person had a reason.

"Miss Zed?"

"Oh, uh, Kristin, could you have somebody bring it here and leave it at the desk?"

"Sure. No problem."

Mary Kate hung up slowly. Maybe it wasn't Alissa. It probably wasn't Alissa. It would have been a childish thing to do. *She'd said she was Avis to my Hertz. Was this how she tried harder?* Mary Kate had a difficult time picturing the beautiful and graceful Alissa Dibiase checking to see if the coast was clear before stealing away with the bag. She had seemed too high-class for something as cheesy as stuffing the notes of her supposed competition into a trashcan. *But if she felt threatened enough* . . . This only muddied her thoughts more. She couldn't imagine anyone feeling threatened by Mary Kate Flaherty of Edgewater, Maryland.

After a nap in which the dreams were dark and surreal, but mercifully unremembered, Mary Kate awoke to dusky shadows. It was almost eight. She could try calling home one more time before dinner. The phone rang a half-ring, and David answered.

"Hi, sweetie. Where've you been? At Grandma's?"

"It's Mom," he said away from the phone. A brief shuffling as the receiver was passed, then she heard Chuck's voice.

"Are you coming home or not?" he said flatly.

"Chuck, something's happened. Alissa . . ."

"Yeah, yeah. Save it, Mary Kate. I don't even want to know."

Her fist squeezed tighter on the receiver as her own anger simmered. There would be no opportunity to explain. She had been tried and convicted *in absentia*. She wondered what he had been saying about her to her children. "I'll be home tomorrow, if I can. You'll have to get the boys off to school."

She heard his teeth grind. He didn't care if she was safe or well, only that she wasn't what he wanted her to be. His seething came through loud and clear. "Fine," he barked, then hung up.

Mary Kate roared her frustration and threw the telephone, clanging and ringing, onto the floor. She stomped her foot and looked around for something else to throw. Conner's voice, accompanied by pounding, came through the door across the room. "Oh, no," she muttered.

"Mary Kate! Open the door!"

She opened it onto a man frightened and ready to fight.

"I'm okay, I'm okay," she said.

"I heard . . ."

She blushed. "That was me," she said sheepishly, glancing over to the phone on the carpet. "I was throwing a temper tantrum."

"You . . . okay, sure. You're overdue for one." He leaned on the doorframe, the adrenaline surge having apparently exhausted him.

"Do you want to come in and sit for a moment?" she asked.

"No." He smiled. "You scared ten years off me."

"I'm sorry. I was just so mad." She broke into a smile herself. He had a way of making her feel she was fine just the way she was. More than fine. That he preferred her the way she was. She ran a hand through her hair and realized it was still sticking out all over from her nap. It didn't matter that she wasn't gorgeous, even though he was good-looking, in a guy-next-door sort of way. If Alissa's perceptions had been correct, then he loved her with all of her faults.

"Mary Kate . . ." Conner stepped into the room and closed the door behind him.

As he moved toward her, she realized what she had been really considering. She put her hand on his chest, stopping him as he came near. "No, Conner." She didn't know what to say next. It was never supposed to become this immediate, this real. "I can't."

"Then you know how I feel."

Alissa had been right. And Mary Kate knew this wasn't a big surprise. She had known, at least since BloodCon. "I can't," she said again.

"Because you love Chuck?" He stood stiffly like a defendant awaiting a verdict.

"Because I'm married to Chuck," she said, hearing the

implications of her words after they had passed her lips. She saw hope leap into his eyes.

"Then you . . ." he began, but she cut him off.

"Don't, Conner. I don't know anything! I don't know how I feel!" Tears began to fill her vision. She trembled with fear. This wasn't supposed to happen. She was married, for better or worse, till death do us part.

"I didn't mean to upset you. I . . ."

She snuffled and cleared her eyes with her sleeve. This had to stop. "You better go, Conner."

His face filled with hurt, and it broke her heart to see him like that. Some part of her, a dreamy, carefree nugget of self buried beneath fifteen years of marriage, believed that asking him to stay would be the best thing she could do for herself. But commitment, family, and responsibility were more than words to her. They were who she was. To deny them was unthinkable.

He stood looking at her as she looked at him, both knowing that the secret had been spoken, and there was no way to hide it again. They were no longer just friends, and couldn't hold up the pretense between themselves. Mary Kate began grieving for the relationship that had been a bright spot in her life, which was now wrong and impossible to continue.

"I'm sorry," Conner said quietly. He turned away from her and opened the door. After a moment's hesitation, he left. Mary Kate stood rooted until the sorrow permeated every bone in her body, then fell onto the bed and cried.

Hunger overtook her emotional misery, and she went out in search of her first meal since she had dinner with Alissa the night before. Not wanting to risk running into Conner at the hotel restaurant, she inquired at the front desk about a place whose service was quick and dirty. The clerk directed her to a deli on the next block. She stopped at the door leading onto the nighttime street swamped yellow by streetlights. *He did say turn right at the corner, didn't he?* Turning back and spotting Conner entering the lobby, she quickly pushed out the door.

The remnants of a light rain earlier in the evening had given the city an oily smell. The warm air held the heavy dampness. Breathing it was like inhaling through a wet towel. Mary Kate hurried down the sidewalk, feeling like a mugger's dream, depressed, distracted, without a lick of city smarts.

She knew she was a child of the suburbs. Houses lined along the streets in neat rows, schools and malls close enough to be convenient, but not close enough to cause traffic problems. Excitement was a grease fire in a neighbor's kitchen. Crime was a bunch of teenagers leaving beer cans and condoms in the middle school parking lot over the weekend. Tragedy was the occasional heart attack death of a husband who put in seventy-hour workweeks to buy the dream house in the burbs. What did she know from murder?

I kill in my mind every day. Once again, she wondered where her bloodthirsty tendencies came from. Her childhood had been ordinary. She had been an ordinary child. She was sure there were no repressed traumas lurking about, though she always had this feeling that she was suffocating. Most of the time, she had done what she was supposed to do, was expected do, working against the current inside her. Her parents had been kept happy, as were the nuns at St. Joseph's Parochial School, then later, Holy Redeemer High School. She had been thoroughly socialized by the time she reached young womanhood. No wonder Chuck thought he had found the girl of his dreams, rather than the girl who dreamed of ghouls.

By luck, she noticed the scent of salami tinting the humid

air and looked up to see the deli wedged between a pawnshop and an adult bookstore. She leaned into the door, and her hungry stomach lurched in both desire and disgust at the rich, meaty odors. The restaurant was hot despite the whirring, clanking fan of the grease-coated air conditioner behind the counter. She shuffled along with the customers waiting to place their orders. Facing a paper-capped old man who seemed too busy to deal with browsers, she ordered a chicken salad sandwich and a ginger ale, wishing she had the option of a plate of fresh fruit instead.

The small table and chair closest to the music of the air conditioner were available. She sat, listening to the rhythmic clanking. There was fresh fruit in her kitchen at home. Home. Her children were there, the loves of her life. And then, there was Chuck. Her husband, till death do us part. He had been the love of her life once. She had been a freshman studying elementary education at the University of Maryland. He had been a junior in the Business Department. Love at age eighteen was easy. If you dated long enough, you assumed you must be in love. If you're in love, you have sex. If you have sex, you have to be in love, right? Those are the rules.

Chuck graduated and went to work for Rightway Insurance. A year later, Mary Kate dropped out and joined him at Rightway. He was an agent. She was the receptionist. It was great, just like playing grown-up. It was time to get married. Everyone was happy. The proper path was being followed. A house was bought. A child was conceived. The children pumped so much life into Mary Kate as she enjoyed them full-time for a few years; she lost the oppressive suffocation until they started school. When Chuck said he could get her a job at Rightway, she knew she couldn't do it. She was too old to play house. She needed some room to breathe.

And she had been having these strange ideas stirring

around in her head. She began to write them down.

And when she wrote, it was like sucking on a tank of oxygen.

After a few false steps of truly crappy writing, she stopped and backed up. She read what others were writing. She studied how they did it. She learned the basics, then tried again. After fourteen rejections, her first novel was bought. For the first time in her life, she felt free. And she felt most alive when she wrote about death.

Chuck hated it. He wanted his Barbie Doll back.

He hates me.

"Chicken salad up!"

Mary Kate blinked her eyes, surprised at finding herself sitting in a stinky New York deli, sweat dribbling down her sides, her head thumping to the tune of the blower blade of the worthless air conditioner. The guy with the paper cap glared at her. "Chicken salad, lady!"

"Yeah, okay. Wrap it to go." She fumbled in her purse for her wallet. *I have to get home. He's alone with my babies.* She tossed the cash on the counter and grabbed the drippy bag. She ran out without waiting for change.

Chapter 12

Thoughts tumbled through her head as she fled onto the street. *Chuck hates me. Chuck hates ME! But how much? Does he hate me enough to send me those notes? No, no, no. I got one here. He's in Maryland. Could he arrange to have someone else deliver it? Sure. No. That's too bizarre. This whole thing is bizarre. I've got to get home to my kids.*

A portion of the seven million of New York flowed around her as she moved along the sidewalk, relying on dumb faith that she had taken the right direction back to the Ramada. She didn't really believe Chuck was involved, but the tiniest of possibilities that her children were in the care of a murderer was enough. She had to get home.

Mary Kate slowed her pace and smoothed her hair as she approached the motel's front door. A phone call or two, and she'd be out on the next flight to Baltimore in no time. David and Ben would be asleep in their beds. She touched her lips as she imagined leaning over them and kissing their cool brows.

A hand clamped roughly onto her upper arm, and before she could register her fright, she stumbled as she was dragged around the corner of the building. Another hand slapped over her mouth as she began to scream. Her eyes darting back and forth, she saw potential rescuers recede as she stepped back with the strong figure behind her. The scents of after-shave and soap filled her nose. He was a tidy kidnapper.

He pushed her against the brick wall and stood in front of her. She felt a strange mixture of dread and relief. "Michael!"

Even in the shadow of the wall, she could sense his rage.

"What are you doing to me?" His fist was balled up by her face as he tried to keep his voice under control. "Why are you doing this?"

Mary Kate's eyes were glued to the fist, inches from her face. He lowered it, and she dared to speak. "What did I do?"

"What did you do?" He laughed and hit himself in the head with the fist. The crazy smile dropped, and he grit his teeth. "You talked about me. To the police. You told them I killed Randall and Alissa."

"I didn't!"

"They said you did! For six hours, I've been accounting for my every movement for the last two months. If the damn lawyer hadn't shown up, I'd still be in there. Why, Theo?"

Michael was dressed in black slacks, turtleneck, and jacket. No beret, but a good outfit for lurking around dark motel alleys. The gray in his hair had grown out more than she had ever seen it before, wide swathes shooting from his temples. "Michael, they questioned me for hours, too. They asked for names of people who knew both victims. I don't know who's doing the killing. I don't know why. What do Alissa and Randall have in common other than writing horror?"

"Walter Truesdale," he said without hesitation.

She hadn't expected an answer, but it was the same one she and Conner had come up with. "The rumors were true, then? Walter had talked to both of them about signing with him?"

Michael looked surprised. "You knew about that? Alissa told me, but only because it gave her so much pleasure to pour vinegar in my wounds. Walter called her a few days ago. I remember thinking that it finally paid off for her."

"What finally paid off?"

"Murdering Randall. I mean, who else had a motive? Then, when she was killed . . ."

"You thought Alissa killed Randall?"

"Or had him killed. She's rich enough. Walter was going to make one writer the next Michael Kazdin. Alissa or Randall. He chose Randall. Alissa tried to buy Randall off, but again she was frustrated to learn that her money couldn't buy a writing career. Then when Randall was murdered, Walter assumed I did it. He's been threatening to tell the police if I don't drop the lawsuit I have against him."

"Blackmail?"

Michael nodded. "Walter had been skimming my royalties for years, but after the divorce I couldn't afford it anymore. When I confronted him with it, he said he'd ruin me and replace me. He was true to his word. Now, all I have left is my name, and if that's connected to a murder investigation, I'll have nothing."

"I'm so sorry, Michael, but if you have nothing to do with the murders . . ."

His anger returned. "Does the press care about truth? I'll be branded Michael Kazdin, murder suspect, long after the real killer is caught. Books are bought on an emotional whim. Contracts are signed based on the public's passing fancy. I'll be paraded about on the evening news as the Vampire Killer, and my name on the cover of a book will pique the curiosity of the morbid few and repulse all others. What have you done to me?"

He leaned over her, and she could see the tears of desperation in his eyes. She understood his fear, but she stood under the same cloud of suspicion, and could just as easily be subjected to the inevitable media frenzy. "I didn't do it to you, Michael, so back off! This is going to be hard for all of us. I'm a suspect, too, but the police wouldn't have let us go if they thought for a second either one of us was the killer. And as far as I know, we both fit the profile of the next victim. So, if we can do anything to help them catch this guy, we'd better do it. There's a lot more at stake here than our names."

Michael leaned back against the wall beside her, exhaling in resignation. His voice was quiet. "I've been so afraid." He sighed, and they stood in the dark for a moment, breathing the warm, damp air. Mary Kate thought about the nastiness of a business that engendered such paranoia.

"Well," Michael almost whispered, "I guess Conner's off the hook."

"Conner?"

"Yes. Alissa didn't live long enough to suck him dry like she did me."

I don't know anything about these people. Mary Kate wondered if she really knew anyone. Her gut told her to let it be, but she knew she had to ask. The only way the identity of the killer was going to remain concealed was under a cloak of secrets. The only way he would be revealed was by looking below the facades until the madness surrounding his heart was exposed. "What happened?"

"Alissa and I had an affair." He seemed eager to talk about it, as if he knew, too, that the time for pseudo-intimacy was past. "I knew it was wrong. Phyllis found out about it, as she had so many of the others. But this time, I thought I . . . I was in love with Alissa. I thought she loved me, at least, I suspected. You know Alissa. She never quite said what she meant.

"She was a vampire, Theo. After she finished with me, I had no blood left." He took a deep breath. "She wanted to be a writer, and she was. A very good writer, eventually. She went through what we all endured starting out: the rejections, the despondency, the anger and fear. As her writing improved, she became less patient with a business in which success has little correlation to talent and effort. She was able to get the small paperback contracts, but after two years, she felt she wasn't making progress. She almost lost that when she tried unsuccessfully to bribe an editor at Doubleday.

"No one could prove anything, so all that was left in the air were the rumors about her. Having failed to get what she wanted using her money, she decided to trot out her other most valuable asset." His sad laugh sounded more like a cough. "I think I was her first victim. Selected, I'm sure, for my known weakness for beautiful women and because my agent was Walter Truesdale. One night with Alissa, and I was at Truesdale's door, falling all over myself about the hot new bestseller I'd discovered. He wasn't interested until he found out how free she was with her money."

Speaking carefully, Mary Kate asked, "What about you, Michael? Were you thinking of her money?"

"I'd be a liar if I said it hadn't crossed my mind. She had inherited millions from her father's ventures into waste management. She didn't like people to know where her money had come from. She referred to her father as the Sewage King. You see, Theo, we became very close. She told me things about herself. I couldn't believe it when she . . ." He choked back a sob.

Mary Kate understood why Walter was convinced that Michael was the killer. The motives were classic—greed, revenge, spurned love. He could still be the one. Alissa might have listened to this tearful confession just before the knife was brandished. Mary Kate stepped away a few steps, stretching and trying to appear casual. She kept her eyes on him. Pieces were still missing. "What about Randall Valentine? If Walter was interested in Alissa because of her money, then Randall was out, right?"

"That would be the case if Walter was only avaricious. He was also a damn good literary agent. After reading Randall's novel, he knew that with proper marketing he had a block-buster on his hands. His fifteen percent would make him rich beyond the Sewage King's dreams."

"Did you know this?"

"I suspected. It seems rather stupid now, in retrospect. I never really believed Walter would drop me. I thought I could get into his good graces once again by bringing potential moneymakers into the agency. He'd start actively selling my work again, and all would be right with the world." Michael dropped his head into his hands and cried openly. Mary Kate patted his arm, thinking about the pool of sewage into which she had wandered.

The kitchen was dark as she closed the door quietly and set down her suitcase. The familiarity of being back on her own turf assuaged the anxiety that had grown worse by the moment during her furtive departure from New York. She had been sure at every step the jig would be up, and the police would nab her.

Everything seemed normal enough. A few dirty dishes in the sink, a jacket hung on the back of a chair, a spill on the floor hastily and incompletely swabbed. The cat stepped through the door, stretching sleepily.

"Have you been keeping an eye on things for me, Lestat?" Mary Kate whispered. Having satisfied himself that nothing of particular interest was happening, he flicked his tail and left. Mary Kate hurried upstairs to check on the boys.

Stepping quietly to Ben's bedside, she held her breath until she heard the gentle intake of his breath. The nightlight he still needed dimly illuminated her baby's sleeping face. She bent over him and pressed her lips lightly to his forehead, resisting the urge to gather him up in her arms. He was safe and well.

She tiptoed out, and entered David's room, where her foot slipped on a stack of books, and she stumbled backwards, cracking her wrist against the edge of the dresser before tumbling into a pile of dirty clothes reeking of dried sweat.

"Mom, you're home," came a voice from the darkness.

Mary Kate sat on the floor, cradling her arm. "Son, I can say with all confidence that your booby trap works."

"Huh?"

"Never mind. I just wanted to check on you before I went to bed." She disentangled herself from a week's worth of crusty undershirts and gym pants and walked over to him. "Give me a hug, good-lookin', and get back to sleep." She sat on the edge of the bed and brushed the hair from her first-born's eyes.

"Dad said you wouldn't be home."

What else did Dad say? "I was able to change my plans at the last minute. Did you have a good weekend?"

He pulled up on one elbow, effectively moving himself away from her touch. "No. I didn't get to do anything fun. Again. Dad dumps us off at Grandma's, and I have to spend the whole weekend with the little fart-face."

"That's no way to talk about your grandmother."

"Mom! I meant Ben!"

She laughed. "I know." She was pleased to see a grin replace the scowl on his face. "Where does your Dad go?"

"I dunno. Work, I guess. He's gone all the time every time you go on a trip."

A chill ran through her. *Means, motive, and opportunity. Isn't that what's required to be a prime suspect?* She pulled the covers up around David's chest, tucking him in as he hadn't allowed her to do in years. Kissing his cheek, she whispered, "Get some sleep now. School in the morning."

"Good night, Mom."

She blew him a kiss at the door. "I love you."

She saw the hump of Chuck's body in the bed as she entered the darkened room and felt a sudden revulsion at the thought of joining him in their bed. Deep in her heart, she didn't believe he was capable of slashing the life out of another human being. That wasn't it. It was something more primal, more immediate. She sniffed the air, and it was like the bedroom had undergone some kind of hormonal imbalance. There was an underscent of wrongness, of molecules out of alignment.

I don't love him anymore, she thought. There was a certain amount of relief in consciously thinking it. The thought had tried to surface in recent days, but she always reburied it in haste and fear. The implications were terrifying. She was a fairly young woman. She would have to spend her remaining years pathetically locked in a loveless marriage. Or she could divorce him and become that pitiable, overworked creature, the single mother. Neither were options she would joyfully choose. *I'll spend some time getting used to the idea before I make any decisions.*

She went into the bathroom and slipped off her clothes, putting on the nightgown hanging on a hook. She stopped at the foot of the bed, hoping this wouldn't be one of those nights when Chuck silently groped for her, mechanically going through the motions of lovemaking, the lack of affection and passion making her feel like a prostitute. Her mind then served up another thought, one she also recognized, but had tried to suppress. The thought had no words. It was the image of her and Conner entwined in an embrace.

"You're back." Chuck rose up under the covers, then turned to face her.

Mary Kate could have been mistaken, but she thought he looked as if he was surprised to see who was there.

Chapter 13

"Here, kitty-kitty!" Mary Kate rounded the corner of the Olsen's house, where she had last seen Lestat hightail it. "Come on, stupid! We're going to catch hell for being in her yard."

While picking up the mail and newspapers that had collected in the boxes over the weekend, she had seen her darling pet squatting for all the world to see in Mrs. Olsen's flower bed. Things were bad enough without a lecture on pet etiquette. She scanned the windows for watchers as she hurried to the Olsen's backyard.

The yard was an unused space. No vegetable garden or barbecue or swimming pool. There were more weeds than grass, in contrast with the orderly front. *Isn't that the way it always is?* Mary Kate thought in her newfound wisdom. A blur of black in the corner of her eye made her turn as Lestat dove into the basement stairwell. Mary Kate followed.

The cat must have known he was cornered at the bottom of the stairs. He slid around the cuff of her jeans in the smarmy way of cats. She picked him up and called him a few choice names reserved for special occasions. "Let's get out of here," she said. Turning to leave, she saw that the window on the door had been soaped.

All of the basement windows had been obscured on the inside by swirls of dried soap. "That's peculiar," she whispered to Lestat. It reminded her of windows in new stores at the mall, blocking the view of shoppers until the renovations had been completed. She chuckled as she imagined a couple of naughty things the Olsens could be doing in the basement that they didn't want the neighbors seeing. *I've got a sick mind.* She carried the cat past the shrubbery to the front yard.

On the other side of an overgrown juniper, Mrs. Olsen stood on the second doorstep, appearing larger than usual. Her gray wool hair stood out in dry tufts, her face quivered, making her jowls sway as in a breeze. She held a cardboard box close to her breast. GOODWILL was scrawled across the side in ink. "You," she breathed.

Mary Kate stepped forward, clutching the squirming cat tighter. She managed a neighborly smile. "I came right over to get him as soon as I saw him in your yard."

Mrs. Olsen continued to stare. Mary Kate found herself staring. Hygiene obviously wasn't one of Mrs. Olsen's top priorities. Her housedress was soiled and wrinkled, the armpits ringed with layers of dried sweat. On her feet, she wore dressy, high-heeled shoes. The vein-striped skin of her bare feet bulged over the tops. She shifted her weight from one side to the other as if her feet hurt. The contents of the box clanked with the motion.

The breakup with Mr. Olsen must have taken a toll, Mary Kate thought. Mrs. Olsen had never been much to look at, but she had always been clean and nicely dressed. *Poor thing. I really ought to make nice with her.* "Is the Goodwill truck coming by to collect today? I have a ton of clothes the boys have outgrown that I could put out," Mary Kate said cheerfully.

Mrs. Olsen wheeled back a bit, teetering on the tiny pegs of her shoes. "No." Her mouth twisted as if she were chewing up and swallowing the rest of the words she wanted to say.

"I just thought . . ." Mary Kate reached out and pointed to the box.

Mrs. Olsen yanked the box to the side and lost her balance. She grabbed the door to stop her fall as clothing and household items clattered onto the walk and spread onto the lawn.

Mary Kate jumped forward, dropping the cat, and threw her arms around Mrs. Olsen's waist, holding her breath against the stench of body odor, halitosis, and what could have been Chanel No. 5. Her arms sunk into surprisingly little flab as she tried to steady the older woman on her itsy-bitsy shoes. Mrs. Olsen panted heavily, a bead of drool running from the corner of her mouth.

"Are you okay?" Mary Kate asked. Mrs. Olsen pushed her away with enough force to make her stumble and bent over to pick up the things that had fallen on the ground.

"Let me help you with those," Mary Kate said, kneeling on the walk.

Mrs. Olsen dragged her hands through the grass, scrambling to make a pile right in front of her. She hovered over it. "No. Go away."

Too weird, Mary Kate thought. She took one last look at the large, hunched back and the hands swiftly tossing silverware into the box. As she crossed the yard, keeping an eye out for the errant Lestat, she heard a more familiar refrain behind her.

"The next time that animal comes in my yard, you'll be sorry!"

Mary Kate turned and saw Mrs. Olsen carrying the box back into her house.

"Well, nuts to you," she muttered to herself, then laughed because that was the only retort she could think of. Giving the landscape one last look for the beast who got her into that mess, she saw Linda Goodman standing in her yard next door, watching. Linda might have seen what happened and

117

could shed a little light on Mrs. Olsen's bizarre behavior. Nancy had said Linda was the resident expert. This would also be a prime opportunity to show Linda that she was normal even though she wrote horror. Maybe, then, Linda would let her kid come over to play with Ben. *Mommy-points!*

"Hi! Terrific weather we're having!" Mary Kate ambled up as if she did this eight days a week.

Linda looked suspicious. "They're calling for rain by Wednesday."

Mary Kate sidled up beside her and checked the sky. "We could use it. The flowers would last longer with a little rain." She waited as her neighbor sized her up. It would be better if Linda brought up the subject first.

After a few moments, Linda said, "Speaking of flowers, your cat got in hers again?" She jerked her head toward the Olsen house.

Mary Kate nodded. "We've got a half-acre of lawn over there for him to pee in, and he still considers her impatiens home. Margaret didn't look well. Has she been ill?"

Linda looked back at her door, then decided to speak. Mary Kate guessed there was a mountain of dirty laundry or a battleground of toys and dusty furniture inside, making chatting with the pervert writer lady a less objectionable choice. "She's been going a bit downhill since Gregory left. Did you know Gregory left?"

"Yes, I did, but not much else than that." Having established herself as an insider in the know, but with missing information, Mary Kate settled in to listen. She felt uncomfortable fishing for gossip right here in her own neighborhood. What goes on in a person's home should be private. But the events of the last few weeks had left her feeling as if she had been living in a pretend world, where everyone knew the score but her. She had always let good manners and the avoidance of uncomfortable scenes keep her from finding out what was really going on. Well, a very large lady in very small shoes had just pushed her and ordered her from her yard, and Mary Kate wanted to know why.

Linda spoke offhandedly, as if she were tossing a bone to the undeserving. "He's had to put up with a lot in the eight years since Tammy passed on. I remember when it happened." She shook her head. "Margaret is my friend, but I knew it was just a matter of time before he left. For the last few years, she's been fine most of the time, but lately?" Her head shook again. "I could hear her carrying on all the way over here."

"Does Mrs. . . . Margaret need help, you know, medical help?"

Linda had caught the slip. The insider identity had been blown. She lifted her chin and pursed her lips. "How could I know that? I'm sure if she needed a doctor, she'd get one."

Mary Kate wanted to know one last thing before Linda got away. "How did her daughter die?"

"She was murdered. An older man seduced her, then killed her. She was only nineteen years old."

"Oh, dear!" Mary Kate was genuinely shocked.

Linda almost sneered. "It's pretty terrible when it happens in real life, isn't it?"

The stab hit home, and Mary Kate's breath caught in her throat. The very idea that a woman's personal tragedy had anything to do with the foolish books she wrote sickened her. She fled toward her driveway. Linda called out to her, the mocking tone still in her voice. "Is your washer working okay?"

Mary Kate stopped cold and turned to see Linda's mouth twitching down a smile. "What?"

"Your washing machine. Did your husband figure out how to work it?"

"Chuck? Why would he want to run the washing machine?" Chuck had never washed a load of laundry in his life.

The smile broke through as Linda turned to her door. "I must be mistaken. I thought Nancy helped him with it. Forget I said anything."

Mary Kate stood in front of her own house, completely baffled. Lestat returned, swishing against her legs. It was, after all, his lunchtime. She picked him up and carried him to the back door. "Let's you and I divorce Chuck, take the boys, and move."

The phone rang as she set the cat's dish on the floor. "Hello."

"Mrs. Mary Flaherty?"

"Mary Kate. Yes?"

"This is Lieutenant Evans of the Anne Arundel County Police. We've been contacted by the New York City Police Department. They've been trying to locate you."

"Oh, no. I'd forgotten all about them."

"You were being questioned as a witness to a murder?"

"Yes, uh, no. I didn't see the murder. I found . . . the body."

"I think they weren't finished with you."

"I had to get home to my children. I told them everything I know."

"Yes, ma'am. They said something about a note you received at your home."

"A note, yes. I got one in New York and in Atlanta, too."

"Could you bring it to the Southern District station on Route Two? We're going to be investigating on this end, and we'd like to fax them a copy."

It was a little past noon. "Okay, but I can't stay too long. I have to be here when my boys come home from school."

"Yes, ma'am. We just need a few minutes of your time."

She was becoming quite an expert on police interrogations. In comparison to the others, this one was a walk in the park. Sitting in a sunny, clean room, she told them about the circumstances of the three notes. She gave them the sheet of paper and envelope, and explained that the New York Police had one and that she had thrown away the first one. No pressures. No insinuations. Mary Kate assumed this was because Lieutenant Evans hadn't seen the mutilated bodies.

She was home in less than two hours. With the dinner cooking on the stove and the boys playing something upstairs that made the light fixtures rattle every few minutes, she turned on the television to watch the evening news. As she had anticipated, the Vampire Killer was the lead story.

After showing pictures of the distinguished, old building where Alissa had lived, the video switched to a mob scene outside of a police station. Michael Kazdin was being ushered through the middle by Detective Malone and a small, well-dressed man.

"Earlier today," the newscaster's voice explained, "popular horror writer, Michael Kazdin, was escorted to the Midtown North Precinct by his lawyer and detectives for questioning. Kazdin is best known for his novel, *Little Terrors*, which was made into a movie in 1988. Also being questioned was Conner Drake, author of *Fiddler's Revenge*. Our reporter, Newt Twomey, caught up with him outside of the Ramada."

Conner towered over the microphone-toting throng, looking tired and angry. His hair was wet, as if he'd just showered. He was cleanly shaven, but he still wore the cheap shoes he had scarfed up on the day before when the police had taken his as evidence. Mary Kate felt a sharp pang of guilt for deserting him.

"Mr. Drake! Mr. Drake! Is it true that you and Alissa Dibiase were seeing each other romantically?"

Conner's jaw tightened. He looked down at the mike poking in his face. "Alissa Dibiase was my friend," he said quietly. "I'll miss her." He turned back to the glass double doors of the motel.

"Mr. Drake! Is it true there was a feud between Miss Dibiase and vampire writer, Theodora Zed?"

Conner stopped, his shoulders hunched. He opened the door and went in without responding. Twomey faced the camera and spoke earnestly. "Both Conner Drake and Theodora Zed were visiting Miss Dibiase on the evening of the murder. Miss Zed . . ." The back cover photo of Theodora from *A Lover's Blood* flashed on the screen. The press hadn't yet uncovered her real identity. ". . . reportedly found the stabbed and bloody body of Alissa Dibiase. Drake, Zed, and Kazdin are also being questioned about a similar murder in Atlanta two months ago."

With shots of the Corinthian Hotel, the newscast droned on about the death of Randall Valentine. Mary Kate watched, a burning emptiness growing inside her. She felt as if they were all sacrificial lambs on the altar of news ratings. More familiar faces appeared on the TV as colleagues were asked to react. Most seemed shocked and uncomfortable.

"Mr. Dee, how do you feel about the recent murders of two horror writers? As the author of a series of vampire novels, have you been personally affected by the grisly way in which the two were killed?"

Ron Dee removed his pipe and stroked his beard thoughtfully. "Alissa Dibiase was a talented writer. This is a great loss, for the world of publishing as well as those of us who were her friends."

"Are you afraid for your own safety? Are you taking any precautions to protect yourself?"

Ron's mouth moved, but a single word was bleeped out. "I can't believe you (bleep) bloodsuckers." He bumped the camera as he pushed by.

The reporter moved over to an elderly man with a baggy, gray suit on his thin frame. "Not everyone believes these murders are the result of senseless, random violence. I have with me sociologist Patrick Henley. Dr. Henley, you were in Atlanta at the time of the first vampire murder."

"Yes, I was," he answered in a depressed tone, his eyes down.

"And you believe these killings were inevitable?"

"Yes, I do. In Atlanta I had the unpleasant task of meeting and studying a group of people who proudly proclaim themselves writers of horror. These people reveled in the worst perversions of the mind, flaunted morality, embraced violence and mayhem." He lifted his eyes, glaring from the television with fervor. "These kind of beliefs degrade the moral fabric of our society and desensitize us to man's worst tendencies. The words they write seduce our children with evil images more insidiously than the television and motion picture industries."

The reporter spoke eagerly. "And you saw the horror writers engaging in perverse and violent behavior?"

Henley looked at him with surprise. "No, of course not. I'm saying that people who can conceive of such things are more capable of committing them than others."

"Oh, I see." The camera moved in on the reporter's face. "Not everyone believes that a horror story is just good clean fun, especially after the real life horror of two writers murdered brutally. Me? There's nothing I like better than a good scary movie on a Saturday night." He laughed as the newscast returned to the anchors in the studio.

This is only the beginning, Mary Kate thought. The latest and the greatest human abominations brought out the worst in the news media. How could writing fiction be more sick than the fun the journalists were having? For all their twisted thoughts, horror writers often embed a core of morality in their stories. The overkill of the news coverage is driven by the need to increase ratings and subsequently advertising revenues. At best, the motivation is to beat the competition to an angle no one else has tried. *Is it okay because it's real?*

Other news of the day took over the broadcast as she sat shell-shocked, reacting more strongly to the publicity than she had thought she would. She rubbed her arms, trying to rid herself of phantom cold. It wasn't bad enough that her life might be in danger and that she was a murder suspect, now her family's peace would be destroyed as soon as the media figured out that Mary Kate Flaherty was Theodora Zed. And it shouldn't take them long.

Across the television screen marched teenagers arrested for spraying automatic weapon fire through an open air market, killing four innocent bystanders . . . the sheet-shrouded, tiny body of a child beaten to death by her mother's boyfriend . . . the smiling wedding photo of a couple murdered during a midnight burglary . . . the red-splashed sidewalk in the aftermath of a neighborhood argument gone berserk.

Mary Kate's eyes filled with tears, sobs broke achingly from her chest. She wept openly for the horror of it all. Her heart broke for all of the dead.

Chapter 14

Red dots on white snow. Blood. Mary Kate looked closer. "Oh, thank God!" They were geranium petals.

She turned to tell Alissa. Alissa lay in the snow, her eyes wide and dry, her blue clothes soaked red. Conner and Chuck stood above her, their arms draped around one another like old friends.

"Theo, darling," Alissa said, her lifeless face unchanged, "don't you have a box to put out for Goodwill?"

Mary Kate poked herself in the cheek with a pencil as she jerked awake. "Ow!" The legal pad with the notes for her next novel dropped off her lap. She stretched as she stood up from the easy chair in the corner of her office. This was the second night in a row she had fallen asleep there. She would have to break down and sleep in bed with Chuck or go downstairs to the sofa. One more night in that chair, and she'd need a chiropractor.

After a few minutes, the dream receded enough for her to feel unafraid to go downstairs in the dark. It was nearly four a.m., plenty of time to fall back to sleep and let her brain concoct a new nightmare. She chose instead to eat.

She savored the quiet. As she had anticipated, the press had learned that Theodora Zed lived in the suburbs of Maryland. The phone had rung all day long. The boys didn't like letting the answering machine get it, especially David, who quite naturally saw the phone as an adolescent lifeline. Most of the calls were from this newspaper or that magazine. One television tabloid offered her an obscene amount of money to dress up as Theodora and tell in vivid detail what it was like finding the body. She hadn't spoken to any of them, and had no intentions of doing so. Her biggest worry was that they would come to her home and upset her children.

Chuck had been unusually silent. Stone silent came to mind. He hadn't spoken a word to her beyond what was necessary in the last three days. She had expected tantrums with the public spotlight, but he only came home later each evening, eating, then going to bed. She found she liked him better that way. She could no longer deny that the writing was on the wall for her marriage. Unless something drastic happened, it was just a matter of when it would dissolve.

Down in the kitchen, she opened the refrigerator door and gazed unseeing at the contents. The cold felt good, but the white light blinded her. This simple motion of pleasant sightlessness suddenly became a metaphor for her life. She had blithely lived for thirty-six years avoiding knowing anything unpleasant, anything unpredictable. Everything had been accepted at face value. Even the mayhem on the news had escaped her notice. It was always other people. People in Mary Kate's world never killed one another.

She closed the refrigerator and pulled out a chair from the table. Sitting in the dark, she became afraid. *How long has Chuck been upset? How long has Conner been in love with me? Who is he really? How many writers have been trading their integrity for book contracts? Am I the only one who doesn't? What else don't I know?*

She stood, clutching her arms around herself, and wandered into the living room. From the picture window, she could see lights on in the Olsen house. "I don't know anything anymore," she whispered.

★ ★ ★ ★ ★

"Mom! Mom!"

Mary Kate rushed down the stairs. She had sent the boys off to catch the bus five minutes ago, and now David was using his scared voice. They stood in the kitchen, their backpacks still on, their faces white.

"Mom, there's a man all covered in blood behind the garage," David said breathlessly.

"Stay here! Lock the door behind me."

She crossed the yard to the detached garage. The weeds by the back fence shuddered. Her knees felt like water. She balled up her fists to give her strength. "Who's there?"

The weeds thrashed against the boards, then a shoulder appeared and dropped back down. She heard a low moan, then, "Mary Kate . . . help me."

"Oh, my God! Oh, no!" she cried, hurrying over. Conner lay in the patch of bear grass and hemp flourishing in the narrow space. The bright red splashes on his clothes, as well as those that had browned, paralyzed her. The ground around him went white. The red fanned out until all went black . . .

She blinked her eyes, then looked into Conner's face, inches from her own. The sky was blue behind his head.

"Are you okay?" he asked, his voice croaking.

"Yeah. What . . . ?" She could see they were both lying behind the garage. She began to remember. "You're hurt."

"I was attacked . . . last night . . . outside your house. I need a doctor, Mary Kate."

She touched his cheek. A fleck of blood came off on her hand. "Yes, of course, a doctor. I'm so sorry." She got up on her knees. "Stay here. I'll call for help. Don't move." As she stood, he lay his head down on the ground and closed his eyes. "Don't die, Conner."

He smiled. "Promise."

The boys' worried faces pressed against the glass of the back door. They plied her with questions as she came in and picked up the phone. "He's a friend of mine. He's hurt. Be quiet, now. I've got to get him some help." She prayed she hadn't wasted precious time by fainting at the sight of his blood.

She could hear the sirens by the time she came back to him with a blanket. She covered him and cradled his head in her lap. He looked like a felled oak. She stroked his brow.

"You and your children get out of here, Mary Kate," he said quietly. "He was waiting for me in your driveway."

"Who?" she asked. He shook his head. She wanted him to talk. He would be okay as long as he was talking. "Where's your car?"

"I left it out on the street. In case you haven't noticed, there's no place to turn around here. I wanted to be able to get away quickly if I had to."

"Why? What did you come to do?"

He closed his eyes and exhaled. Afraid he was dying, she grabbed his shoulder and shook. "Conner! Conner!"

He reached his arm up, and digging his fingers into her hair, he pulled her face close to his and kissed her lips. "I might have been planning to do that," he said weakly, as if that movement had taken the last of his strength. "But I hadn't thought it through that far. I was worried about you. I came here instead of going home from New York. You disappeared . . . and I had to see you again."

The flashing lights of an ambulance turned into the driveway, followed by two police cars. She turned back to him. "Conner, I don't know what to say."

He closed his eyes and smiled. "If you want to, you can attribute my behavior to loss of blood and delirium."

★ ★ ★ ★ ★

She didn't have much to say to the police this time. As she waited for Lieutenant Evans to finish with Conner, she paced the hallway. David and Ben sat on the floor reading comic books she had picked up in the hospital gift shop. There was no way she was going to let her sons out of her sight. A murderer had been at her home.

The doctor wouldn't tell her much because she wasn't family. Conner would recover fully from his wounds was all she could get. She considered calling Chuck at work, then changed her mind. The odds of him being helpful were close to nil. She'd have to let him know before he came home this evening. The driveway was now not only hard to turn around in, but was also a potential deathtrap.

The door opened, and three police officers came out. Evans was the youngest, looking like a tall Boy Scout beside the others. Mary Kate caught up with him as he left. "Lieutenant, how is he?"

"He's going to be all right, Mrs. Flaherty. He was asking to speak with you."

"His wounds, were they like the others?"

"Others? You mean, the murders? There are similarities, but I can't say for sure yet. Are you going back home?"

She looked at her sons. *How can I protect them?* "I don't know what to do. I don't know where it's safe."

"You should be okay at home through most of today, anyway. We have investigators on the scene. I'd like to talk to your husband. Where was he last night?"

Chuck. *Chuck is now in the clear!* Thank God. "In bed," she said eagerly. "He went to bed early."

"He didn't get up during the night?"

"No, uh, I don't know. I mean, he went to bed around eight, and I got the boys off to bed around nine, nine-thirty.

But, after that, I was in my office down the hall."

"You didn't go to bed?"

Mary Kate blushed. She didn't want to tell this clean-cut, young man that she'd do anything to avoid sleeping with her husband. "I worked late, then fell asleep in a chair. I woke up around four and went downstairs."

"Could you have heard him if he got up?"

This isn't fair. Chuck is a jerk, not a killer. Reluctantly, she said, "No. I wouldn't have heard him. The office door was closed."

She gave Evans the address and phone number of the Annapolis branch of Rightway Insurance where Chuck worked. After checking on the boys and warning them that no foolishness would be tolerated here in the hospital, she entered Conner's room.

"You look better," she said. He sat up in the bed, his face whiskery, his hair hand-combed, but with more color in his face. "Would you like for me to come back later?"

He shook his head and patted the sheets beside him. She walked over and sat on the bed.

"I'm glad you came," he said. "I guess we have to talk."

"You could have been killed."

He smiled. "Don't I know it." Becoming serious, he said, "I didn't see who it was, Mary Kate. I was hit from behind, then somebody jumped on my back and started stabbing. At first, it felt like something was pushing on my side. It wasn't until I twisted around that I felt the pain."

"Could you see anything?"

He shook his head. "It was dark. He was dressed in black. I got tangled in something when we were fighting. Maybe a cape. He wasn't very strong. I was able to push him off and get one good punch in. That's when he ran away. I was getting weaker and knew I couldn't make it to your door. I was afraid he'd come back to finish me off, so I crawled behind the garage. It's so overgrown back there, you could hide a Sherman tank."

"He was at my home, Conner." Her voice trembled, and he squeezed her hand.

"Mary Kate," he said softly, "nobody knew I was coming to your house. I didn't know until I decided to turn south at the last minute. Do you know what that means?"

She nodded. "He was looking for me." She rubbed tears from her eyes with her fists and dug in her purse for a tissue. Wiping her nose, she said, "You were looking for me, too. What in the world did you think you were going to do?"

Conner looked sheepish. "Really, I don't know. I was going to ask you if you were all right, then I'd take it from there. It was stupid."

"It was stupid. I'm a married woman with children. It's not fair putting me in this position. And you kissed me! Right in my own yard!"

"That I can explain," he said. "I was lying there in the dark all night, falling in and out of consciousness. I kept telling myself that I had to make it because I've never kissed you, and I had to do that at least once before I died."

She looked at him, surprised, then started to giggle.

"What's funny?" he asked, and she laughed harder.

"That's . . . so sweet," she barely got out before she doubled over, howling.

Conner smiled, then joined in the laughter. "You're something, Mary Kate," he said, wincing from the pain in his side.

Chapter 15

Taking the yellow legal pad, Mary Kate flipped over the page with her notes and touched the pencil to her tongue. SUSPECTS, she wrote across the top of the fresh sheet. "There." She underlined it twice.

The police had left her home two hours earlier, with promises to cruise the neighborhood all night. The pressure of fear she felt for herself and her children was almost palpable. If she didn't do something, she was sure she would burst a blood vessel in her brain. She remembered reading the Lord Peter Wimsey mysteries by Dorothy Sayers. The sleuth, Harriet Vane, always started with a list of likely suspects.

She drew a line down the middle of the paper. On one side, she wrote WHO, and on the other, she wrote WHY. "Now we're getting somewhere." She thought for a minute, started to write, and stopped. She felt much less comfortable with this exercise than she had anticipated. This wasn't someone else's murder that she had been called in to solve like in the books. Most of the names she could produce were friends . . . or a husband.

Tentatively, she wrote "Chuck." On the WHY side, she wrote "Doesn't like writers. Is mad at me for unknown reason. Leaves the boys with Grandma when I'm out of town. Could have left the bedroom unobserved last night." She read back over it. Factual and concise.

She tried another. WHO: "Michael Kazdin." WHY: "Proximity to both murder scenes. Jealous of Valentine.

Dumped by Alissa. Alissa dating Conner. Career in the toilet. Recently divorced." This doesn't look good for Michael.

"Conner." She took a breath, then let it out slowly. "Proximity to both murder scenes. Angry with Valentine for heckling me. Had relationship with Alissa. In love with me." She stopped and looked at the last line. Speculative and irrelevant. She erased it and wrote, "Wounds possibly self-inflicted." No. He couldn't have done that to himself. She remembered how he had looked, so helpless, so bloody. *I never really saw the wounds,* her mind offered suspiciously. And the doctor was awfully optimistic.

Her emotions split in separate directions, as they often did when she thought about Conner. She wished he had deep, madman gouges in his side; the more life threatening, the more innocent he could be. She wished he hadn't come here at all, he wouldn't be hurt, but she would still feel alone. She wished he hadn't kissed her, then closed her eyes and imagined again what it had felt like. Her breath caught in her throat, warmth flooded her face.

"Uh-oh." She opened her eyes and patted her cheeks. "Snap out of it, girl. Don't even start to think that way." Waving her hand to cool off, she picked up the legal pad and read back over her lists.

This wasn't working. It was all speculative at best and probably irrelevant. The attacks had been senseless and brutal. No one had a good reason. But it did help in a way. She felt more proactive, less like a sitting duck. "Okay, who else?"

"Walter Truesdale" she wrote. "Playing Alissa and Valentine off one another. Could have gotten into something he couldn't get out of. Was stealing from and blackmailing Michael. Is a lizard." She laughed. *I'm losing my objectivity.*

Let's go for it. WHO: "Me." WHY: "Proximity to both

murder scenes and attack on Conner. Angry with Valentine for heckling. Jealous of Alissa's talent, beauty, and relationship with Conner." Not true, but makes a good argument. "Afraid Conner might make a scene with husband at home."

"That does it. I'm guilty. I'll turn myself in in the morning." She tossed the tablet onto the desk, then picked it up again. Laughing, she wrote "Mrs. Olsen." WHY: "My cat pees in her flower bed." Dropping the list on the desk, she went downstairs to check on the boys.

David and Ben sat on the living room carpet in front of the television. "Look, Mom," Ben said, smiling, "we're on TV!"

She looked. He was right. There was their house on Linden Lane. A reporter stood in the foreground, speaking into a microphone. ". . . a quiet neighborhood, rocked by terror. This is Patricia Mulrone for NewsCenter 4. Back to you, Chet."

Mary Kate pulled back the drapes, just enough to peek out. "Oh, holy cow!" Strangers milled around the street, held back from the house by officers of the Anne Arundel County Police. Vans with satellite dish headdresses blocked out her neighbors' homes. A snake pit of black wires covered the ground.

"Speaking of cows," David said, "Mrs. Goodman is on the news."

Mary Kate groaned as she turned around to watch.

Linda Goodman stood at her front door, a phantom hand holding a microphone in front of her. "The Flahertys were always a little strange. They don't keep their home up as nice as the rest of the neighborhood, and the parents aren't as involved in their children as much as you'd expect . . ."

Mary Kate felt the heat growing in her face. "You self-righteous, pug-nosed, saggy butt . . ."

The boys stared at her, David with a wisp of a smile. She decided not to finish the sentence. Aloud. Linda had more to say.

". . . and the mother writing that . . . that pornography! Violent, filthy books!"

"Have you read any of her books?" the phantom asked.

"Me? No, I'd never! But, I've heard. All about vampires and killing and sex." She smacked her lips in self-satisfaction. "You reap what you sow."

Mary Kate walked over to the set and turned down the sound. "I'm sorry this is happening," she said to her sons. "How are you guys feeling?"

"It's scary," Ben said. "The Vampire Killer might come back tonight and try to get in the house."

"Come here, sweetie." She sat on the sofa, and he climbed in her lap. Stroking his downy, white hair, she said, "We're sticking together tonight. You, and David if he wants, can sleep in bed with Dad and me. Okay?"

David peeked out the drapes. "Dad's really going to be pissed."

She let the language slip pass. Dad was going to be pissed. "Let's act like they're not out there. I'll tell you what. You know that computer game I got for Christmas?"

"Doom?" David asked, turning from the window.

"Yep. You guys can play it on my computer. If . . . I repeat, if . . . you promise not to mess in my work stuff. Deal?"

David and Ben high-fived each other and ran out. Mary Kate sighed and thumbed the remote on the table, turning off the television. She agreed with Ben. It was scary. And nothing was ever going to be the same again.

The alarm clock on the nightstand said it was ten minutes past eleven. When Mary Kate had looked at it two minutes before, it had said eight minutes past eleven. Sleep was something that just wasn't going to happen. David slept soundly on Chuck's side of the bed, hogging most of the covers. Ben sprawled in the middle, such a little guy requiring so much room. Slowly, she moved until she was sitting on the edge of the mattress. As she stood, the bedsprings squeaked. David rolled over, but didn't awake. Mary Kate tiptoed from the room.

She went down to the living room and looked past the drapes. Linden Lane was deserted, except for Conner's car. The news crews and trucks had taken off after the last of the evening broadcasts around seven-thirty. They hadn't returned for the late news. Throughout the day, only one reporter had made it past the police barricade by cutting through neighbors' yards and approaching by the back door. He had given up after Mary Kate thumbed her nose at him through the window and walked out of his line of sight.

As she watched, a pair of headlights turned onto the street, pausing at the end of her driveway before turning in. Chuck was home. *It's about time.* She was more worried than angry. He wouldn't be the first man to lie bleeding in the driveway all night.

She found herself nervously fiddling with her hair as she waited for him in the kitchen. They hadn't spoken to each other in days. Knowing the police were going to talk to him, she hadn't called to tell him what had happened. She knew she should have. It would have been the wifely thing to do. She just couldn't find a point in the day when she was up to being snubbed and rejected. As the key rattled in the lock, she considered running back upstairs and pretending she was asleep.

His eyes met hers through the windowpane, then the door opened. She walked to the sink and busied her hands picking black cat hairs off her nightgown. She looked up into his hard face. "I was starting to get worried," she said. "It's late."

Chuck took off his sports coat and threw it on the table. He grabbed the knot of his tie and loosened it violently. Then placing both hands on the back of a chair, he seemed to sag, his head drooping between his shoulders.

"Chuck . . ." Mary Kate began.

He picked the chair up over his head and swung it against the wall, a leg cracking, the wallboard caving in as it hit. Mary Kate cried out, her hands crossed on her breast over her thumping heart. The chair dropped to the floor, and Chuck stared at it, breathing heavily. He turned slowly to face her.

"How much more can I take?" he growled, then spinning around, he slammed his fist into the refrigerator door, creasing it. "How much more?"

Mary Kate slid her back along the counter toward the door. The concept of being afraid of her husband was difficult to grasp. He looked like Chuck, but larger. He had a wild, feral, out-of-control glint in his eyes. She had seen him angry many times in the past. This was different. She felt small, vulnerable.

He dipped his head toward her. "Are you going to keep this up until I go insane?"

"Chuck, please, the children."

He danced around in a circle, his arms thrown over his head. "Now, you think of the children!" He shook his head and mimicked a laugh as if this was the most absurd thing he had ever heard. "Your lover is stabbed in my driveway, and now, you think of the children!"

She forgot her fear in her surprise. She took a step towards him. "My what?"

Chuck almost shrank back from her. He tried to recover his momentum. "Conner Drake. Don't think I didn't know about him." His head bobbed. "I knew, I knew."

Mary Kate felt relieved. *It's a misunderstanding. He's feeling insecure.* She smiled. "No, no, Chuck. Is this what you thought? Conner and I are friends, that's all. It was never like . . . what you thought."

He prowled around the room, avoiding her gaze. "What was he doing here?"

"He said he was worried about me. I left New York without telling anyone. A friend of ours was murdered. He was concerned for me."

Chuck ran his fingers over the knobs on the oven and picked up the decanter from the coffee maker and set it back. He drummed his nails on the counter, then slapped his palm down. "The police came to my office, the place where I work. Everyone saw them."

She knew this was important to him. "I'm sorry."

He wheeled around. "Our house was on the news!"

"I'm sorry! How many times can I say it? I'm sorry! But I didn't do it! I didn't make any of this happen! I'm as upset as you are! I'm scared, Chuck! Maybe if you talked to me once in a while . . ."

His mouth turned up into an evil grin. "Innocent, little Mary Kate, nothing's ever her fault," he purred maliciously. She stepped back, but he followed, leaning closer into her face. "She writes dirty books and goes prancing around in public in tight little dresses, her boobs poking out one end and her butt the other, and she still expects everybody to believe she's so sweet and innocent." His forefinger poked hard into her collarbone. "Well, you don't fool me for a minute . . . Theodora."

"Chuck, that hurts." She glanced towards the door and saw a shift of shadows, probably the cat lying low during the fight. This was getting too scary. She sniffed for any sign of alcohol, but he was just mean sober. "Maybe we can talk about this in the morning."

He grabbed her arm and swept her across the room. "No! Let's talk now!" He pushed her against the counter.

"You're hurting me!"

"Let's talk about how you shame your family and abandon your children! How you dress like a slob and a slut! And how about this pigsty you call a home or the slop you feed your family? How about it, Mary Kate?"

She pushed him as hard as she could, and he stumbled backwards. "Get away from me!"

Chuck snagged her arm before she could make it to the door. She saw his hand cutting through the air toward her before the smack hit her jaw, knocking her to the floor. She drew her arms over her head.

The floor was cold on her bare legs. She heard a ringing in her ears.

"Mary Kate? Are you okay? I'm sorry. God, I'm sorry."

She opened her eyes and saw Chuck kneeling over her. She tried to scoot away.

"No, I'm not going to hurt you. I'm sorry, Mary Kate. You've got to believe me. I'm sorry." He took her arms and helped her sit up. She touched her cheek and it stung all the way into her teeth.

"Go, Chuck. Don't . . ." Talking hurt. "Don't come back."

Chapter 16

The ice pack had taken down most of the swelling, but there wasn't much Mary Kate could do about the black bruise running across her lower right jaw. Her eye was puffy and bloodshot. She patted some concealer under it, then dabbed it with face powder. Turning her head to see how she looked in the mirror, she groaned from the pain shooting through her jaw. David appeared in the bathroom mirror behind her.

"I don't want to go to school today," he said.

She turned around to face him, brushing her hair forward over her cheek with her fingers. "I really think you should, sweetie. You'll be glad you did once you get there."

He hesitated, then looked down at his shoes. "I don't want to leave you alone," he mumbled.

She swallowed hard and blinked her eyes. Her baby was feeling responsible for her welfare. *What a burden for a thirteen-year-old!* All she had ever wanted was for her children to feel safe and loved. She reached out and touched his brow. "David, I'm going to be just fine, and so are you."

He looked up. A tear escaped from the corner of his eye. "Mom . . ." His voice cracked, and he tried again. "Mom, do you think Dad is the killer?"

"Dad? Why do you say that?"

He wiped his nose and eyes on his sleeve. "In your office. You wrote some stuff."

My suspects list. Why did I leave that out? Stupid, stupid, stupid. "That was nothing. I should have thrown it out. I was just trying to . . . to think through some things. That's all. I wasn't being serious. Okay? Your Dad's not the killer." She hoped, looking into his glistening, brown eyes, he believed this more than she did.

"I saw," he said.

"Saw what?"

He pointed to her face. "The yelling and stuff woke me up."

The world slipped from under her for a moment, and she felt she was in freefall. He saw. The violence of last night came back to her, with the added horror that her son had witnessed it. She was overcome with guilt. "I-I'm sorry. I'm sorry you saw that."

"He hit you! I thought he killed you!"

"No, no," she pleaded, wanting desperately to erase the picture from his head. She wrapped her arms around him. "Dad was angry, too angry. I think he was scared, too, and frustrated. And he was sorry, David. He said he was sorry." She heard his muffled crying and began to cry herself. *What have we done to our child?*

The phone rang again, and Mary Kate let the machine pick it up. The boys were in Ben's room building with Legos. She sat at her desk, unable to start or finish anything. The yellow suspects list lay shredded in the waste paper basket.

"Mary Kate, it's me, Conner."

She picked it up. "Hi."

"I thought you might be screening your calls. The hospital's keeping the jackals away from me."

"I'm glad."

He paused. "Uh, I'm going to be released from the hospital tomorrow. I was wondering if you wanted to come by and pick me up."

It was a logical request, but under the circumstances,

probably not a good idea. She tried to think of a way to say no. "I don't think I can, Conner. I have to . . . the boys are . . ."

"What's wrong, Mary Kate?"

"Nothing. Everything's fine, I just can't . . ."

"Something's wrong."

"No, listen, I've got to go. Uh . . . will you be all right? Can you take a cab or something?"

Silence. "Sure. No problem. I'll, uh, see you around then," he said.

"Yeah, sure."

He hung up.

After driving the boys to school the next morning, Mary Kate continued into Annapolis to the public library on West Street. As a writer, she had always found the answers to her questions there, be it the population of a small town on the Romanian border or the amount of blood one would have to lose before going into a coma. Her fiction was always well researched. She thought it was about time she gave the real world a closer look.

She parked, and once inside, went straight for the listings computers. The library was nearly abandoned on a Friday morning, so she didn't have to wait her turn. One by one, she typed in the names from her suspects list and of the murder victims, scribbling on scratch paper the titles of books found by each search. She didn't find much. Not too many horror writers became popular enough to warrant biographies.

The only one who had a whole book devoted to him was Michael Kazdin, and he had two: *Writer of Horror, Interviews with Michael Kazdin*, collected by Leo Djorsky, and *The Art of Fear* by Michael Kazdin. Another book, *Profiles of Horror*, had chapters devoted to Michael and Conner. There was nothing on the vampire ladies, Alissa Dibiase and Theodora Zed. She went to the stacks and collected the books, then sat down at the computer reserved for magazine and periodical searches.

The same names produced thirty-seven articles about Michael, fourteen about Conner, three about Theodora, two about Walter Truesdale, and one about Alissa. And oddly enough, one about Margaret Olsen.

Mary Kate hit the keys that called up the abstract. She had put Mrs. Olsen in as a joke. *What could anybody have to say about her?* The summary came up on the screen.

The Mid-Atlantic Inpatient Care Journal
Volume XXVI, January 1996
"Stress Screening for Peripheral Inpatient
    Care Providers"
by Nadia V. Bellows, R.N., Chief Surgical Nurse,
    City Hospital, Daleville, NJ
Seven cases are described in which direct care providers in hospitals endanger convalescent patients while exhibiting stress reactions to personal problems unrelated to hospital operations. Procedures to detect and treat employees under stress are outlined. Included are the cases of orderly, James Otfrey, and nurse, Margaret Olsen.

"I'll be a monkey's uncle." Mrs. Olsen had been nuts enough to make it into a medical journal. *If it's the same Margaret Olsen.* This was written after her daughter had died. Stress reaction. *I wonder what kind of stress reaction she had back then.* Her curiosity getting the better of her, Mary Kate inserted the compact disk with the article into the drive and made a copy of it on the laser printer with the others.

Driving over the South River Bridge delineating the line between the city and the rural south county, Mary Kate felt her growing need for information surge. She felt empowered by her back seat full of references, but knew in her heart that the majority of it would be carefully constructed publicity for the authors' own works. She needed to know what wasn't available to the general public. Signaling right, she turned off Route 2 into the Southern District Police Station in Edgewater.

"I want to see Lieutenant Evans." He had been accommodating to her in the past. She could convince him to fill her in on the investigation's progress once she explained how frightened and vulnerable she and her family felt. He'd understand that they needed to know if it was almost over.

The officer at the desk put down her pen and slid her glasses down her nose. "He's in a meeting right now."

"Yeah, but, I'm Mary Kate Flaherty. He's working on a case I'm involved in, and he said he'd answer any of my questions. If he could talk to me for a few minutes . . ."

The officer rolled her eyes and stood. "Wait here."

Several other uniformed officers sat at desks around the room, leafing through manila folders or studying a computer monitor. A young man in sweats leaned against the wall, shifting from foot to foot as if he'd been waiting an awfully long time. A door down the hall opened, and the desk officer came out, followed by Lieutenant Evans. He crooked his finger at Mary Kate.

He ushered her in, and her aching jaw fell. She faced her second worst nightmare. Detective Malone of the NYPD smirked at her. Atlanta's Detective Pumphrey growled, "Who slugged you, Mrs. Flaherty?"

Too stunned to speak or do anything else, she allowed Evans to lead her to a chair.

"We were going to be contacting you again anyway, Mrs. Flaherty," he said. "The investigation keeps leading back to you." The three of them looked at her as if they were waiting for her to break down and give it up.

She mentally kicked herself in the butt for coming in. "I can't stay all day, you know. I have to pick up my children from school."

The bullfrog croaked again. "Who punched you?" The toothpick slid into the corner of Pumphrey's mouth.

"This?" She touched her chin. "Nobody hit me. I fell. I slipped on the basement steps and hit my face on the rail."

"You sure you didn't walk into a door?" Malone asked.

That had been her first story, but she thought it had sounded familiar. She tried to look ingenuous. If they knew Chuck had hit her, they would have even more evidence that he was the murderer. She wasn't going to help them convict Chuck. He was, first and foremost, her children's father. They loved and needed him. She couldn't take that away from them. He had to be innocent.

She didn't miss the looks they exchanged among themselves. They knew she was lying.

Malone gave it another shot. "Did your husband hit you when he found your boyfriend at the house, Mary Kate? May I call you Mary Kate?"

"No, you may not call me Mary Kate. And Conner Drake is not my boyfriend."

Evans tried to smooth things over. "We're just trying to work with what we've got, Mrs. Flaherty. Your husband was very upset when we questioned him yesterday. He became kind of agitated when we said it was Mr. Drake in his driveway."

"He's found this whole situation . . . difficult to deal with," Mary Kate said. "As we all have. Can you tell me more about the investigation? Is there anything new or something I should know about? I have children, and I don't know if it's safe for them to go out and play in the yard."

Pumphrey stared at her. "Your neighbors don't like you

much, do they, Mrs. Flaherty?"

"Huh? I don't know, some don't. Have you found out something about the neighbors?"

"Just that they don't like you much," Pumphrey said. He and Malone laughed.

Evans smiled and said, "A couple of your neighbors believe you're getting the grief you deserve."

"You guys aren't going to tell me anything, are you?" she asked.

"I wouldn't count on it, Mary Kate," Malone said. They all burst out laughing as she walked out the door.

Dimitri pointed his finger at Ursula. "Come with me." His dark eyes were commanding. His deep voice frightened her with its authority. She had done everything he had asked, had given up everything to be with him. Yet still, he wanted more. She had no more to give.

"I can't, Dimitri! I love you, but I've given up the light of day and the warm touch of a living hand for you! I walk the underworld, my existence is but a shadow. How can you ask me for more?"

His eyes glowed red with anger. As he slowly crossed the room towards her, she saw for the first time what he really was. A monster!

Mary Kate leaned back from the computer, looking at what she had written, pressing her fingers against her lips. "It's true," she whispered. Tears fell down her cheeks.

Wiping her eyes, she shut down the computer and trudged downstairs to make dinner. Hesitating at the front door, she looked through the glass at Linden Lane. Margaret Olsen pumped her arms at her side as she passed, her body stuffed like plump pillows into her pink exercise suit.

Chapter 17

Mary Kate squeezed her eyes shut until the burn stopped. Picking up another magazine article from the pile on the kitchen table, she began to read, the words rocking in her head at a singsong pace. The main thing she had learned from reading the materials from the library is that writers are a self-serving bunch. Most of the interviews had been designed to convince someone to plunk down hard-earned cash at the local bookstore for the interviewee's newest novel. They had all begun to sound the same after awhile.

Michael had the most written about him, but little of it was new. He had been a public figure for a long time. Alissa and Theodora had been mentioned in one article about the new interest in vampires, and Mary Kate as Theodora had two promotional interviews. Walter Truesdale had been profiled in *National Business Digest* as a mover and a shaker in the literary world. The article was very positive, with no suggestion that he had been capable of something as underhanded as skimming profits from his best clients.

Conner had been a published author as long as Michael, but was nowhere near as well-known. The articles on him weren't revealing, but a paragraph in his one-chapter biography intrigued her.

"Conner Drake doesn't know where or exactly when he was born. His childhood in Indianapolis was a blur of foster homes, and he learned to be a scrapper and a fighter in his teen years, just to survive. No one would guess from the big, gentle man he is now that, in his youth, he did a stint in the State Prison for assault. The anger from his early years seems to have been channeled into his insightful, individual-against-the-system fiction."

Her feelings for Conner were mixed, as usual. She felt sorry for the boy he had been, for the fears and unhappiness he must have felt. On the other hand, this showed that he had a history of violent behavior. She wished she knew more, but the biographer hadn't elaborated.

And Conner never told me. She had shared everything about her life with him during long evenings of conversation, probably boring him silly. And he had never breathed a word about his past.

The bulk of the medical journal article was as dull as ditch water, but Mary Kate was convinced that the Margaret Olsen in the case study was her own screwy neighbor. The first sign that Mrs. Olsen had returned too soon to her work as a convalescent nurse after the death of her daughter was her severe reaction to the sight of blood. She was then assigned to patients who had no external bleeding. This worked for a short time before her superiors began to receive reports that she was accusing male senior staff and elderly male patients of making sexual advances on young female nurses. She was released on administrative leave after being caught shaking a post-operative patient, demanding that he tell her what he had done with her daughter. The case made local headlines when Nurse Olsen returned to the hospital and hid in the underground garage, leaping out from behind a parked car and attacking anesthetist John Burchram.

The slant of the article was that the hospital had been partly to blame because they failed to see the warning signs of stress. Mary Kate wondered how anyone could predict such extreme behavior. With an unprovoked attack on another human being in her background, Margaret Olsen could be a suspect in the murders, but only with a stretch of the imagination. Alissa was female and Randall Valentine was young. She would have no reason to hurt them.

A tap on the back door made her turn and see Conner through the panes. Her hand flew to her jaw, where the bruise had spread out into a smoky shadow. *What is he doing here?* At least the boys were in school. After what David heard his father say, seeing Conner might upset him. She walked over and opened the door. "Hi."

Conner smiled. "Hi, yourself. I left a message on your machine that I'd be picking up my car this afternoon. I'm glad to see it's okay after sitting on the street . . ." He took her hand away from her jaw. "What's this?" He held her chin gently in his fingers, tipping it to the light.

She winced as she answered. "Nothing. I slipped on the basement stairs and . . ."

Conner's face clouded over with anger. "Chuck hit you, didn't he?"

She couldn't lie to him. She wanted to, but knew he'd never believe it. "Don't do anything, Conner, please. For my sake. It's never happened before, and he's gone now. You can only make it worse."

His face reddened as he transformed into something frightening. He spoke through clenched teeth. "Damn it, Mary Kate. Why would you want to protect him? If he wants to hit somebody, I'll give him somebody that can fight back."

She turned her back on him, feeling tears and not wanting to cry. "This doesn't have anything to do with you, Conner, and you're scaring me worse than him." She turned around in time to see him clutch his side in pain. "Look at you. Your first day out of the hospital, and you're trying to be a tough guy." She took his arm. "Come in here and sit."

He allowed her to lead him into the living room and make him comfortable in Chuck's big TV chair. "Mary Kate, I can't stand the thought that someone would hurt you. Just the idea that he could hit you hard enough to make that bruise . . ."

She sat on the sofa. "Then don't think about it. I admit it was terrible. But it's done, and you can't undo it. Maybe it was a long time in coming, and I just didn't see it. I'm finding that's the case with a lot of things in my life."

"You always see the good in people. That's one of the things I've always loved about you."

"There's a difference between seeing good and not seeing at all, Conner. My whole life has been a series of happy accidents up until now. It's like I never saw what effect I had on other people. I assumed everything was okay because nobody kicked me in the butt and said that it wasn't. Now the murders and Chuck and . . . and you . . . and everything. Well, my butt's been kicked, and I don't know how to react."

He listened intently, and she could tell he was thinking, but not speaking his thoughts. She was grateful to him for that. She knew it would take very little to make her forget Chuck and fall into his safe, protective arms. Safe, as far as she knew, and she didn't know much about him. "To change the subject, I found out recently that you grew up in Indiana. I didn't know that."

"Yes," he said.

"Well?"

"Well, what? I grew up in Indiana."

She tried again. "Don't you think it's funny that we could know each other so long, and I wouldn't know where you came from?"

"Now you know."

He doesn't want to tell me. It wasn't only that the subject never came up. He was actively dodging it. She felt hurt.

Conner ran his hand over his chin. "There's nothing to tell. Don't look at me like that, Mary Kate. It was a long time ago. I don't even remember a lot about it."

"Okay," she said, standing and walking over to the window. She casually glanced out to the street, seeing Nancy kneeling over her flowerbed. "You don't have to tell me anything you don't want to. I mean, it's none of my business really."

"Mary Kate. You know I don't mean it that way."

She turned back to him. *I don't know what you mean at all.* She decided to let it drop. She didn't want to argue with him. In fact, a tiny seed in her mind told her to be wary. He had a temper, she'd seen it. *You don't want him mad at you.* He could break a jaw with one pop from his big fist. "Have you had any more thoughts on who could have attacked you?"

He seemed glad to talk about something else. "I know it wasn't Michael. He might be ten years older than me, but I'd never be able to knock him off so easily. I've seen him working out at hotel gyms. He's pure muscle."

"That's a relief," Mary Kate said. "I didn't want it to be Michael. I've always liked him despite his, uh, excesses. With all of his accomplishments, he's still a sad, frightened man. He'd be afraid to kill." Conner seemed to be mulling over her evaluation. "I've been thinking . . ."

"Uh-oh." Conner smiled.

She was not amused. "As I was saying, whoever it was, it had to be someone consumed with passion. I mean, if you just want to get somebody out of the way, then you shoot them or poison them. But when you come up to them and hack at them with a knife, then you want to feel them die. It has to be

151

something personal. And the fork marks, that's a message, a statement. It should explain why."

"Vampire bite," Conner mused. "The killer thinks he's a vampire. No, he stabbed first. He knows he's not a vampire, but wants us to make a connection."

Mary Kate picked up the train of thought. "He kills horror writers, and he leaves them with a mark of their profession. Okay, it's somebody who hates what we write. He thinks it's wrong, and he's trying to do something good. That doesn't sound like enough to murder for, Conner."

"People have killed for less, Mary Kate. If he's really a fanatic, then . . ." He tipped his head as if he were listening to voices. "The ex-priest guy, from the panel in Atlanta, what's his name?"

"Henley? Patrick Henley, the sociologist?"

"Yeah, that's him. Do you know what he's been up to since then?"

"Well, no. I saw him in Atlanta after Randall Valentine was killed." She remembered the tall, lean man speaking to the reporter as the church women chanted. "Leading a rally against the godless horror writers. And he was on the news right after Alissa's death, talking about immorality and violence. Oh, holy cow!"

"Holy cow is right. I saw in the newspaper a few weeks ago that he'd teamed up with DC, the Decency Coalition, you know, that group that goes around trying to get television shows and movies censored through advertiser boycotts."

"One of my favorite cop shows was watered down so much after they got hold of it that it ended up looking like 'The Brady Bunch.' Yeah, they're right wing, but I never saw them as dangerous."

"They don't have to be," Conner said. "All it takes is one extremist."

He left after making her promise to call him if Chuck showed up and gave her any trouble. Conner had taken a room at the Holiday Inn in Annapolis for a few days until he was well enough to drive back to Westport; at least, that's what he'd told her. Mary Kate suspected he was just staying near.

Nancy was still out in her yard. It was close to time for the mail, so Mary Kate strolled down the driveway to wait. "Hi!" she called across. "Whatcha planting?"

Nancy turned around, brushing her gardening gloves together to knock off the soil. She gazed into the distance as if she'd been disturbed from deep thoughts. Taking off the gloves as she walked over, she pulled on an unconvincing smile. "Just marigolds. The irises are fading, and I wanted some color there until I made up my mind what I wanted to do. I really should divide the irises this year. They're not blooming well and need to be divided." She sounded much too distressed about the irises.

"Are you okay?" Mary Kate asked.

"Me?" Her laugh was hollow. "Why, of course, I'm okay. Don't be silly. What happened to you?"

Mary Kate shrugged and touched her bruised jaw. "I'm a klutz. I slipped on the basement steps."

Nancy nodded. Mary Kate was relieved she didn't ask for more details. They looked at the dying irises for a few moments.

"What's with Chuck and the washing machine?" Mary Kate asked. "Linda Goodman told me you had to help him with it."

Nancy's face twitched. "Oh, that. Yes, Chuck called when you were away because he was having trouble with the machine. You know men. The boys were out of underwear or something, and he couldn't get it to drain."

"Left the lid up?"

Relief flooded Nancy's laugh. "Yes, exactly! It must be the same mind-set that makes them leave the seat up on the toilet." They both laughed.

"Miracles never cease," Mary Kate said. "Chuck never would have tried to do the wash before. Maybe there's hope for him yet. I wonder why he didn't take the dirty laundry over to his mother's the way he usually does. They spent the weekend there."

"I think it was before they left," Nancy said quickly.

She's upset about something. A helpful, perceptive friend would make her talk about it, but Mary Kate felt too burdened by her own problems to look for more.

"Mom! Dad's on the phone!"

She took the receiver from Ben as she continued to stir the spaghetti sauce on the stove.

"When's he coming home, anyway?" Ben asked. "We never get to see him."

"I don't know, sweetie." She paused before she spoke into the phone. Chuck had been leaving messages on the answering machine for two days. "Hello."

"Oh, good," he said. "I finally caught you. I suppose you weren't returning my calls on purpose. I don't blame you, Mary Kate. I crossed the line, and I'm sorry."

Her anger flared, and she swallowed it back. Ben sat at the table doing homework. "I don't know what you want me to say, Chuck."

"I want to come home. I made a mistake, okay? You've made mistakes, too. Let's start over."

"Chuck, it was . . . Just a minute." She put her hand over the receiver. "Ben? Dad and I need to talk privately. Could you finish that in your room, please?"

"I'm almost done."

"Upstairs, please." She waited for him to leave before speaking. "Chuck, what you did was more than a mistake. Leaving the top off the toothpaste is a mistake. Socking your wife in the jaw is unforgivable."

"I didn't mean to do it, Mary Kate." Anger seeped into his tone. "I was just so frustrated."

"And what's going to happen the next time you get frustrated?"

"I promise I'll never hit you again. I never did before, did I? Look, I'm trying to make up now, even though I know Drake was at the house today. See? I'm trying to understand here, Mary Kate."

"How did you know Conner was here?"

"It wasn't a secret, was it? Listen, I want to come home. I miss my children, and I don't have any clean clothes. It's my home, too, Mary Kate. We have too many years together to throw it out over one bad night. I'll come home, and we can talk. We can work this out, Mary Kate, if you'll give me a chance."

Too many years. She felt as if the destiny of her family depended on what she said next. Too much was at stake to be selfish. "Dinner will be ready in an hour. I'll set you a plate."

Chuck turned down the sound on the television as a commercial came on. He reached over and refilled Mary Kate's glass of wine. "Not bad, huh? I thought you might like it."

The flowers gawked at her from a vase across the room. Another sip made her head fuzzier, and the evening more bearable.

"I suppose you heard about that last Vampire Killer attack," he said matter-of-factly.

She was stunned. "No, what?"

"Some guy, a writer you might know. He lives in Colorado. Moss. That's it."

"George Moss? Is he all right?"

"According to the radio, all he got was a few scratches. Didn't even need stitches."

"Thank God. Where did it happen?"

"I said Colorado. Last night, at his home in Denver. Sssh, show's back on." He pointed his remote and turned the volume up. Mary Kate drained her glass and filled it again.

An hour later, she lay in bed behind Chuck's back as he slept. Her head throbbed from too much wine and what it made her do. Chuck had seemed braced for rejection of his advances upstairs after the news. If she had been sober, she would have said no. Now, she was left with a headache, wide-eyed in the dark, and he slept peacefully, believing that everything was back to the way it was before.

Chapter 18

"You've got to get out there, Mary Kate. The time is now, and it'll slip away before you know it." Donna Brook's voice was always too loud over the telephone. Mary Kate held the receiver on her shoulder to protect her eardrums. "You're in the news, and the interest is there. This is no time to hide out."

"Donna, I can't. It's . . . wrong." She knew her editor would not be deterred so easily.

"What's wrong? Nothing's wrong. You don't see George Moss peeking from behind the living room curtains on the evening news."

No one could have missed George on the television as he pulled up his shirt for the cameras, showing off the bloody bandages wrapped around his flabby, white belly. "I'd have to flash my breasts, Donna. I don't have any wounds."

"You miss my point, Mary Kate. George knows a promotional opportunity when he sees one. All I'm asking you to do is what you've always done—readings, interviews, signings, conventions. The Vampire Killer has people out there buying books, but they're buying anybody's books. We want them to buy your books."

"How's it going to look, Donna, if I'm actively trying to make money on the backs of two families' tragedies?"

"I'll tell you how it'll look. It'll look like Theodora Zed has an income two years from now. You've heard the rumors that the mid-list horror novel is going the way of the dodo bird.

The buyers are going for guaranteed returns on big name authors—King, Clancy, Steele. It won't be long before you might as well be writing in a diary with a little brass key. If you plan on being one of the few to survive, you have to cross that river into the mainstream. I don't mean to be cruel, but you're not going to make it on your literary talent, Mary Kate. If your intention is to make a living as a writer, you're going to have to fight for a spot."

Donna had never been one to mince words. Mary Kate wished she had. Cold, hard reality hurt. She wasn't a good writer, just a passably entertaining one. There had been enough of a following of fans to make Freeman Publishing a respectable profit, but any reductions could make her dispensable. What would she do? Mary Kate loved the writing and loved the lifestyle.

She saw in her mind two scenarios. In one, she worked as a receptionist at Rightway Insurance, driving home with Chuck after work. In the other, she continued to write. No Chuck. "Okay, but no cheesy tabloid shows."

Donna laughed. "I thought you'd gone to sleep. It's a deal, nothing beyond the usual." Her joy in winning made her even louder. "There's a convention in Cleveland a week from Saturday. What is it? Here . . . The Ohio Valley Writers of Speculative Fiction Association Convention . . . say that three times fast. And we'll line you up some signings and readings. Close to home, if we can, so you don't have to deal with child care too much, okay?"

"Thanks, Donna." Mary Kate entered the information into her calendar. *It's show time.*

David pushed Ben as they got out of the car. "Hurry up, fart-face! God, you're slow."

"I'm getting out as fast as I can!" Ben whined. The school

papers he held to his chest began to slip onto the floor again.

"David, just get out the other side." Mary Kate's patience with their bickering and fussing was wearing thin. Having their dad home hadn't been a positive influence.

"I can't! You parked too close to the damn wall!"

She closed her eyes and grit her teeth to the count of ten, just like the child abuse public service announcements said. She still wanted to clobber him. "I've about had it with the two of you! Either you get your little butts out of this car and in the house or . . ."

"Okay, okay. God, Mom, chill." David followed Ben out of the garage door, leaving her in the car to stew. She said, "I love motherhood," three times before getting out. She wasn't convinced, but it gave the kids a couple of minutes to get out of her way before she went in.

David and Ben stood in the front hall at the bottom of the stairs, looking at something on the floor.

"What is it?" she asked, walking up to them.

"Blood," Ben said.

Round, shiny red spots dotted the wood floor. Three to six inches apart, the trail led up the stairs. It hadn't been there a half hour ago when Mary Kate left to pick up the boys at school.

"Did you hurt yourself, Mom?" David's smart-mouth demeanor was gone. He looked scared.

"Uh, no, it's not mine." She checked her hands for an overlooked paper cut. "No, maybe it's the cat. I thought I put him outside after he ate, but he might have slipped back in when I went out." She felt increasingly uneasy. There had been too much human blood spilled lately to assume any-thing rational. "How about you guys waiting at Nancy's while I check this out?"

David put his hands on his hips, at least, the approximate

location of hips. Two-thirds of his body was long, skinny legs. "I'm not leaving you."

Ben took the same stance. "Me, neither."

As touched as she was by the sentiment, she felt a rising urgency to get her babies out of the house. "Come on. Don't argue." She took their arms and marched them through the kitchen. "I'll come and get you in a few minutes."

She walked with them across the street, ignoring David's pout, and at the door, Nancy's quizzical expression. On the way back, she saw the pink puff of Mrs. Olsen on the next block. Feeling eyes on her neck, she turned around. Curtains were peeled away at Nancy's front window, and two houses down, at Linda Goodman's. She wondered if either of them knew something she didn't.

Her suburban two-story with detached garage loomed above her as she approached, its ordinariness imbued with a sense of menace. The red drops weren't geranium petals this time. She felt no guilt at hoping Lestat got his nose shredded by a reluctant paramour.

First checking the yard and around the garage, she went in, the house closing around her like the inside of a whale. There were so many places for a murderer to hide. She ran over and locked the basement door, then looked at the knife rack. Deadly weapons, defensive weapons. Slowly, she extracted the largest, gripping its wooden handle. The blade caught a flash of sunlight and reflected it into her eye. In that blinding second, she saw Alissa, the gaping rips in her skin, the blood splashed everywhere . . . the red. "No," she whispered. "I couldn't." She put the knife back.

Straddling the drips on the treads, she followed them upstairs. Every part of her being was girded for the discovery of another body. The blood was there; the deed must be done. And only one person in the family was unaccounted for, though his car wasn't in the driveway.

At the top, the path was more difficult to see on the green floral runner, but she crouched down and found it soaked in to the right. It stopped outside of Ben's room. She opened the door and threw it back until it banged on the wall. Stepping in, giving the closet across the room a wary glance, she looked down. The trail resumed, plop, plop, plop, along the floor, onto the rug, to the side of the bed. On the bed, the spread was stained irregularly, a plate-size red splotch on the spaceship design. In the middle of it was a white business envelope, no address.

She whimpered at the abomination of seeing her tormentor's note on the place where her baby boy rested his head. Taking one hand away from her heart, she picked it up. The front was lightly smudged, the back had absorbed the liquid beneath it. Using the tips of her fingers from both hands, she removed the sheet of paper.

THIS IS REAL.

Lieutenant Evans held the plastic zipper bag with the note in it. "How are we supposed to know which smudges you made and which were already there, Mrs. Flaherty?"

"I'm sorry, but it was on my baby's bed. I had to know what was in it."

"And this was done between three and three-thirty?"

"Thereabouts. I've been taking them to and from school since Conner, uh, Mr. Drake was attacked. Anyone watching would know when and how long I'd be gone."

"Does anyone have the key to your house?"

She laughed ruefully. "Everybody, anybody. Up until the first note, I kept a key under a flowerpot by the back door."

Evans shook his head. "Mrs. Flaherty, you are a walking cliché."

"Yeah, that's been said about my books, too. Listen, this has always been a safe neighborhood. Everybody knows everybody. These are nice people." Her defense elicited a smirk from Evans. "Well, mostly." One of these nice people might have befouled her child's bed and left a threatening note. "Okay, so you can't know everybody, but we never had any trouble before."

"Before what?"

"Before the murders. The notes and the murders started at the same time."

"They're not necessarily related."

"Well, it's a peculiar coincidence. You interviewed my neighbors, right? I've done a little research on my own." Mary Kate warmed to her subject. "Mrs. Olsen across the street has a history of violence. She attacked a guy. And she's nuts. She hates me. My cat pees in her flowerbed."

"Your cat pees in her flowerbed," he repeated.

"It's more than just that. We leave the trashcans out overnight and let weeds grow up around the mailbox. And she's always lurking around. She spies on everybody."

Evans smiled. "Do you think it might be time to change your locks, Mrs. Flaherty?"

She realized he was blowing her off but she nodded. She really didn't believe that poor lawn care could elicit this kind of reaction from a neighbor. She just wanted to help make it over. She would change the locks and the boys would go to Grandma's. She had hoped she could keep their lives as normal as possible, but it was too dangerous now. "Where are your out-of-town buddies?" she asked. They were missing an opportunity to laugh at her again.

"Pumphrey and Malone? They've gone to Denver to check out that other attack."

"I know George Moss. Is he all right?"

162

"He looked pretty healthy on the news. You know, that was the first one where you weren't nearby."

Nearby. She remembered what she wanted to ask him. A real lead. "Maybe you can check something for me, a theory." He appeared interested, so she continued. "There was a guy at BloodCon in Atlanta who seemed pretty upset by what we horror writers write. Patrick Henley. He's been heard using the murders as a rallying point with his new friends in the Decency Coalition. He was interviewed on TV in New York right after Alissa Dibiase's murder. It would be interesting to see if he's had any recent stops in Denver, or if he's been seen around here."

"Is that it?"

"Well, yeah. Henley might be killing off horror writers as some kind of crusade. Conner and I were discussing it . . ." She noted his raised eyebrows. ". . . and we both feel that the murderer must have some strong emotional and symbolic motivation."

Evans' interest receded, but he made a note in his pad. "Sure, anything helps."

They both turned as Chuck appeared at the top of the stairs. Mary Kate had called him right after she called the police, both to see if he was okay and to let him know what was going on. She didn't want a repeat of Monday night's outburst. Evans eased her back with his arm as one of the crime scene investigators pushed by them in the hallway, carrying Ben's bedding in a bundle.

Chuck stood aside, then looked at Mary Kate. "What's going on this time?"

Evans spoke. "Didn't your wife tell you?"

"Yes, she told me. I just can't believe it. Does somebody have some kind of vendetta against me and my family? And you, what are the cops doing about this? Can't people leave their homes for a few minutes without weirdos breaking in?"

Evans squared his shoulders, then bit his lip before he responded calmly. A lesser man would have lost his cool. "The investigation is ongoing, Mr. Flaherty. I was just telling your wife that it was time to change the locks. 'Leave It to Beaver' is dead, and you can't let Eddie Haskel just walk into the house anymore."

Chuck turned on Mary Kate. "You've given out keys to half the neighborhood, haven't you? And probably some of those sicko writer friends of yours, too. Damn it, Mary Kate, do you see what it's all coming down to?"

She could see what Chuck couldn't. In his propensity for underestimating others, he couldn't see that Lieutenant Evans was losing patience.

"Mr. Flaherty, did you hit your wife?" Chuck reared back as if he'd been punched. As he reddened and searched for words, Evans asked the next loaded question. "Where were you between three and three-thirty this afternoon?"

Please, don't do this. Mary Kate knew she'd take the flack from this later on. Evans was kicking the hornet's nest and handing it to her. "Chuck was at his office," she interjected. "I called him there. He wouldn't have had time to get back."

The lieutenant met her eyes, his expression caving into regret as he realized what he had done. "Yes, of course. These are routine questions, Mr. Flaherty. You were concerned about security. Do you want us to post an officer here for a couple of days?" He asked the question as much to Mary Kate as to Chuck.

Chuck was still twitchy, but he had settled down. "No. We'll get somebody out here to change the locks. Just don't be handing keys out like candy," he said to Mary Kate.

Evans looked at her, and she said, "I'll be fine. Thank you." He nodded.

One of the other officers called up the stairs. "Lieutenant?"

Mary Kate followed Evans down the hall to the top step.

By the front door, a perspiring young officer held his hat in his hand. "Sir, we found some more blood outside. The trail went from the kitchen to the back yard and across the rear neighbor's yard. We're trying to pick it up on the street behind here, but no luck so far."

"Keep looking, Grossman," Evans said, going down to meet him.

Chuck took Mary Kate's arm and spoke quietly in her ear. "At least that jerk, Drake, has gone back to Connecticut and doesn't have anything to do with all this."

She cringed inwardly. Conner was five miles away at the Holiday Inn.

"Things are going to change around here, Mary Kate. Like it or not, you're going to have to stay home more often."

She decided this was not a good time to tell him about the publicity plans she had made with Donna.

Mary Kate packed overnight bags for the boys and gave them to Chuck as he went over to Nancy's to pick them up and take them to his mother's house. She had convinced him to stay with the children for their peace-of-mind and protection. She would stay behind to wait for the locksmith and to guard the house. Chuck had no problem with this. She wasn't as scared as she had anticipated. The alternative of spending the evening with Chuck must have made bloody intruders pale in contrast.

By seven o'clock, the locksmith truck was backing down the driveway, and she was the only one in the world with a key to her home. It was a good feeling. The sun was getting low, casting long shadows across the lawn. She opened the back door, expecting to find Lestat. She hadn't seen him since lunch. He usually disappeared if there were strangers around, but everyone was gone now. "Kitty, kitty! Come on, stupid!" It was spring, and she regretted once again not having the carousing beast neutered.

Back in her office, she looked up a number and dialed. The phone on the other end rang, and a Hispanic woman's voice answered. *"Hola."*

"May I speak with Mr. Moss, please?"

"Si, uno momento."

Mary Kate heard the receiver being put down, then a couple of minutes later, picked up again. "It's your dime."

"Hi, George. This is Theodora."

"Theo, you love goddess, how are you holding up with the police presence?"

"Me? I'm fine, George. How about you? That must have been terrible."

He laughed. "Folded and spindled, but not mutilated. Seriously, Theo, a little touch of death goes a long way. After the initial trauma, I had time to think. I believe now that being assaulted by a raving lunatic was good for me. A part of me, the sleeping animal, has been awakened. Survival instincts I never knew I had have risen from the depths of my brain tissue."

He's been working on his article for People Magazine. "I'm really glad you came through it okay. What was it like, I mean, what do you remember about the Vampire Killer?"

"Aren't you a curious little vixen? Looking for some vicarious fear?"

"Yeah, George, something like that."

"Where can I start? Hmmm. At first, it was nothing more than a sense of unease, like something wasn't right. The creature's aura preceded him in my consciousness."

Mary Kate realized she would have to sit through his literary excesses before she could get a description, if he ever got around to that at all. He went on. And on. Eventually getting to the actual attack.

"Lying in the dirt, his knee digging my spine, I saw the cape swing out and fall over my face. I heard a jangle of metal hitting metal, then the weapon being drawn from its sheath. Knowing I would die within moments, I acted with the adrenaline pumping through my chest. You might know me as a short, fat, middle-aged man with a ponytail, Theodora, but that night, I became Tarzan, Conan, the Lone Ranger, all my childhood heroes rolled into one. I fought like I never knew I could. And I prevailed."

If he were at the podium, she knew she would be expected to applaud. "How exciting! George, I am impressed. Besides the cape, did you see anything else?"

"Like what?"

"A face, maybe?"

"No, no, no. Nothing that specific. Images. Impressions."

"How big was he?" Someone kneeling on your back should give you some idea of weight.

"Big, Theodora. Tall, strapping, superhuman. I can tell you, Theo, the only way this killer will be stopped is with a fusillade of automatic weapons."

Mary Kate extracted herself from the conversation as gracefully as possible, wishing him well and knowing that his account of the incident would improve with the telling. George had been an arrogant blowhard from the time she had first met him, and this particular story was custom-made for embellishment.

Still, she couldn't shake the feeling that he was not only exaggerating, but lying.

★ ★ ★ ★ ★

Having the house to herself for a full day was a rare plea-sure. The next afternoon passed quickly. With no dinner to prepare, no homework to supervise, and no chauffeur service to soccer practice to provide, she was able to focus com-pletely on her writing. Mary Kate listened as the answering machine picked up a call.

"Mrs. Flaherty, this is Lieutenant Evans. I've got some of the lab tests back, and I'd like to . . ."

She picked it up. "I'm here."

"Oh, hi. I was just saying about the lab tests . . . uh, Mrs. Flaherty, do you have any pets?"

Where are you, Lestat? She had called him, then combed the neighborhood when he didn't show for lunch. "Yes. I have a cat."

"Damn. Have you seen it lately?"

"No."

He took a deep breath. "Mrs. Flaherty, the blood we found in your house wasn't human."

Aliens? "What are you saying, Lieutenant?"

"The blood came from an animal."

Chapter 19

The impatiens looked really bad. Lestat had certainly left his mark. The leaves were yellowed and the flowers rangy and sparse, despite the perfect shady location under the arching boughs of the spruce. The shredded bark mulch had been scratched like kitty litter. The soil beneath was probably toxic. Mary Kate gave the Olsen yard one last glance, then went up to the front door and knocked.

She had some reservations about this action, but she hadn't thought about them until her knuckles had already rapped on the wood above the doorknob. Marching right over and asking Mrs. Olsen what she knew about the cat had seemed like a darned good idea after Lieutenant Evans told her about the animal blood. He had told her not to worry, that it could be any kind of animal. It could just as likely have been blood from a leg of lamb or a pork butt. But Lestat had missed his noontime meal. Fat, spoiled Lestat. Mary Kate had entertained a logical progression of thoughts. Animal blood . . . cat . . . impatiens . . . pee . . . Mrs. Olsen. As logical as one can be in thirty seconds.

Impulsivity has its price. Other thoughts impinged as she stood on the door step. Notes . . . knife . . . blood. She tallied up what she knew about Margaret Olsen. She was a documented crazy. She had been open with her dislike of Mary Kate, and the cat had been a point of contention since the Flahertys moved in. Mrs. Olsen had only to look out her front window to monitor their comings and goings, and like so many others in the neighborhood, she had access to the house with her very own key. If she truly wanted to avenge the impatiens, she would have the means and the opportunity.

This is dumb. Mary Kate turned to leave. It had been years since Mrs. Olsen jumped the anesthesiologist in the hospital garage, and becoming a bit eccentric after one's husband has taken a powder didn't make one capable of murdering absolute strangers. As she took the second step down, she turned at the creak of the door behind her. It had been cracked open. "Mrs. Olsen?"

The door opened further, and Mary Kate could see a large shape in the gray shadows of the foyer. "I'm looking for my cat again."

The shape moved farther back. "Come in."

"Yeah? Oh, yeah, sure." Puzzled, she stepped up to the door and peeked in. The sunshine from outdoors made a bright crescent on the dark floor. Like most of the houses in the development, a staircase went up from a small entryway. Blinking away bubbles in her vision, Mary Kate followed the shape into the living room to the right, swinging the front door shut behind her.

The heavy, brown drapes were closed, and Mary Kate guessed from the stale air that all of the windows in the house were closed, too. The leftover scent of this morning's bacon drifted by, along with a sickly sweet odor and eau de mildew. "It's getting hot out there, isn't it?" Mary Kate said to get things rolling. "I suppose keeping the drapes closed cools things down some, but I just love the sunshine, you know?"

Mrs. Olsen filled the corner of the room, either her height or her formal demeanor making her seem as if she dominated the space. She wore a simple dress that was too small for her, with a cheerful flowered print that clashed with her stiff broad face. The short sleeves choked her thick arms, and when she stepped forward, Mary Kate could see the open zipper in the back making room for six inches of extra skin. Her shoes were a much better fit this time, brown leather brogues, very suburban, very matronly. Her white-gray hair had been combed back from her brow. Mrs. Olsen clasped her hands at her waist. "Have a seat, Mrs. Flaherty."

"Thank you." Mary Kate sat on a worn, but well-kept sofa. The matching cherry end tables and coffee table had been swiped recently and incompletely with a dust rag.

"Would you like some tea?" Her congeniality had a forced quality.

"No, thank you. I've been drinking coffee all day. I know it's too hot for coffee, but I've got to have it. It'll probably catch up with me some day. It can't be good for you." *I can't stop talking. What am I doing here? Why does she want me here?*

Mrs. Olsen sat on a little, velvet Victorian chair, her rear end completely engulfing the dainty cushion. Her back perfectly straight, her hands gripped each other in her lap. Her jowls jerked as she attempted a smile. "How is your family?"

A normal question. Okay. "Everybody's fine. The boys have always been disgustingly healthy. We've been fortunate." Mary Kate smiled pleasantly and let Mrs. Olsen take the lead. She didn't know where this was going, only that it wasn't likely that Mrs. Olsen had decided to be her friend.

"That's . . . good." Her eyes darted around the room and her thick, rough fingers twisted together until they whitened. "So . . . you're a writer."

"Yes."

"You write books. Fiction books."

"Novels, yes." *She's not going to ask me for my autograph, is she?* After the tension of the last few minutes, this idea was disproportionately humorous. Mary Kate sucked in her cheeks and blinked her eyes to keep from giggling.

"Is something funny, Mrs. Flaherty?"

"Ah, uh . . ." *Caught.* She felt as if she were back with the nuns at St. Joseph's. She covered her mouth with her hand and coughed. "Uh, no, of course not." The giggles were vanquished, at least, for now. "No. You were saying?"

Mrs. Olsen cleared her throat. She seemed more comfortable, as if she'd won a round. "I've read your . . ." Her nose creased. ". . . novels. How did you come to choose your subject matter?" She leaned forward, staring into Mary Kate's face with smoky gray eyes.

"You read them? Thank you, I . . ."

"I didn't say I liked them."

"Oh." *Definitely unexpected.* "You read them, but you didn't like them?"

"Linda Goodman recommended that I read them. Why do you write what you do?" She focused on Mary Kate, her eyes wide, her mouth working slightly as she ground her teeth.

Oh, holy cow. The giggles were dead and buried. The sweat breaking out on her back made her shiver. Mary Kate felt they were heading toward some unpleasantness, and her first impulse was to get out. She could utter some excuses and be out the door in less than a minute if she really wanted, but then she would have lost what could be her one chance to understand this woman, even if it wasn't what she wanted to hear. "I, um, don't know exactly where my ideas for stories come from. I just, you know, start writing. It's kind of like pretending."

Mrs. Olsen stared a moment longer, her eyes glazed over as if she were thinking. Her lips moved as she muttered softly to herself. Mary Kate had never met a really crazy person before, with the exception of one uncle who ran into walls when he was off his medication. She found it interesting, and a little sad.

Refocusing, Mrs. Olsen spoke again. "Do you enjoy it?"

"What?"

"Writing . . . what you write." She couldn't even speak the words.

Vampires! Vampires! Mary Kate shouted in her head. "Do I enjoy it? Yes. Yes, I do. It's creative and challenging and fun. And where else are you going to get a job where you can work in your bedroom slippers?" She smiled. Mrs. Olsen didn't. "What do you think of my novels?"

Mrs. Olsen sat back suddenly, then stood. Disengaging her fingers, she turned her back to Mary Kate, muttering and rubbing her palms together, making a dry swishing sound. Mary Kate's own palms were damp and clammy. *Oh, jeez, I've done it now.*

A table behind Mrs. Olsen held framed family photographs on a lace doily. One was a black and white wedding picture, the others were color photos of a little girl growing into a young woman. Toddler, first grade, braces, high school graduation. One picture in a crystal frame caught Mary Kate's eye. The same girl around age twenty, smiling prettily and wearing a size eight dress identical to the one Mrs. Olsen was crammed into.

Mrs. Olsen swung back around, standing over her. "You have sons."

"Uh, yes, two. You know that. I'm sure you've seen them around the neighborhood."

"No daughter?"

"No daughter."

"Ah. I see." Mrs. Olsen nodded. Mary Kate could hear her whispering to herself, "I have a daughter." Then nodding again as if she'd gotten instructions from an invisible friend, she asked, "What does it mean?"

"What does what mean?" Mary Kate felt she could follow

173

the conversation better if she could talk directly to Harvey the Giant Rabbit, or whomever Mrs. Olsen was consulting.

Mrs. Olsen pursed her lips impatiently. "What do your books mean?"

"What do . . . ? Nothing. They mean nothing. They're stories. I make them up, people read them for fun. Just for fun. There's no deep meaning. Really."

Mrs. Olsen took this in, then tipped her head to the side and listened. "Thank you for stopping in, Mrs. Flaherty." She held her arm out toward the front door. "It was . . . nice of you to visit."

Mary Kate felt as if she were getting the bum's rush. Walking to the door, Mrs. Olsen hurrying her along, she said, "Are you okay? I mean, do you have any family or anybody who can come stay with you?"

"I have all that I need," she answered quietly.

As Mary Kate was ushered through the foyer, she turned back, trying to think of something more to say, something to help her understand what had happened.

Past Mrs. Olsen's shoulder, she saw the carpeted steps, badly in need of vacuuming. The beige dust bunnies matched the pile, but one step was tufted with short black threads. *Cat hair?* She leaned sideways to look closer, but Mrs. Olsen's body barreled forward, propelling her out the door.

On the doorstep, Mary Kate asked, "Have you seen my cat? He's been missing for a couple of days."

"No."

"I thought you might. He likes to hang around in your yard."

Mrs. Olsen looked thoughtful, her fingers tugging at the thick wattle below her chin. Her eyes glinted mischievously. "It might have been hit by a car. It could be lying beside the road someplace, dead." She seemed to enjoy the thought.

Hateful old cow. "I hope you're wrong. He's a pest, but we're all very fond of him."

Mrs. Olsen pressed her lips together, as if she were the one who thought something was funny. She was a homely woman. Her face was big and rubbery, and her body, thick and boxy like a lady wrestler. Mary Kate supposed that physical strength had come in handy when she had been a nurse and an incapacitated patient had to be moved as dead weight.

The sun illuminated the flowers stretched across Mrs. Olsen's girth. Pink and turquoise on white, bright and youthful. "That's a lovely dress, by the way," Mary Kate said.

Mrs. Olsen touched her breast and smiled. She seemed almost soft. "My daughter gave it to me."

The door closed, and Mary Kate gulped the warm fresh air. The lack of oxygen in there might have contributed to the weird feeling that followed her out into the sunlight. She wondered if Mrs. Olsen had found out what she wanted to know. She sure as heck hadn't gotten anywhere. As Linda Goodman had said, Mr. Olsen had definite grounds for abandonment. Mrs. Olsen was Looney Tunes.

As Mary Kate crossed to her driveway, she saw Nancy driving out of hers in her van. She waved Nancy over. "Have you seen Lestat?"

Nancy rolled down her driver's side window. "Lestat?"

"Yes, he hasn't been home to eat. I just had a bizarre visit with Mrs. Olsen, and she said he probably got run over."

"What a mean thing to say, even if she is . . . you know. I don't remember seeing him, Mary Kate, but he's such a fixture roaming around here that I wouldn't pay too much attention if I had."

"If he shows up, will you give me a buzz?"

"Sure. You must be worried sick."

Animal blood. "I am. Where you off to?"

175

"The hospital. The kids have after-school activities until evening, so Doug's going to pick them up and take them out to dinner." She seemed distracted. "I decided to do a double shift, you know, double shift at the hospital. Doing my volunteer work, the volunteer work I do."

"Such dedication."

Nancy turned sharply. "What do you mean?"

"That you must be dedicated to work so hard for free. What did you think I meant?"

She laughed awkwardly. "Nothing. I'm just in a hurry. Late. I've got to go." She zoomed away up Linden Lane.

Mary Kate watched her go through the stop sign without braking. "Is everybody getting weird?"

"No, sweetie, not yet. Just a couple more days, okay? You're having fun at Grandma's, aren't you?"

"I want to go to school," Ben whined through the receiver. "There's nothing to do here."

"Hey, I thought this was a kid's dream, skipping school and playing Nintendo all day."

"I thought so, too, until I did it."

Mary Kate laughed. "Hang in there, slugger. Let me talk to your brother."

David came on the line. "This sucks, Mom."

"I know, darling. It should be over soon."

"Why should it?" he shouted. "The police don't know anything! The only way it'll end is when you get killed, too!"

"David, stop that right now. I'm not going to get killed. There are detectives from three states working to catch this kook, and they have lots of clues to work from. It can't go on much longer. Don't worry about me, I mean it. I'll be there with you guys tomorrow, and we can go out to lunch and a movie if you want."

He was quiet a moment, then spoke softly. "Mom, don't open the door for anybody, okay? Not anybody."

"Sure, sweetie." She wished there was some way to make his pain magically disappear.

"Dad called Grandma and told her he'd be late from work. You're the only one with a key to the house, right?"

"Yes, baby, I'm the only one. Don't worry."

Chapter 20

Shielding her face with one arm, Mary Kate spritzed her hair with red tint from the aerosol can. The color was unnatural, but so were the thick, black lines drawing up the corners of her eyes and the pale powder whitening her skin. The leather skirt pinched her waist uncomfortably, and the silk tank top showed more cleavage than she thought it should this early in the day. She stepped into the four-inch spikes. Her calves let her know immediately that they weren't used to stretching this way.

Theo looked back at her from the bathroom mirror. "Hello, darling."

She puckered her blood red lips, then brushed on a little more rouge for that totally consumptive look. Taking in the whole picture from frizzed-out hair to long, black-stockinged legs, she stuck out her tongue. "Who are you, Theodora Zed?"

Theodora responded with a question. "Who are you, Mary Kate Flaherty?"

Frightened because she had no answer, Mary Kate hurried out to the car for her book signing at Barnes & Noble.

The grungy windows of the garage let in diffused daylight, just enough for her to pick her steps over the junk without tearing her nylons. Her fingers fumbled along the wall for the switch to the automatic opener. As she hit it, the cables creaked and the big door rattled as it opened grudgingly. With the additional light, she found her way through to the car. The door banged against the handles of the bike Ben had outgrown, the one she had planned on giving away, if she could remember to do it. She squeezed in, promising herself that she would clean out all this stuff as soon as life returned to normal.

Twisted around in her seat as she backed out onto Linden Lane, she saw a large truck heading for her, broadside. Throwing the car into drive, she lurched forward. As she leaned out the window, the man in the passenger seat of the Goodwill truck wolf-whistled. She watched as he hopped out and picked up the cardboard box at the end of Mrs. Olsen's driveway, the same box that had distressed her so much before when it had spilled. Mary Kate considered the coincidence of almost being run over by a Goodwill truck right after committing to clean the garage. It had to be an omen.

Ten a.m. on a Tuesday isn't a good hour for vampire fans, especially when the signing is at the back of the store, yards away from the story time for three- to five-year-olds. Customers seeking Theodora Zed's autograph were few and far between, and when she wandered near to listen to the stories out of boredom, the children began to cry. The low-cut blouse brought a couple of men over to her table out of curiosity and lust. She was able to tease them into buying copies of *A Lover's Blood*. By noon, she had sold six books. She walked out to the parking lot, disheartened.

She still had grocery shopping to do. It had been four days since she had found the blood in the house, and nothing more had happened. The boys were eager to resume their lives, and she couldn't survive another weekend with Grandma. If she tried to help out around the house, she had been "taking over" and if she let Grandma do everything, she had been "treating me like a maid."

That was how Grandma voiced it to Chuck, who relayed her complaints to Mary Kate. Of course, Mary Kate didn't have a leg to stand on when she had said it wasn't fair.

"How can you say that when Mother's done so much for us?"

High on today's priorities were restocking the larder, collecting her children, and not letting killers or Grandmas or anybody disrupt her family anymore. She also wanted to find out more about Mrs. Olsen. There was something about their conversation last Friday that nagged at her like an itch between the shoulder blades, just out of reach. She had gone over and over Mrs. Olsen's words in her mind, trying to decode the message. Was she just insane, or was she extracting information for an unknown purpose?

The lot had filled with cars in the two hours she had been in the bookstore. Mary Kate ignored the stares of passing shoppers as she inserted the key in the door. Before she could climb in, she heard a car horn blatting.

"Mary Kate! Wait a minute!"

She turned to see Conner leaning out the window, his car blocking traffic. He pulled off to the side and waved the cars by. She walked over. "Hi. Is this a coincidence, or are you following me?"

"A little of both. I saw in the newspaper a few minutes ago that you were doing a signing here, so I drove over hoping I'd catch you before you left."

Mary Kate sighed. "You should have been here earlier. Then I could have sold seven books."

"Hometown signings are always small. People don't believe you're special unless you come from somewhere else."

"I was getting desperate. I got two guys to buy books by leaning forward so they could look down my blouse."

Conner raised an eyebrow and smiled. "You don't have to

180

lean forward in that blouse."

"Which is why I need to go home and change. I've got a lot to do today."

"How are things at home?" he asked. It was a question that could be interpreted different ways. She decided to take it literally.

"Quiet. The children have been at my mother-in-law's for the last few days. We had another break-in." Seeing the concern in his face, she didn't want to make it worse by explaining how awful it really was. "I've had the locks changed, and I'm bringing the boys home tonight. So, we're okay. Okay?"

"You should have called me, Mary Kate. You shouldn't be there by yourself. Was there a note this time?"

"Yeah. I gave it to the police." Her hand rested on the open window. Conner covered it with his hand.

"I'll come over tonight," he said. "You shouldn't be alone, Mary Kate."

Don't do this to me, Conner. Seeing him looking up at her expectantly was like dangling a carrot of possibilities. She didn't have to pick up the kids tonight. She could pick them up tomorrow.

What am I thinking? She had a husband and kids, and a home that had been turned inside out because of the madness of the last few weeks. It was all she could handle trying to put it all back in order. Conner had become a complication, a factor that threw her whole life out of whack. She didn't know what to do with him. He wasn't just a friend anymore. "That's not a good idea, Conner. Chuck is . . ." *Is what? Is never where he says he's going to be? Is as obnoxious as ever?* ". . . back home. We're trying to work things out."

Conner's face darkened. "Oh. Are you going for a broken jaw this time?"

The shame she had felt at being beaten came back to her. His words hurt more than he could know. She straightened her shoulders, knowing she looked ridiculous in her Theo get-up. "You might not understand this, but I have obligations to more than just myself. I'm not only talking about the children, either. I have an obligation to my husband. We're married, which means more to me than staying together until times get rough. We've made a lifetime commitment to being responsible for each other. I take my marriage very seriously, Conner. I can't end it until I know without a doubt that there's nothing left to save."

Conner looked at her for a moment longer, his anger barely concealed. "I see. That's it, then."

It sounded so final. She nodded.

He shifted his car into gear. "It's time I was heading home, anyway. Take care of yourself, Mary Kate." Lifting his hand in a casual wave, he drove away, tires squealing. She waved back, but didn't think he saw. Opening her car door, she saw her reflection in the window.

Who are you, Mary Kate?

Ten minutes later, she was backing into her driveway so she could head straight out after she changed into less conspicuous attire. She left the car outside and spent a few minutes calling the cat, as she had each day, although with less enthusiasm as time went on. Animal blood. Missing cat. It didn't look good. She had told David and Ben that Lestat hadn't been home, but she hadn't told them about the blood. The police had withheld the information from the public police reports because it was part of a continuing investigation, so nobody knew but Chuck, herself, and the cops. And whoever did it.

A warm shower took the goop out of her hair and the

make-up from her face, but didn't help with the guilt she felt about Conner. She hadn't meant to encourage him into believing she was leaving Chuck for him. She had never seriously considered it. *I fantasized about it. Do fantasies show? Did I leak secret messages telling him what I really want? That would make it real.* She wrapped her arms around her breasts, lifting her face into the spray. *I'm not ready for real. Not yet.*

"Oh, holy cow," Mary Kate whispered as she read the newspaper article on the computer screen. A librarian walking by the row of information access computers gave her a passing glance, then went on. The lady muttering to herself wasn't notable in any way. Theo had transformed into the unremarkable Mary Kate Flaherty.

She read on:

The body of nineteen-year-old Tammy Lee Olsen was discovered by Louise Overheart as she walked her golden retriever along the wooded road near her home in Fulton. Overheart said the dog had been sniffing around the trees, then ran back to her, barking excitedly. Expecting to find a box turtle or bird's nest, Overheart went to the side of the road. When she saw a naked foot sticking out of the dirt and leaves, she hurried home and called 911.

The Howard County Police uncovered the body of a nude female in her late teens to early twenties. Bruises and other trauma could be seen on the head and torso, but the cause of death was not immediately apparent. No identification had been found on the scene and she was listed as a Jane Doe.

Gregory and Margaret Olsen filed a missing person's report on Friday, two days after the body had been found. They had expected their nineteen-year-old daughter,

Tammy Lee, for dinner Wednesday evening. When she did not arrive, they assumed she was with the man she had been dating. Gregory Olsen said that Tammy occasionally stayed out all night without telling them where she would be, but usually contacted them the next day. "She would never worry her mother like this," Olsen said. "I should have known something like this would happen."

Police are trying to locate Jules Kingston, the man Tammy's parents believe was with her the night she was killed. Kingston, forty-three, has been missing from his Gaithersburg home and has not been to his office at the northwest Washington branch of Abelard and Sons since Tuesday, coworkers say.

The autopsy report distributed today attributed death to asphyxiation by strangulation. Blunt force trauma to the head and abdomen and forcible sexual intercourse had taken place prior to death.

"A parent's nightmare," Mary Kate said, looking at the grainy, black-and-white photo of the smiling teenager in the flowered dress, the same picture she had seen on the table in the Olsen's living room. She was painfully aware of how much was not said in the clinical news report. The shock, the tears, the emptiness, knowing one's only beloved daughter was gone forever. Then there was the anger over the terror Tammy must have experienced before she died and the guilt for not acting sooner. *I would have gone crazy, too.*

Mary Kate paged down to the next article found by the search words, "Tammy Olsen." It was a short report, describing the murder and the continuing investigation of Jules Kingston. The photograph alongside was of a handsome, dark-haired man with a distinguished beard, expensive clothes, and eyes full of promise and mystery. He was frightening and intriguing, the kind of man found in romance novels. Dominating, sexy, just out of reach. A vampire lover. *Did he kill this girl?* Mary Kate looked through several more articles of dead-ends and cold leads. No one knew. The murder of Tammy Lee Olsen had been officially unsolved for eight years.

Mary Kate typed in another newspaper search. "Margaret Olsen." Three articles from different papers told about the attack on the anesthesiologist, Dr. John Burchram, in the hospital garage shortly after Tammy's murder. Mrs. Olsen had accused him earlier in the week of trying to seduce the young, female nursing students. After she had left her job on extended personal leave, she had returned and waited for him near his car. As he was getting ready to go home, she jumped out, a sheet cut with eyeholes over her head. She scratched and slapped him, but he was able to get away with minor injuries. She later explained to the police that she had been wearing a shroud.

The next article had Mrs. Olsen in court pleading guilty by reason of temporary insanity to the charge of assault with intent to maim. Because of the extenuating circumstances regarding the recent brutal death of her daughter, she had been remanded into the custody of her husband and ordered to obtain psychiatric treatment. That was it for the next seven years.

Mary Kate's eyes opened wide at the recent dates on the next few reports. All of them were short filler stories or community police beat reports. Mrs. Olsen involved in a dispute at the Annapolis Mall. Mrs. Olsen tampering with someone's car. Mrs. Olsen loitering in someone's yard. Mrs. Olsen shoplifting in a hat shop on the waterfront. Mrs. Olsen disorderly at Saint Anne's Cemetery. *She's out of control. Why now?*

What was special about now? Murder, that's what. Mrs. Olsen was crazy and Mrs. Olsen was violent. She pinched a hat from a milliner and a woman in New York wore a hat. Nobody knows where she's been and when she went there. Mary Kate grabbed her purse. She would stop at the police station in Edgewater. She would tell Lieutenant Evans . . . what?

Of course, nobody knows what Mrs. Olsen has been doing, Mary Kate thought. Her daughter is dead and her husband has abandoned her. *And stop the presses because a woman in New York wore a hat. Now, that couldn't be a coincidence.* Mary Kate could see the lieutenant's condescending little smile already. He would call her "Mrs. Flaherty" in that just-a-housewife tone and tell her he will look into it. He might even laugh at her again. *The murders are in my life,* she thought. *Mrs. Olsen is just a fat, mentally ill woman in a teeny tiny dress.*

"I'm going to the grocery store," she said.

The trip to the Superfresh Store after leaving the library lifted her spirits. Under ordinary circumstances, grocery shopping was a hated chore, but today it symbolized reuniting her family. She was being Mother, Giver of Food. Fabulous, home-cooked meals were in store for them. Hot, hearty, nurturing meals. Turkey and pot roast, meat loaf and pork chops. And desserts. Ice cream, homemade chocolate chip cookies, Jell-O. "Leave It to Beaver" is not dead. *For us moms, food will always mean love.*

The walk from the car trunk to the back door was shorter from the driveway than it would be from the garage. She hauled bag after bag into the house, smiling at the bounty she was bringing. As the kitchen table filled up, she wondered where she was going to put it all. She packed the cabinets full of cans and jars, and the refrigerator with milk and cheese and fresh produce.

Half of the freezer section of the refrigerator had been taken up with frost-covered unknown entities. She stacked the meats and frozen vegetables into the available space, fitting one to the other like a jigsaw puzzle. The odd-shaped, twelve-pound turkey almost didn't make it. She balanced it on end and closed the door before it could roll out.

A five-pound bag of flour and a box of macaroni had to stay out on the counter, but, all in all, Mary Kate was pretty satisfied with herself. She had taken the first step. All she needed now was a husband and young'uns to start the rebuilding process. It was going to take a lot of work on her part. And sacrifices. She would call Donna tomorrow and tell her that the convention in Cleveland this weekend was out. There were steaks in the freezer screaming for a family barbecue.

Glancing out the back door window, she saw she had left the trunk open. She pressed her fists into her back as she walked out to close it, debating on the way if she should bother to drive the car into the garage. *Yeah, I better.* Chuck would get upset if he had to park farther away from the house than usual. She slammed the trunk closed and got in, turning the key with one hand, while pressing the remote opener on the sun visor with the other. Thirty feet forward and she was in the dark hole of the garage. Cutting off the engine and opening the car door, she stopped and sniffed. A familiar odor underlay the oily car and lawn mower smells.

Though she didn't know why, Mary Kate's heart fluttered as if a less evolved, instinctual sense had been triggered. She could see nothing out of order, meaning everything was out of order. The garage had been the main junk depository for years. Her eyes hadn't completely adjusted from outside. The walls were black shadows between shapeless hulks. She stood very still. No sound. No breathing. Nothing alive. She sniffed again, this time shivering as the sharp odor hit her nostrils. Blood.

Where? The heat of the day had been trapped in the garage, making it ten degrees warmer than outside. The smells had been baking. Hot blood. Spoiled meat. She would vomit if she didn't get some air. She lurched forward toward the door. Throwing it open, a low shaft of evening sun came through. Beside the light switch, Lestat's body hung suspended on the wall, his eyes wide and blank, white teeth bared, his coat damp and dripping. On the concrete floor . . . blood.

Mary Kate screamed.

Chapter 21

The weak, yellow circle from the flashlight zoomed by the spot where the cat's body had been nailed to the wall, then settled on the hook near the corner. Mary Kate hung the dirty shovel on the hook, then got out before she became ill from the lingering odor of death, faint but still there after four hours of airing out.

Her clothes were soiled, and she was sweating from the exertions of grave digging. Even such a little grave. The ground back in the weeds behind the garage had been soft and sandy, but the job had taken a long time. She had needed many breaks to cry.

"Poor Lestat, you stupid cat." Mary Kate dragged herself into the house and locked the door. Her brain hurt from too much thinking, and even though she thought she had it worked out, she knew there were flaws in her plan. *I can't think anymore tonight.* She went upstairs and peeled off her clothes, dropping them on the bathroom floor. She turned on the hot water and stepped into the steaming spray. The mud ran off her skin, going down the drain like a chocolate swirl.

The house was quiet. Too quiet. Mary Kate lay in bed, not able to close her eyes, aware moment by moment of her own breathing. *I'm the only living thing in the house.* The thought of a cockroach or even a spider creeping around in the dark made her feel a little better. She hadn't realized before how much Lestat filled in the spaces as the members of the family came and went.

That he hadn't been home for days made no difference. There had been the constant hope he would be sitting outside the back door, flipping his tail impatiently as he waited to come in. That hope was gone. Mary Kate tried closing her eyes again, opening them as the image of white teeth curving out from black lips filled her head. In death, Lestat's mouth had drawn back from his teeth, leaving him with an eternal snarl. Knowing it was rictus, Mary Kate still found it frightening and accusing.

It had taken her two hours to decide what to do. Right after she had found him, she ran out screaming, then peeked in every few minutes to see if it had been real. After a short stage of true hysteria, she had pulled herself together enough to think. She was glad she had. She had given herself time to realize that her first impulse to call for help was wrong. The police could only look in from the outside. Their investigations after something dreadful had happened seemed to encourage more of the same. Chuck would just get angry. She would end up wasting energy attending to him. And Conner . . . He was probably gone. She would have liked to have someone to hold her and make her feel safe, but she knew she was on her own now. She had to make her own decisions. Alone.

Burying the cat had been the first step in her plan. Only she and the sick individual who did this would know what had happened to him.

Lestat had seemed to be magically floating three feet above the floor. Mary Kate had to turn on the lights and dig through the black fur to find the method of attachment. She had almost lost her nerve as her fingers touched the hard metal of the nails driven through his shoulder joints. The only way to get them out was with the claw end of a hammer.

After releasing the body, she had held the remains of her old buddy a moment before placing him gently on the concrete floor. She couldn't have followed through with her plan if she had allowed herself to feel all of her grief. She swallowed hard and grit her teeth, then proceeded to make mental notes of his condition.

His legs and tail had been warm and limp, but his torso was cold and hard. She had forced herself to look closer still and found the killing wounds on his belly. Touching the skin around them was like touching an ice cube. *Death's not this cold,* she had thought. He had been frozen. The hard lump inside his abdomen was the only part that hadn't defrosted in the hot garage. Mary Kate's teeth chattered, having nothing to do with the cold. The perversion and desecration, the heat, the smells—she couldn't go on. Running down the driveway screaming had been the only thing she could think to do. For about ten seconds. Then she reminded herself that she was the only one who could end this once and for all. She picked up Lestat and carried him to his burial place.

Cleaning up the blood hadn't taken long. There wasn't much there. Mary Kate grimly remembered the large red stains on Ben's spaceship bedspread. The most difficult part was throwing the first shovel full of dirt onto Lestat's snarling face. She had tried to think of an appropriate prayer, but instead vowed to him that she would find the monster who did this.

Now lying in bed, sleepy and exhausted, her eyes fluttered shut. Alissa glared at her, her lips drawn back from her curved teeth in an eternal snarl. "Theo, darling, what do you think you're doing?"

Mary Kate jerked awake, shuddering. Pressing her hands against her thumping heart, she whispered, "What am I doing?"

★ ★ ★ ★ ★

Mary Kate closed the zipper bag and handed it to David. "Share them with your brother."

"Grandma always makes cookies when we come over. We don't need yours."

"Mine are better," Mary Kate said, then after a pause, added, "Be sure to tell her so." She hated sending them back after being home only four days, but there was no other way to do it.

"Mom," Ben said, "what if Lestat comes home this weekend when nobody's here?"

She hadn't told them what happened to Lestat. It broke her heart to see them out calling him each day. She put her arm around his shoulder. "I'll put some food and water by the back door before I go. Okay?"

He nodded sadly. She kissed his cheek, then reached over and grabbed David. She kissed him before he could object. "I love you, you know," she whispered in his ear. He shrugged away from her, but managed a nod of acknowledgment.

Chuck came into the kitchen in an odd, good mood. "Come on, soldiers, move on out!" The boys skulked out the back door. "I wish you didn't have to go," he said to Mary Kate after they had gone.

"I promised Donna I'd be there. This is the last convention I have scheduled. I'll be home more after this."

Chuck took a chocolate chip cookie from the plate. "I should stay and watch the house. We're setting ourselves up leaving it empty for two days. I could eat those good leftovers from all that cooking you've been doing."

What has gotten into him? He's almost . . . likable. "The boys need you, Chuck. I'll feel better knowing you're looking after them." *If you stay with them at all.* "I've asked Nancy to keep an eye on things for us. You've got the new key?"

"Yeah, right here," he said around a mouthful of cookie as he patted his pocket. "Well, that ought to do it. Mm, this is good, Mary Kate." He swallowed and approached her, a sprinkle of crumbs on his upper lip. He held her arms awkwardly, leaning forward to kiss her and smelling of chocolate. She gave him a quick kiss. He smiled, brushing cookie crumbs from her lip with his fingertips. Mary Kate smiled. *Hello. Aren't you the guy I married fifteen years ago?*

"I'll get out here." Mary Kate took the money for the cab out of her jeans pocket.

"Here?" The driver pulled the taxi to the side of the dark road. "Isn't there someplace I can take you? You get killed or somethin' and I'll feel responsible."

She handed him the money and opened the door. "I'm fine, really. Thanks for caring."

"Be careful then." He waved as she stepped back into the brush. She watched as the red taillights disappeared around a curve, then walked in the shadows of the trees until she could see the back of her house across the yards.

She felt invisible in her black jeans and black sweatshirt, skirting across the edges of the lawns. Barking dogs were dispatched quickly with a chocolate chip cookie. She had thought of everything. The car with the packed suitcase was in a twenty-four-hour parking garage in downtown Annapolis. All the world thought she was on her way to the Ohio Valley Writers of Speculative Fiction Association Convention in Cleveland.

The weeds smothering her own back fence were the final obstacle. She crept up to the basement door, unlocked it, and slipped in. The trap was now set. She had told everyone who might be involved that her house was going to be unoccupied this weekend. Whatever devilment was going to take place

193

was going to have a witness this time.

Emerging from the basement door into the silent, black kitchen, she could smell every part of their lives from the chicken she fried two days ago to the mildew on the shower curtain upstairs. She felt like a stranger invading her family's home, intruding on their privacy, being where she did not belong. *Did the person who broke into my house feel like this?* She stepped quietly to the front of the house and looked out the living room window.

Lights were on in Nancy's house across the street and two doors down at the Goodmans'. The Olsen house was as dark as her own. As Mary Kate watched, she thought she saw movement in Mrs. Olsen's driveway. A moment later, the interior light of a car came on, then went out as someone— she couldn't see who—slipped in and slammed the door shut. Through the closed window, the start of the engine was muffled. The taillights glowed red, and the headlights cast a broad beam on Mrs. Olsen's hedge. The car backed out onto Linden Lane, then roared away.

The blue numbers of the VCR clock showed that it was eight-forty-three, and one of her prime suspects had just taken off. *What if nothing happens?* She hadn't found notes and blood and murdered kitties every time she left home. *I'll feel stupid . . . not the first time.* She had been hoping that the lack of a reaction to the cat would prompt the perpetrator into escalating the activity. She had imagined the sicko standing back and laughing as the police failed repeatedly to discover his—or her—identity. She was sure her own emotional outbursts had added to the fun. So, this time . . . Nothing. *You butchered a sweet, little animal and nailed it up for me to find and . . . nada.*

She didn't need lights as she walked from room to room, depressed and angered by a family driven by fear from their home. She went into each boy's room upstairs and looked at their empty beds. *We could move away. And not tell anybody where we went.*

She knew Chuck would never move. He had his whole adult life tied up in the insurance company, and he'd never get out of mooching distance of his mother. Mary Kate wandered back into the hallway, imagining what kind of house she would buy if she could select it herself. A log cabin or a sea cottage with gray weathered siding. Anything different. Chuck had wanted this house as a testament to his success. Solid suburbia with no identifying characteristics distinguishing one owner from the next. If it weren't for their overgrown lawn, she could easily walk into the wrong front door. No, she wanted a house that said loud and clear, Mary Kate Flaherty lives here.

Going for another pass downstairs, she took the first step, then stopped as she heard a jingling of keys. The back door in the kitchen opened and a paralyzing fear ripped through her. *It's happening!* She realized she wasn't breathing and took a gulp of air, sounding to her own ears like a bagpipe wheeze in the dark silence of the staircase. Footsteps crossed the kitchen and a light came on. Trying to regulate her breath and ignoring the pulse pounding in her ears, she padded quietly down three more treads.

She listened and heard the soft suck as the refrigerator door was opened. *Wait a minute. Would an intruder stop for a snack? Maybe.* Glass clinked. The refrigerator closed. She leaned precipitously over the banister. Light fell on the floor outside the kitchen door. All she could see was a shadow moving across the counter with the coffee maker.

Then he coughed. It was like music. The relief loosened the tension in her muscles so quickly she had to sit on a step to keep from falling. *Chuck came home anyway!* He must have been too concerned to leave the house empty. Smiling, she slapped her hands onto her knees in preparation to stand and stopped as she heard a gentle knock on the front door. The footsteps crossed the kitchen to the foyer. Puzzled, Mary Kate rose to her feet and shrank back into the shadows of the upper staircase.

Chuck opened the front door and laughed softly. "I brought wine, too," he said, stepping aside.

Nancy Reiner came into the foyer, holding a wine bottle. "We can drink both." She laughed and leaned into Chuck's chest. They kissed.

At least, Mary Kate thought she saw them kiss. It certainly looked like kissing. She rubbed her eyes and looked again. His arms were around her. Their faces were pressed together. Yes, they were kissing. And moving toward the stairs.

OhmyGod! She backed up the rest of the stairs, started to go into her bedroom, realized what she was doing, and dove into the hall bathroom just as their heads became level with the floor. As she had feared, they went into Chuck's and her bedroom. Mary Kate peeked into the hall. They had left the door open. She could hear their voices. Giggling. She couldn't remember Chuck giggling once in the seventeen years she had known him.

The only thing keeping her in the bathroom was her doubt of her own perceptions. *I must have it wrong. This can't be what it looks like.* Chuck's interest in sex had been minimal since she had met him, and for the last few years he had claimed he was too tired most of the time. And Nancy . . . Mary Kate could have believed her children were the result of virgin births. *And I always thought the television was my competition.* She knew she had to see it with her own eyes.

She tiptoed into the dark hallway and slid up to the bedroom door. Flattening her body against the wall, she leaned toward the opening just enough to see.

The lights were off, but it was not too dark to prevent her from seeing the clothes strewn on the floor and Chuck and Nancy standing beside the bed in a naked embrace. She pulled her head back, but the image of their bodies continued to float in front of her.

She felt sick with the torrent of emotions pummeling her. Anger . . . betrayal . . . grief . . . frustration . . . shame. The force of it took her breath away. She couldn't bring herself to confront them. She didn't want anyone to know what a fool she had been. She didn't know what to do . . . until Nancy moaned.

She hurried down the stairs as if jabbed with an electric prod and ran into the kitchen.

She paced the kitchen floor, her fists bunched. *What do I do? What do I do?* No answers came, just an overwhelming feeling that she was going to explode any moment. *Can't stay here. I have to go.* She headed for the door, put her hand on the doorknob, and stopped. Looking back at the refrigerator, she said, "Why not?"

Mary Kate took the wine bottle from the refrigerator and the corkscrew from the drawer. She unstopped the cork as she walked down the driveway, throwing the corkscrew out onto the lawn. *Don't have a car.* Walking up Linden Lane, she took a long swig from the bottle and set it down on the pavement. By the light of the streetlamp, she dug in her purse for her cell phone. When she turned it on, she was immediately accosted by low battery beeps. The phone cut off before she could call Information for the taxi company number. "Damn."

The nearest pay phone was two miles away at a convenience store. *I'll walk to the phone and call for a taxi to take me back to my car.* A long walk in the dark in the company of a bottle of zinfandel didn't sound so bad. She took another drink.

"Son of a bitch," she muttered as she wiped her mouth with the back of her hand.

Chapter 22

The bartender paused as he passed Mary Kate at the bar. Seeing that her glass was full, he moved on to the next customer. She lifted the wine glass and sipped. Her lips tingled, numbness setting in. "Wait a minute," she said louder than she had intended. She looked at the glass. "How did I get white wine?"

The young lady on the stool beside her laughed. "Don't you remember? You asked for something that didn't look like blood."

As Mary Kate smiled, she felt the corners of her mouth reaching her eyes. "Oh, yeah! That's right." She leaned over the bar and saluted the bartender with her glass. "Thank you!" she called down to him. He nodded.

As the late panels broke up, the bar began to fill. No one had recognized her without her Theodora costume. She still wore the black jeans and sweatshirt she had been wearing when she walked to the Jiffy Mart five hours earlier. The bottle of wine from the refrigerator at home had been half gone by the time the cab arrived to take her to her car. She had driven to Baltimore-Washington International in fear of being stopped for driving under the influence. Sitting on the edge of a toilet in the airport ladies' room, she polished off the bottle while waiting for a commuter flight to Cleveland.

Mary Kate spun around on the barstool to see who had come in since she last checked. She fell off, landing on her feet. "Whoopsie!"

She let the turbulence in the air around her head settle before picking up her drink. She scanned the tables and booths. This was one of the smaller conventions and leaned heavily toward science fiction. Few of the horror writers would be in attendance. Mary Kate had every intention of partying all night long and didn't care if it was with new friends or old friends. She only wanted to make it through the night without thinking.

Walking between the tables, she sipped from her glass, looking for a likely party to invite herself to. As she passed the booths along the wall, she saw the back of a brown, shaggy head lifted higher than the others. She came up on his side, first seeing George Moss on the vinyl bench across from him. George gave her an odd look, then Conner turned to see her at his shoulder. He also looked puzzled, but slid over on the seat. "Join the party, Mary Kate," he said.

As she sat, George clasped his hands on the table, one eyebrow lifted suggestively. "Theodora," he said, "this is the most clothing I've ever seen you wear. Or do you prefer being called Mary Kate when you're not in masquerade?"

She looked down at her clothes, having forgotten what she was wearing, then shrugged. "You can call me Phil."

George laughed, and she gave him a wink. Conner drank from his beer glass, watching her over the rim. She felt as if he were disapproving, as if she were lowering herself by drinking too much, as if she had no right to go out on a toot. *No-o-o, you can do it, everybody can. But not Saint Mary Kate, mother and keeper of all virtues.* She couldn't handle being judged this way tonight. She would have fun with George instead. "Have you recovered from your Vampire Killer attack, George?"

He tugged on his ponytail in his excitement. "The wounds are healed, thank you for asking. The scars itch occasionally, but nothing a little salve won't relieve."

Mary Kate drained her glass and smiled. "I never got to see those infamous slashes. How about a peek?"

George huffed self-consciously. "There's nothing to see really. It has been some time."

"Aw, come on. Lemme see."

He glanced at Conner for help, but Conner lowered his eyes to his beer mug. Tentatively, George lifted the bottom hem of his cotton crew neck. He held it up for Mary Kate's inspection.

She leaned forward, scrunching her eyes dramatically. "Where is it, George? All I see is an incredibly furry belly-button."

He waved his hand around his stomach. "Right through here . . . somewhere."

"I can't see anything." Mary Kate practically climbed across the table. "Point or somethin', will ya'?" George pulled down his shirt. She had seen what she expected. Nothing. She lowered her voice. "Okay, Georgie, just between you and me . . ." She crooked her finger, and he brought his face close to hers. ". . . there's nothin' there, is there? You were never attacked, were you? You see, George, I've seen the Vampire Killer's handiwork up close, and believe me, you'd have noticeable scars. Alissa . . . remember Alissa? She was attacked for real. It was real, George. She had blood all over. All over. Everything was . . . red. I saw into her body, the cuts went into her body . . ."

"Mary Kate. Stop." Conner's fingers dug into her shoulder, bringing her back into her seat. "Stop."

George's face drained of color. His lip jittered. "I . . ." he said, then stood quickly. "You're horrible, Theo!" He strode stiffly from the barroom.

Mary Kate closed her eyes and the room jilted wildly. She opened them before her stomach revolted. Conner was

looking at her. She touched his cheek. It was warm and a little
stubbly.

"What's wrong?" he whispered.

She smiled stupidly. Everything was wrong. The world
was wrong. "I'll tell you what's wrong, Conner. My glass is
empty." She held it up for him to see.

"You've had enough for tonight."

"No, I haven't. I haven't had near enough."

A shadow fell over her right side. She turned to see an
impeccably dressed vision with gleaming teeth.

"Do you need a refill, Theodora?" Walter Truesdale
asked. He waved to a waiter. "What are you drinking?"

She held up her glass. "Fruit of the vine, my dear man."

He ordered drinks for the table and sat across from Mary
Kate. "How is the promotion for *A Lover's Blood* going?" he
asked her.

She giggled. "How the hell do I know? I just write the
damn things." Truesdale's hand moved, and the diamond on
his pinky ring caught a passing light, throwing out a glittering
aurora. He was a wealthy man and wanted everyone to know
it. She stared at the ring.

"You're usually working these conventions like there's no
tomorrow," Truesdale said. "Are you taking it easy this
time?"

"Huh?" She looked up. His teeth were too long. "Oh,
yeah. Taking it easy. Relaxing. Right, Conner?" She turned
to him. He met her eyes and went back to contemplating his
drink. "What about you, Walter? Are you working?"

He smiled, and the full display of his teeth reminded her of
Lestat's death grin. "I'm always working, Theodora." The drinks
arrived. "On my tab, please," he said to the waiter. "As I was
saying, I'm always open for business. And it's been rough lately. I
guess you've felt the effects of the declining horror market."

Conner said nothing. Although his mug was dry, he didn't touch the one paid for by Truesdale. Mary Kate took a couple of gulps from hers before speaking. "Not me. My books sell out wherever they're sold. You know why? Because they're trashy. Pure crap. Sweet, young thing moves away from home and meets older mysterious stranger. He seduces her with sexual maneuvers I haven't personally experienced in fifteen years of marriage." Conner turned from his drink, long enough to look at her with a raised eyebrow. She shrugged and continued. "Having the poor wench completely under his domination, he reveals that he's a . . . You guessed it! A vampire! He kills people and this is supposed to be romantic."

"Women love the fantasy," Truesdale said. "You're filling a need."

"I'm filling a septic tank."

He laughed. "Maybe so, but the real tragedy is what you're being paid for it. Freeman Publishing is wasting your potential. I think you have enough of a following to rise above the mid-list."

"You do, do you?" She watched him run the tip of his tongue over his teeth and wondered how he did it without drawing blood. He wanted a piece of her. A fifteen percent agent's commission, to be exact. He would mesmerize her with shiny rings and seduce her with promised riches to get it. Then what? Would he reveal that he, too, was a vampire?

"I have some ideas, Theodora." He narrowed his eyes as he looked into hers. "We could talk about them some time."

A shiver ran through her. One of the most successful agents in the country was promising to give her the career she had always wanted, and all she could feel was fear. She knew she was out of her league. He could chew her up and spit her out before she knew she'd been bitten. "There's a little problem, Walter."

He raised his eyebrows. "What?"

"The writers you talk to have a funny habit of turning up dead."

Truesdale drew back in his seat, his lips closing over his teeth. Conner shook his head.

"How does that happen, Walter?" she asked. "What is it about you?"

He hissed as he spoke. "You're a sloppy drunk, Theodora. I liked you better when you showed your boobs and kept your mouth shut."

Conner touched her arm as she was about to answer. He looked across the table to Truesdale. "I think you'd better go," he said in a low voice.

Truesdale recovered his composure and smiled. "Call me when you sober up, Theodora." He threw his business card on the table and left.

Mary Kate sighed and leaned on Conner's shoulder. His arm around her waist kept her from slipping off the seat. "Conner," she said, "get me out of here before I start talking again."

Conner sat Mary Kate on the bed, then went to the phone. She couldn't remember how she got to the room. "Are you calling down for drinks?"

"No, coffee. Lots of it."

She had an audible buzz between her ears and the room dipped when she moved her head. "I'm plastered, aren't I?" she muttered to herself.

"Yes, you are." Conner appeared, standing over her. "What brought this on, Mary Kate? I've seen you a little tipsy before, but never like this."

"Oh, you know . . . things. I don't want to think about it."

She reached out and touched the side seam of his jeans with her fingers. "One thing, then another. It's all too much sometimes." She ran her fingertips over his thigh and looked up at him. She felt so rejected and alone. He could make her feel safe. She stood and put her arms around his neck. Tentatively, he encircled her waist. She rested her head against his throat. *Better. Much better.*

"Mary Kate," he whispered, "we shouldn't . . ."

She turned her face to his. His warm breath on her skin smelled of beer, his eyes were smooth, deep brown. Being near him felt right. She rose up on her toes and touched her lips to his. She kissed him again, and this time he met her kiss. Looking into his eyes, she could see him succumbing. His arms tightened around her. He lowered his mouth to hers and kissed her hungrily.

She relaxed into the silken protection of his arms, so tight she could barely breathe. She didn't want to breathe. She closed her eyes and tasted his mouth and tongue with hers, melting into his body, the pounding of her heart the loudest sound. His hands slipped below her waist, making slow circles on her bottom, pressing her closer. She dug her fingers into his soft, thick hair.

Conner broke away from her, breathing heavily. "No, Mary Kate," he said hoarsely.

Though the room was lit with a single lamp, the brightness stung. Her eyes had become accustomed to a soft, black, exciting place. "Wha'?" she managed to say between gasps.

"I'm sorry, Mary Kate." He backed away a few steps as if he knew he couldn't resist falling into the sexual whirlwind around her. "You're not yourself. You've been drinking too much. I want you . . . God, I want you, but not like this."

The rejection and shame were amplified by her inebriation. She stood dumbfounded on shaky knees, wishing she could disappear. Instead, to her greater embarrassment, tears rolled down her cheeks.

Conner rubbed his chin. "Damn," he mumbled, taking a step toward her, then stopping, afraid to come within touching distance. "No, don't cry. It's all right. It's my fault."

His clumsiness made her feel worse. She had screwed up another relationship. *No man wants me. Not Chuck, not Conner, nobody. I'm repulsive. I'm a horrible person!* She covered her face with her hands and sobbed. She heard Conner mutter, "Oh, no," then felt him lead her to the bed. She sat and cried as he patted her back.

A few minutes later, she came up for air. Conner had tissues waiting. She wiped her eyes and blew her nose. The post-bawling hiccups made it impossible to speak for a couple of moments. She took a deep breath and exhaled. "I guess I've made a total horse's patoot out of myself tonight."

"No, I wouldn't say that." He sounded as if he were being careful. The crying jag must have thrown him off. He turned as they heard a knock on the door. "I forgot all about the coffee," he said.

Mary Kate went into the bathroom and threw cold water on her face as Conner attended to the room service. He met her with a cup of hot coffee as she came out. They sat at the table, and she sipped. The high from the massive wine consumption was wearing off, and she was feeling just plain sick. "I suppose I ought to explain why I, you know . . ."

"You don't have to." He sat across from her, looking for all the world like a man who has dealt with too much female emotion for one evening.

"Yeah, I do. I'm not so potted that I didn't notice how much of a sacrifice it was for you to stop when you did." He returned her smile. "You did the right thing and I thank you because if you'd waited for me to say stop, it wouldn't have happened."

"Mary Kate, under other circumstances . . ."

She nodded. "I know. That's why I wanted to explain. You see . . ." She swallowed hard in preparation of saying it out loud. ". . . I caught Chuck in our bedroom with another woman tonight."

"In your bed?"

"They didn't make it that far. I saw them butt-naked beside the bed before I ran out. It was Nancy from across the street. They say charity comes back to you a hundred-fold. I guess all that volunteer work she does paid off."

"I'm sorry." He was quiet a moment. "Man, I don't know what to say, except that I'm more certain than ever that Chuck needs his ass kicked."

"Be my guest." She savored for a moment the image of Conner punching out Chuck, then the awful reality settled in again like pond scum. "Thinking over the last few months, I'm sure this has been going on a long time. I feel so dumb. He didn't want me. We lived in the same house, slept in the same bed, and I didn't know. If I hadn't buried the cat, I might never have found out."

Conner stopped mid-sip and looked at her. "If you hadn't what? Back up, Mary Kate. I think you left something out."

"Oh, I guess I did." She started with the blood and note found on Ben's bed, then told him about finding Lestat nailed to the garage wall and her plan for catching who did it.

As she finished, Conner shook his head wearily. "Where is your brain, girl? What if the killer did come?"

"I had to do something! Anyway, I really didn't consider being seen. I just wanted to catch the guy in the act. Then the police could do something because we'd have a witness."

"The next time you get a great idea, Mary Kate, check it

with me first. Okay?"

She sulked, but nodded. The coffee wasn't mixing well with the wine in her stomach. She closed her eyes against a rush of nausea. Her abdomen cramped. "I don't feel too good."

Conner jumped from his seat. "Oh, jeez. Are you going to throw up?"

"I don't think so. Not yet. If I could lie down for a minute, I'll be fine. I think." Conner helped her to the bed. Her eyes closed as she stretched out. "Thanks. You're sweet." As she drifted off, she felt him removing her shoes.

"Yeah, I'm a regular sweetheart," she heard him say.

Mary Kate awoke face down. A painful cannon blast went off in her skull as she lifted her head from the pillow. She groaned, then turned to the sound of laughter.

"I used to dream about what it was like to spend the night with you." Conner laughed again as he combed his wet hair.

She rolled over and threw the other pillow at him. She could see herself in the dresser mirror, and it wasn't a pretty sight. "I'm not a woman to trifle with right now. My mouth feels like the underside of a lawn mower." She had slept in her clothes in what she assumed was Conner's room. "Where did you sleep?"

He pointed to the bed. "Right beside you. You're a mattress hog." He put down the comb and put his wallet in his pocket. "Come on, get up. You'll feel better. Do you remember if you have a room? You didn't know last night."

She thought a moment. It hurt. "Yeah, I have a room. I registered when I came in. And I dropped my bag off before I went to the bar. I should have a key card on me somewhere." She checked pockets. "Here."

"Good. As soon as you get your sea legs, we'll get you

there and you can begin recovery."

Mary Kate threw her legs over the side of the bed. Pieces of the previous night flashed into her mind. "I drank too much."

Conner shook his head. "That's an understatement."

"I can't remember too much else." She looked up at him and her cheeks blushed hot and red. She knew exactly what it felt like to kiss him. *Did I dream it?* "Conner, did we . . . do anything?" His sheepish look told her it hadn't been a dream. "Just kissing, right?"

"Just kissing, Mary Kate." He drew a cross over his heart. "I swear."

She remembered. It was wonderful and humiliating all at once. "We'll have to talk about that if I ever feel human again."

"You will. Come on."

The ride up the elevator almost jarred her stomach into her mouth. Mary Kate read the door numbers as they looked for room 312. "I don't know why you had to walk up with me." At an adjoining hall, she said, "This way."

Conner grabbed her arm and pulled her in the opposite direction. "Your sense of direction is lousy without a hangover. Once I get you to your room, you can be on your own." They approached a door across from a stairway exit. "This is it."

Mary Kate took the card from her pocket. "I feel like I've been wearing these clothes for years." As she reached to insert the card in the slot, Conner grabbed her hand. Looking up at the steel door, she saw deep gouges in the paint—long, angry slashes.

Chapter 23

Conner flung the stairwell door open and looked up and down the steps. Mary Kate checked other doors in the hall, hoping but not expecting that the scratches were an act of random vandalism. Hers was the only damaged door. "It could have happened any time during the night, Conner!"

He re-entered the corridor, angry and frustrated. "What if you had been here?" He touched one of the gouges, then pounded his fist on the door, the metal reverberating loudly. "You could have been here."

She put the card in the slot. "Well, I wasn't here."

"What are you doing?" He jerked her back by the elbow. "Get back from there!"

The sudden move detonated an explosion of pain in her head. She contained it by squeezing her hands on her temples. "Ow! Holy cow, Conner! What's your problem?"

"You're going to walk right in? The person who did this to the door wasn't delivering Candygrams, Mary Kate. What if he's in there?"

She leaned against the wall and closed her eyes. She hadn't known how debilitating hangovers could be. "If he got in, then he wouldn't have gotten mad and attacked the door." She opened her eyes, and his lips were pressed together into a tight line. She gave him a moment to finish counting to ten. "I really need a shower and fresh clothes, Conner, even if I have to fight the boogeyman to get it."

He turned and re-inserted the card, removing it when the

green light blinked. "I'll go first," he said as he turned the knob.

The room was fresh and unused. Conner checked the closet and bathroom. The telephone message light flashed red on the nightstand. Mary Kate lifted the receiver and punched the button. The recorded voice said, "You have three messages."

Dead silence followed the first electronic tone. The next message was from Chuck. "Just seeing if you got in all right. Everything's fine here. I'll see you Sunday evening." She wondered if Nancy was with him as he called.

The tone sounded once more. In the ensuing silence, Mary Kate thought she might have heard the faint intake of breath, then the recorded voice concluded, "That was your last message."

Conner stood at the bathroom door. "Anything?"

"A message from Chuck. He said everything was fine at home. He was probably calling from the bedroom. Then there were two messages with nobody there."

"Somebody was there." He rubbed his chin. Her suitcase sat on the floor where she had left it. He grabbed the handle and picked it up. "Come on."

"What do you mean, come on?"

"You can get cleaned up in my room. The killer knows where you're supposed to be staying, Mary Kate. I'm not letting you out of my sight."

"I'll get another room. I can't stay with you."

"He could find that room as easily as he did this one. If you want your clothes, you'd better come with me." He opened the door and went into the hall.

"But, Conner . . ." she whined, following.

Two boys chased each other around the chairs in the small

lobby. Passersby on the busy sidewalk outside the windows glanced in as they walked along. Mary Kate squinted in the bright sunlight. "Somebody pull the shades." She shielded her eyes with her hand as she followed Conner to the front desk.

"Excuse me," he said to the back of the clerk. "We'd like some information."

The clerk turned a frantically freckled, young face toward them. "Good morning," he sang. "How may I help you?"

I hate perky, Mary Kate thought. The long, hot shower and clean undies, blue jeans and oversized blouse improved her appearance, but not her disposition. Her stomach gurgled loudly.

Conner seemed unfazed by the young man's bright personality. "Has anyone been inquiring about room 312 overnight?" he asked.

"Well," the young clerk said, "I'd love to help you, but I can't. The night staff left at eight this morning, and I can only tell you what's happened since then."

"What's happened since then?" Mary Kate asked.

"Not a thing," he sang. "I've had a nice cup of coffee and a Danish, and I even had time to call my mom."

"Bully for you," she said. Conner nudged her with his elbow. She sighed and tried to smile. "Could you do a couple of things for me?"

"I'd be delighted." He looked delighted.

"Peachy." She inched away from Conner's elbow. "Could you leave a note for the night staff, telling them that Mary Kate Flaherty in room 312 would like to know about any inquiries last night?" He wrote as she spoke. "And could you check to see if I have any messages?"

As the clerk turned to check for messages, Mary Kate whispered to Conner, "They're going to want to know about the damaged door as soon as the maid comes to clean."

"Tell them the truth. You don't know who did it."

"Miss Flaherty? You have a letter." The clerk held out a white, business-size envelope.

Mary Kate took it. "This looks familiar." The paper was white and clean, but felt like filth in her fingertips.

"Do you want me to open it?" Conner asked.

"No, of course not." *I want to burn it.* She pulled out the unglued flap and removed the single sheet of paper. Two words had been typed in the center of the page.

IT'S REAL.

She handed it to Conner. "The killer's here," she whispered.

Conner leaned on the front desk and spoke to the clerk. "When did this letter arrive?"

He smiled in his freckled face. "I wish I could tell you. It was sometime between when I left promptly at four yesterday afternoon and my arrival at precisely eight o'clock this morning."

Mary Kate hurried over to the chairs abandoned by the frolicking boys and sat heavily. Her head felt light and her stomach heavy. Conner sat beside her. "He followed me here," she said. "What are we going to do? What if someone gets hurt?"

"We could call the police."

She grimaced. "We'd have to start from scratch with a whole new police department. I've made a terrible mistake, Conner. I thought he'd go to my house, not here. I've put all the writers' lives in danger."

He took her hands in his. "You haven't done anything wrong, Mary Kate. At least now we know he's around here somewhere. Maybe we can stop him this time before he does anything."

★ ★ ★ ★ ★

Mary Kate hung up the phone as Conner finished packing. "They're on the way. I hope they take my advice and call Lieutenant Evans. Murders in Atlanta and New York might not mean much in Cleveland."

Conner locked his suitcase and put it beside Mary Kate's by the door. "They must be interested to come before a crime's been committed."

"That we know of. Any one of these rooms could hold a body that hasn't been discovered yet."

Fifteen minutes later, Conner answered a knock on the door. A stocky, thirtyish man wearing a shirt, tie, and green polyester, no-belt slacks stood outside the door. A plaid sports coat was draped over one arm. His forehead was beaded with sweat; his round cheeks flushed bright pink. "I'm Detective Hedstrom. I'm looking for Mary Kate Flaherty."

"Come in," Conner said. "This is Mrs. Flaherty. I'm Conner Drake."

"Nice to meet you," Hedstrom said. "It's a hot one out there today, isn't it? The air conditioning isn't very good in here either."

Mary Kate thought the young detective looked absolutely withered. "May I get you a glass of water?"

"Yes, that would be nice. May I sit?"

Conner showed him to a chair, then sat on the bed. Mary Kate gave Hedstrom his drink and sat at the table across from him. They waited while he drained the glass.

"Ah, better," Hedstrom sighed. He seemed less apoplectic. "Okay, down to business. I talked to Lieutenant Evans of the Anne Arundel County, Maryland Police Department. He was familiar with the case and felt the latest note . . . May I see it?" Mary Kate handed it to him. He took it out of

214

the envelope, then put it back after a glance. "Good," he said. "The lieutenant thought this was cause for concern. He was particularly concerned about your safety, Mrs. Flaherty."

"I don't know why," she said. "The killer hasn't harmed me. I'm just at the center of some kind of terror campaign."

"Don't rely on that continuing, Mrs. Flaherty," he said ominously. "These things have a way of escalating."

Conner gestured to the suitcases. "I'm taking Mary Kate to another hotel. She'll keep her room here to throw off the killer."

"Good idea," Hedstrom said. "I wouldn't let her go any-place by herself, if I were you. If he can't get to her in her room, he might stalk her until an opportunity presents itself."

Mary Kate felt as if she had no more say than the suitcases. She knew she was well protected having these two supermen watching over her welfare, but didn't believe that was the crux of their meeting. "What are you going to do about all the other writers at risk? I get notes, but others get murdered."

"We can get a description of the person leaving the note from the night desk clerk, and we can station extra officers around the hotel. That'll be it for right now. Without a description of the perp, we can't do more than that. The safest place for you, Mrs. Flaherty, might be home."

"I'm not leaving," she said quickly. "If I go, we'll lose him. I want to stay at the convention and make sure everybody sees me." She looked at Conner.

He chewed his lip, but nodded. "Okay, Mary Kate, but we stay together, every minute. Don't get any of your bonehead ideas."

"I'll be good," she said.

"How much longer are you going to be in there, Mary Kate?"

She pinned up her hair, ignoring Conner's most recent bellow. Transforming into Theodora Zed took time. Her only panel was at six o'clock, the dinner hour. Few would be attending, simplifying Conner's bodyguard duties. There was plenty of time. She didn't hurry as she teased her hair high and spritzed on the red stuff.

Looking in the bathroom mirror, she adjusted the front of the leather dress to show more bosom. "Let's go for broke, Theo." Whatever she was hated for, she wanted to accentuate. The killer had to make his move tonight, or she would be left in limbo again, not knowing where he was, not able to go on with her life.

Her make-up was in place, the dress tight and short. She lifted her left foot onto the toilet seat and straightened the seam in her black stocking before slipping on the spiked heels. As she stepped out of the bathroom, she bent over to pull up the ankle strap that had slipped under her heel. She looked up to see Conner gawking. His Adam's apple jumped as he swallowed hard. "Oh, for heaven's sake, Conner, you've seen me in this dress before."

"I know," he said in an uncharacteristically soprano voice. He cleared his throat and said lower, "I know." His eyes cut over to the two queen-size beds in the hotel room. They had moved to the Holiday Inn after speaking with Detective Hedstrom.

Mary Kate looked, too, and sighed. "I don't know why we couldn't get separate rooms."

Conner turned to the dresser and studied the knobs. "I'm trying to keep you alive this weekend, Mary Kate. It's either this, or you go home."

"Let's go, then. It's show time."

They drove several blocks back to the convention hotel.

As they entered the lobby, Mary Kate said, "Let's go to the bar."

Conner stared at her. "Haven't you had enough?"

"The good Lord knows I want nothing stronger than ginger ale. I just want to see who's here."

Most of the tables were unoccupied. Three people sat at the bar. It looked smaller than it had the night before. She remembered it as an endless sea of potential parties. A table in the back had a group of young people in costume. Wearing gowns and tunics, chain mail and leather helmets, they were easily identified as sword and sorcery, rather than horror, fans.

Mary Kate approached them. "Hi, I'm Theodora Zed. I was wondering if you've seen a tall, heavyset person around, wearing a long, black cape with a hood."

"Subtle, Mary Kate," Conner whispered out of the corner of his mouth.

She shrugged as the medieval warrior questioned the judgment of the stout princess as to whether a particular minstrel's cape was black or midnight blue.

"This cape covers everything," Mary Kate said. "And the hood is . . ." She thought a moment for a term they would grasp. ". . . like an executioner's."

"No, nothing like that," they all agreed.

Conner led Mary Kate away. "If the word gets out that you're actively looking for this guy, Mary Kate, he's going to bolt."

"Well, he's not going to come up and introduce himself. I want to know where he is."

"So do I, but I think you ought to leave the investigating to the police."

On the way out, they ran into George Moss coming in. He blanched as he saw Mary Kate.

"George," she said, "I want to apologize for last night. I had too much to drink. I didn't know what I was saying."

"You called me a liar," he whined.

"It was a reprehensible thing for me to say." *True, but reprehensible.* "I was being mean. I'm having some personal problems, and I got drunk and took them out on you. I'm sorry." She leaned on his arm and twiddled his ponytail. "Could you ever forgive me?" she cooed.

George grinned sheepishly. "The light was bad in here last night. I guess you couldn't see the scar."

"I saw it," she lied. "I was just being evil. I would deserve it if you never spoke to me again."

"I couldn't do that, Theodora. If I didn't have you, who would I have dirty dreams about?"

"There," she said, kissing his cheek. "I knew I had a purpose in life." She batted her eyelashes at him over her shoulder as he went into the bar. She turned to Conner, but he had stepped away and was leaning against the wall, laughing.

He batted his eyes at her. "I knew I had a purpose in life," he mimicked.

"Stuff it in your hat, dear," she said, passing him by. He jogged to catch up.

Chapter 24

The leather dress felt as if it were seared onto her skin. Mary Kate fanned herself with a copy of *A Lover's Blood*. The panel discussion had been going on for forty-five minutes and was winding down even though another forty-five minutes had been scheduled. Four drowsy spectators sat amidst empty folding chairs in the small conference room. Not even the three speakers at the table up front seemed interested in the topic, "I Love You To Death: Romance in Horror." Mary Kate watched Conner rub his eyes and yawn. She wished they'd put this panel out of its misery. She had to go to the bathroom desperately.

"Any last thoughts before we conclude, Theodora?"

Mary Kate hadn't been listening. She didn't know or care if her remarks were redundant. "Briefly, Vanna," she said to the moderator, "I'd summarize this discussion by saying, you can find love in the most bizarre places, even in real life, but be careful out there."

The skinny guy in the front row laughed too hard at her pathetic humor. The rest left without bothering to applaud. Conner stretched as he walked up to the table. "Let's go get some dinner. I could use a cup of coffee. It's going to be a long night."

They walked out into the crowded corridor. Several tables had been set up for book signings, and the well-fed fans were out in force. Mary Kate craned her neck until she saw a rest room sign. "I'll be back in a minute," she said.

Conner dropped his hand on her shoulder. "What do you mean you'll be back in a minute? Whither thou goest, so goest I."

"Not here, Conner. I'm going to no-man's land. I've got to pee."

He seemed uncomfortable. "Well, wait."

"Yeah, sure." She rolled her eyes. "I've got a calling, Conner, and I must answer. Soon. I don't have the luxury of discussing this further." She started walking away, then turned and called back, "This might be a good time for you to go, so we don't have a similar problem an hour from now!" She laughed at herself as she turned the corner and pushed open the ladies' room door. How many times had she said something like that to her kids?

The skirt of the leather dress crumpled around her waist, she sat and relieved herself. Not for the first time, it crossed her mind that her motivation to stay in Cleveland had more to do with avoiding the problem with Chuck than snaring a serial killer. She still had no idea what to do about the home situation, but at least she was no longer reeling from the shock. She knew she'd think of something.

The outer door from the hallway opened, and footsteps crossed the sink area, stopped, then walked past the stalls, too far back for Mary Kate to see shoes. They sounded like leather bottom flats. The shadow came back to where she sat on the first commode, paused again, and went into the stall beside her. Mary Kate listened. Something about the way the new arrival moved made her uncomfortable. There was no rustling of clothes, no telltale sounds of expected toilet activities, no squeaking toilet paper dispenser, no flush.

Mary Kate finished, but didn't get up. There was more to this than what could be explained by a normal occurrence, like a woman hiding from unwanted attentions from someone who wasn't welcome in this denizen of females. It wasn't the sound of the clunky shoes or the lack of sound in the next stall that unsettled her. Something else. A smell. One beyond the usual aroma of antiseptic cleaner and hair spray. Mary Kate sniffed. Perfume. Chanel No. 5.

Quietly and slowly, she slipped off her shoes and began pulling up underclothing and pulling down her skirt. Many women prefer that particular scent, but this was one intuition Mary Kate didn't want to ignore. She listened. Still no sounds from next door. Leaving her spiked heels and purse on the floor in front of the commode, she crouched down and slipped under the side of the stall by the sinks. There was fifteen feet of open space to the door. She glanced back to the stall doors and was horrified to see herself looking back in a wall-length mirror directly in front of the occupied booth.

Oh, holy cow! She threw herself forward, her stockinged feet skidding on the tile floor. She heard the metal door of the stall bang open as she pummeled through the outer door into the passageway leading from the rest rooms. She could see the crowd milling around the main hallway ahead. Conner faced the opposite direction, watching a queue of fans waiting for autographs, short yards away at the corner. She sped towards him and was whisked off her feet by an arm wrapped around her chest.

"I know about you," a low voice breathed in her ear.

"Conner!" she screamed. She twisted around, trying to dislodge octopus arms. She looked up into the face of Patrick Henley. She screamed again.

Henley looked as professorial in his bland gray suit as she remembered. He held her arms and spoke softly. "The downfall of civilizations has been caused by women like you. The decay of morality, the degradation of human life can be held in a single word. You must stop what you're doing. I must make you understand."

Mary Kate struggled. *He won't hurt me,* she hoped. *He used to be a priest.* He was thin and wiry, but strong. He pinned her against the wall, and she screamed.

Large hands appeared from behind on his shoulders. He was ripped away from her and flew against the far wall. Mary Kate stumbled backwards. Conner grabbed Henley by his shirtfront, drew one elbow back, and hammered his fist into Henley's nose in a spray of blood.

"My nose! My nose!" Henley cried as he fell to the floor. Conner jumped onto his chest, clamping his hand on the thin man's throat, pulling back his right fist for another blow. Henley moaned and cried, choking on the blood sheeting into his mouth. Conner held back. "Move and I'll splatter your face across the floor."

Mary Kate collected herself enough to help. "I'll find a cop!" she called as she pushed into the throng. The people in the hall had pushed forward to see what the commotion was. A woman wailed at the sight of splattered blood. Two men joined Conner, holding Henley's legs, even though the sixty-year-old appeared much too distressed about his broken nose to want to escape.

Working his way toward Mary Kate in polyester splendor, the Green Hornet Hedstrom brandished his detective's shield. "Step aside! Police! Coming through!" Around him were three more plainclothes officers.

She waved her arms over her head and pointed. "Over there! Conner's got him!" She watched from a distance as the reinforcements broke through the crowd and took over. *Is it really over? It was Henley all along?* She wanted to believe, but it didn't feel right.

Among the gawkers was George Moss, his ponytailed head a few feet ahead of her. He turned, and his red face was bathed in sweat, his eyes rolling. He pushed a young woman out of his way in his rush to the exit. Mary Kate followed him, winding through the bodies, breaking into a run as he reached the door, twisting his neck around, his eyes bulging. By the time Mary Kate opened the door, she had lost him.

The sky above the buildings was smeared orange as dusk fell over the parking lot behind the hotel. A chain link fence surrounded the space, weeds and daisies sprouting at the base. Mary Kate stood on the cracked sidewalk, looking for George, wondering why he had fled. *Could he have been telling the truth about being attacked? Was he afraid to confront the Vampire Killer a second time? Naw. He lied. I know it.* Then what was he running from? She walked around to the corner of the building, the heat of the day held in the concrete burning the soles of her feet. *Exposure!* The police would want him to identify Henley as his attacker. The same reporters who had written his startling account of survival would ask him why he couldn't add anything to help convict Henley. "George, you wuss," she said to herself.

And could I? Her gut told her Henley wasn't the killer. She denied her gut because events told her differently. He had been caught red-handed. *Then why am I going after George? Why am I worried about him?* She walked faster, then began to trot. "He shouldn't be out here by himself." He's a horror writer, and two have died already.

The sidewalk ended. The chain link fence continued around the back of the hotel, leaving a narrow, weedy passage. Twenty feet away, George's head popped out of a recess in the brick wall. A large, black shape floated out of the shadows of the far corner and overtook him.

"George!" She ran in the overgrown thatch, a sharp edge tearing the length of her foot. She heard his high scream and ran faster. "George, I'm coming!"

Chanel No. 5! I smelled Chanel No. 5! I know who it is! She needed to save George. She needed to bear witness.

The screaming stopped. She slowed, then waited, the first real thought of her own safety hitting her like a freight train. She looked beyond the fence to a steep, littered hill leading up to the deserted rear areas of buildings on the next street. Evening had removed the crisp lines from everything, turning all into gray, nonspecific blobs. An especially big, black blob came out from the place she had last seen George. "Oh, my God!" Mary Kate backed away, then turned and fled the way she had come. Heavy footfalls pursued her, moving fast.

Stones and spears abraded her feet. Perspiration washed red dye from her hair into her eyes. She pumped her legs as high as she could in the tight dress, whimpers escaping from her throat. As she broke into the parking lot, she saw the door where she had come out. The sound of clunky shoes on concrete came up behind her, another shadow joined her own. She smelled perfume. Chanel No. 5. The door up ahead opened. Mary Kate felt fingers grasp her hair and pull her backwards. As she fell, Conner flashed into sight at the door.

A red-hot pain slipped across her neck. A hard body pressed close behind her. *I'm dying.* Rank breath panted into her ear. A black-gloved hand in a black-sleeved coat held the bloodied, serrated knife in front of her. Kitchen knife. Goodwill. The blade plunged into her midriff and scraped across the surface of the leather dress. Conner called her name a million miles away, perhaps in another galaxy, and she was discarded roughly onto the ground. Her attacker ran away, heavy shoes thud-thud-thudding back through the narrow passage.

"It burns," she whimpered, holding her throat as Conner fell onto his knees beside her. He gingerly took her hands away from the wound. Blood coated her fingers. "How bad is it?" she cried.

He cleared his throat. "Not bad, Mary Kate. Not too bad."

"She cut my throat, Conner." Images of wide, gaping slashes filled her head. Squirting arterial blood. "I'm going to die!"

He held her hands in his. "No, baby, you're not dying. It's a scratch. A big scratch."

"Oh." Mary Kate sat up. "Oh, my God. George! She got George! Over there!" She pulled her hands out of Conner's and stood with him steadying her. "Come on!"

"Who got George?"

"The Vampire Killer!" She grabbed his arm and dragged him along.

The recessed doorway was difficult to find in the growing darkness. Her fear grew. George might not be the only one there. Conner was a head taller than Mary Kate with broad shoulders and a good right punch, but even he had been laid low by the killer's knife. The danger was as much his as hers.

Her foot slipped in something wet on the ground. "Eew, what's that?" She looked down and saw the puddle trailing across the path. It led to George, lying on his back in front of a door, his round stomach splashed dark red. Conner caught her as her knees collapsed and lowered her to the ground. "Is he dead?" she asked fearfully.

A strained, whiny voice came from the door well. "I will be if you don't get me to a hospital, Theo."

"George, you're alive!" She tugged Conner's pants leg. "He's alive!"

"Can you get up?" Conner asked him.

George groaned. "Not without losing vital organs."

Conner rubbed his chin thoughtfully. "I'll take Mary Kate

back with me to get help. I'll be back here in two minutes."

"Don't you dare leave me!" George cried. "What if she comes back to finish me off?"

"Good point," Conner said. "What we need is a cell phone."

"I've got one," Mary Kate said without thinking.

They looked at her expectantly.

"But it's in my purse. In the ladies' room. And the battery's dead." She shrugged.

"Okay . . ." Conner said, not sure how to respond. "I'm going for help." He reached into his jeans pocket and took out a pocketknife and handed it to Mary Kate. "It's not much, but you probably won't need it anyway. I'll be back in a minute. Less than a minute."

As he took off in a long-legged run, Mary Kate pulled out the blade from the knife. "I could never do it," she said.

"Then give it here, Theo," George said. "I'd have no problem slicing that bitch."

"You saw her?"

He nodded. "Her perfume preceded her. That Chanel bilge water just reeks of tacky." He glanced away, a tear twinkling in his eye. "I saw her," he whispered.

Mary Kate looked away so George could cry.

Conner came running back, followed by an army of police. A distant siren heralded more help to come. "Are you okay?" he asked, breathing heavily, his hair sticking wet to his forehead.

"Yeah," Mary Kate said. "She got away, you know. It's not over."

"I'll never let you out of my sight again." He slipped one arm across her back and the other under her knees and lifted her up, holding her close, kissing her hair.

Hedstrom took in the scene. "You ought to wait for the ambulance."

"I'll take care of her," Conner said. He carried her back into the hotel. She wrapped her arms around his neck and did not object.

Mary Kate stepped out of the bathroom, tugging on the bottom of the tee shirt she had packed to sleep in, trying to cover up more of her legs. From now on, she promised herself, she would pack flannel pajamas. Conner lay in his bed, covered to the waist, bare-chested above. She hurried over to her bed and slipped under the blanket, wondering what was under his.

His arms were crossed behind his head on the pillow. "So George lied about that first attack. I can't believe he'd do that."

Mary Kate turned on her side toward him. "I knew he was lying from the start. He seemed to be enjoying it too much."

"How's your neck?" Conner asked.

"If you hadn't shown up, she wouldn't have lost her grip. It's just a big, ugly scrape." She touched the white bandage around her throat. The wound began under one ear and stopped below her chin, not deep enough to require stitches. She had gotten the bandage slightly damp taking a bath. The doctor in the emergency room had instructed her not to shower for a couple of days, but she had to clean off the dirt and dried blood, not to mention the Theodora hair and make-up. Her other injuries were less serious. Some minor scrapes and contusions on her feet. A single round bruise on her tummy.

Conner turned toward her. "Damn it, Mary Kate. Why'd you go out there? I thought we'd agreed to stay together."

She shrugged and smiled. "It seemed like a good idea at the time?"

"It's not funny. When I came out that door . . . I thought I was too late. I thought . . ." He fell back onto the pillow and looked at the ceiling.

"I'm sorry. I didn't even think it was dangerous until I got out there. I mean, you had Henley. And George looked so scared, I was curious, then worried about him. If I'd gone to get you, I would have lost him. And he'd be dead now."

He shifted his eyes to her. "I know," he said grudgingly. "And, all I did was beat up an old man."

"With good cause. I thought he was going to kill me. Mrs. Olsen sure had him riled up thinking I was the devil incarnate."

Conner sat up on the edge of his bed. Mary Kate watched, fascinated as the blanket slid and shifted, wrapping around his waist, leaving his lower body decently covered, his legs bare. "That was a smart move on her part. Are you sure she's insane? She made it her business to find out who could be a possible suspect, then wrote and called him, telling him about you and your depraved books, knowing he'd have to confront you sooner or later as part of his censorship campaign."

"She's crazy all right," Mary Kate said. "I've talked with her. It was bizarre. She wore clothes way too small for her, said they were from her daughter. Her daughter died, was murdered, actually, years ago. I think she was wearing the girl's clothes. And when she talked, I felt as if she was trying to find out something, like something I could say would explain everything. I didn't know what she wanted. I still don't. Why would a middle-aged, retired nurse from the 'burbs want to slash up writers with a knife? Where would such rage come from?"

"She's still out there, Mary Kate."

A chill ran through her. She gathered up the blanket to her chest. "I've got to get home to my kids, Conner." She had called them at Grandma's as soon as she came back to the Holiday Inn from the hospital. They were fine, but itchy to get home. Their dad wasn't there.

"I'll come with you," Conner said.

"You can't do that."

"Then, you and the boys come with me to Connecticut."

The offer was tempting. *I could tell Chuck that I know about the affair with Nancy, and, by the way, I'm leaving and taking the kids to live with Conner.* She shook her head. She didn't want to live with Conner. She wanted her own life. She wanted her children safe and loved, and she wanted to bring some order to her life before she could think about including another person.

"Are you going to stay with Chuck?" Conner asked softly.

"No, I don't think so," she answered.

He looked at his knees. "When you kissed me . . . was it just to get back at him?"

She hesitated. "No, I don't think so."

He looked up. Their eyes met across the space between the beds, such a short space. She felt a longing to be near him. How easy it could be. Conner held out his hand to her. She could almost feel what it was like, taking his hand, leaning into the soft hair on his chest, his arms wrapped around her, lying warm in the bed beside him. "I can't," she said.

He nodded and climbed back into bed under the covers. Turning out the lamp, he said, "I'll see you in the morning, Mary Kate."

"Good night, Conner."

His voice said in the dark, "I am going back with you to Maryland."

"Thank you, Conner."

Chapter 25

The room was dark, except for the pale halo of light surrounding Alissa.

"Didn't you forget something, Theo?" she said quite clearly, despite the long fangs protruding from the corners of her mouth. Lestat purred loudly, curled up in her lap. He had a little wool scarf tied around his neck.

"It's possible," Mary Kate said. "I'm always forgetting something."

" 'Leave It to Beaver' is dead," Alissa said with a sigh. "And so am I." Lestat meowed. "Yes, dear, and so are you."

"What did I forget?"

"The same thing I did, Theodora, you twit. The doorman is only the first line of defense. The door is the last."

Alissa and Lestat fell dead on the floor, their bodies torn and bloodied as Mary Kate had seen before.

The sound of her own cry startled her as she awoke. Mary Kate looked around the dark hotel room, her hand on her beating heart. She couldn't see a thing.

The bedspring across the room creaked, and she whimpered again. A black figure stood over her.

"Mary Kate, are you all right?"

She let out her breath. "Conner, yeah, I'm okay. Nightmare. I've been having a lot of them lately."

"Me, too," he said. "Shouldn't be surprised." His voice was deep and sleepy. She couldn't see his face as he sat on the edge of her bed. "I'll sit up with you awhile, okay?"

"No, get some sleep. I'm okay now."

"You sure?"

"Yeah." She watched as he returned to his side of the room. Knowing he was near took the fear out of going back to sleep.

Mary Kate hesitated at the door. "You go ahead and check out. I'll be down in a minute."

Conner smiled. "What happened the last time I left you for a minute?"

"I have to make a phone call," she said seriously. "You can wait outside the door, then. Okay?"

"All right, but I want to get out by eight a.m. sharp. We have a long drive."

After he closed the door behind him, Mary Kate sat on the bed and picked up the receiver. She dialed her home number.

Chuck answered on the second ring. "H'lo," he mumbled.

Oh, good, I woke him up. It'll be even better if Nancy's there. "Chuck, I thought you might be there. Watching the house?"

"Uh, Mary Kate. Uh, yeah, the house."

"I was worried about leaving it alone, too. I forgot to tell you. I rented a bunch of camcorders and hid them all over the house to record any break-ins."

"Wha'? How many, Mary Kate?" He sounded very concerned.

"Three or four. Maybe five, I don't remember. You know how ditzy and forgetful I can be. We can find them when I get home this evening. We'll watch the videos together. Okay?"

His breath quickened. "Sure, Mary Kate, sure. We'll do that. I've got to go."

"Bye-bye," she sang and hung up. *That ought to keep the son of a bitch busy for a while.* She knew it was a cruel trick, but she promised herself she would be mature and responsible later in her dealings with him. She had earned this one shot. Even though it was a hateful thing to do, she felt quite cheerful.

She opened the door to the hallway, smiling. "I'm all ready to go home."

Seven hours later, they were coming off Route 50 onto Aris T. Allen Boulevard toward Parole, then Edgewater. They had talked about many things for most of the way, the novels they were working on, her kids, the state of the union, but had fallen silent as Mary Kate neared home.

"What are you going to do?" Conner asked.

She put her feet up on the seat and hugged her knees. "I don't know. I might've made things worse."

Conner glanced over at her. "How?"

She rested her forehead on her knees. "Something I said when I called him this morning." She turned back to Conner. "You're going to wait in the car, right?"

"Do you think he'll hurt you?"

"Keep the engine running."

As the car turned onto Linden Lane, they could see the police cars on the street in front of the Olsen house. The neighbors stood on the front lawns, watching. News crews had set up their trucks for remote telecasts. Mary Kate saw Nancy beside her husband, Doug. "That's her," she told Conner. "Martha Stewart gone bad."

He stopped the car at the end of the driveway. "Do you think they caught Mrs. Olsen?"

"George gave a pretty good description of her, even if she was wearing men's clothes. And Detective Hedstrom told me they found the guy she paid to deliver the message to the front desk at the hotel, and he identified her, too. She's pretty sharp. I don't think she'd come back home." An officer came out of the front door carrying evidence bags, just as a car from the coroner's office drove up.

"I'll bet she killed herself," Conner said.

Mary Kate watched. "We can only hope."

The police presence on Linden Lane helped her face her next task. If anything went wrong, they would be readily available. At the back door, she turned and gave Conner a little wave and a nervous smile before taking a deep breath and going in. Chuck was home. She had seen his car in the driveway. She looked for him in the living room, then went upstairs.

Chuck sat on their bed, his shoulders hunched, wearing only boxer shorts. The dresser had been emptied onto the floor, the closet door stood open, hangers and clothing strewn everywhere. He noticed Mary Kate moments after she entered the doorway.

"There are no cameras," she said.

His eyes widened as he realized what she had done. And what she had known. Mary Kate felt awful. All these years together had come down to this, an ugly, humiliating scene. She tried to think of a way to take it all back. Not only what she had done, but his transgressions, too. Could everything be a misunderstanding? He had never hit her, but had only tried to get her attention. He and Nancy weren't having an affair, they were only checking each other for scorpion bites. *This won't work.* She had to accept the degrading role of wronged wife, right down to the last remaining shred of personal pride.

"Bitch," Chuck spat.

"Thank you," Mary Kate said, "that makes this a little easier. I'm going to leave for a couple of hours, and when I come back with my children, I want you packed and gone."

He stood over her, his right eye twitching spasmodically. His face was whiskery with an oily sheen. His breath was rank; he stunk of dried sweat. "How long have you known?"

She stepped back. "I don't want to talk about this, Chuck. I don't want to know more than I do. I only want you out of my house and out of my life."

He reached out and held her arm. "We need to talk, Mary Kate. You see, I . . ."

She jerked away. "You don't seem to get it, Chuck. This is it. I . . . I don't love you." She had said it. The monkey was out of the cage. She felt both freed and bereft.

Chuck didn't grasp the significance. He attempted once again to explain, but she turned and hurried down the stairs.

"Mary Kate!" he called after her. She paused, but he didn't follow.

Stopping at the back door, she pressed the heels of her hands against her eyes to stem the flow of tears before it could start. When she felt somewhat under control, she walked out to the car where Conner waited. She slipped into the passenger seat. "Let's get out of here," she said, her voice cracking.

David stared daggers at Conner across the kitchen table. Ben dug his fingers into the open bun of his cheeseburger, picking out diced onions.

"Use your napkin, honey," Mary Kate said. Ben wiped ketchup and mustard-covered hands across the front of his shirt. She sighed, but let it pass. Temporary concessions would have to be made in the name of the new home-world order. Ben balanced a chunk of onion on his fingernail and flicked it into David's hair.

David howled and punched Ben's shoulder. Ben screamed, "That hurts, fart-face!" and dumped his soda into David's lap. Both boys fell to the floor, arms flailing.

"Stop it! Stop it!" Mary Kate shouted.

Conner picked up one boy by the back of the shirt in each hand and sat them in chairs on opposite sides of the table. They panted and snuffled, but stayed put. Ben's lower lip trembled. Mary Kate looked at them in disbelief. "What is going on here?"

David glared at her angrily. "Why does he have to be here?"

"I told you, David. Because there's still some danger. Mr. Drake's only staying until they catch Mrs. Olsen."

"Why not Dad? Dad could protect us better than him."

Mary Kate took a deep breath and prayed for patience. "I told you, darling. Dad can't be here right now." Dealing with the children had been as bad as she ever thought it could be. After picking up her car at the airport, she had driven to her mother-in-law's with Conner following. On the ride home, she had explained to the boys that she and their father had to be apart for a while. They became quiet and sullen, even with the promise of a McDonald's dinner.

The situation had deteriorated from there.

A giant tear sprung from Ben's eye. "Are you going to marry Mr. Drake?"

She gathered him up in her arms. "No, sweetie, no. I'm not marrying Mr. Drake. He's our friend, that's all." She turned to Conner. "I'm sorry. We're going to need some time alone."

He thought, then nodded. "Okay. I'll stop at Olsens' and tell the cops there to keep an eye on you, then I'll come back in a couple of hours."

She held the sobbing little boy close to her breast. "Thank you, Conner." She knew how concerned he was. She appreciated his understanding how important it was that she take care of her children right now.

After he left, she pulled up a chair close to David's and positioned Ben on her lap. "Okay, guys, let's talk."

Chapter 26

Mary Kate walked down the hall and peeked into her room. David and Ben sprawled on her bed, sleeping the peaceful sleep of the innocent. She, on the other hand, felt like a tightrope walker with a nose full of pepper. Her slightest move could have tremendous repercussions, and the next sneeze could come at any time and blow everything away, regardless. If she had said the wrong thing to the children, they could be traumatized for life. If she had made the wrong decision, they could face financial disaster. And on top of that, there was a murderer out to get her, and her feelings for Conner were growing stronger while Chuck's smell still permeated the house.

She sighed and went back to her office down the hall. A page of her latest novel filled the screen on the computer. "When all else fails, write," she said, sitting down.

Ursula crouched behind the oaken wine casks until Dimitri had passed out of sight. "How could I have been so foolish?" she thought. She remembered how swept away she had been, just a girl, attaining the undivided attention of one so mature, so wise. She was older now, if not in years, then in experience.

She would use the wiles and trickery he had taught her to bring about his end. Her plan included her own destruction, but death was sweet when faced with an eternity of blood and deception.

"Good for you, Ursula." The phone rang. Mary Kate

answered, expecting it to be Conner checking to see if it was all right to come back.

"Mrs. Flaherty?"

"Yes?"

"This is Mark Evans. Is everything okay there?"

The voice sounded familiar. "Who is this?"

"Uh, Lieutenant Evans, Lieutenant Mark Evans."

"Oh, yeah, Lieutenant. Mark, huh? If you'll call me Mary Kate instead of Mrs. Flaherty, I'll feel less like your great aunt."

He laughed. "It's a deal, Mary Kate. I guess you haven't heard from Mrs. Olsen since you've been home."

"Nope. All quiet here. Your officers come up the driveway every twenty minutes or so and knock on the door. What's going on?"

"We haven't found her, if that's what you mean. The Cleveland police think they might have traced her to the airport, boarding a plane for Chicago using an alias. It makes it hard because she's so ordinary looking. She could be anybody's mother."

She was Tammy's mother. Her little girl, seduced and betrayed. "Seduced and betrayed," Mary Kate said.

"Huh?"

"Mark, have you ever read any of my books?"

"No, uh, I haven't," he stuttered, "but, uh, I could, I guess."

"No, that's all right. What I meant was that Mrs. Olsen told me she read my books and didn't like them."

"That's too bad."

"No, my point is that I think I know why she doesn't like them. Or like me. My books are all the same. The heroine is a young woman seduced and betrayed by an older man, a vampire. He kills her, but they live forever as the undead. Her daughter was killed by an older man."

Evans uttered a noncommittal hmmm. "I found out about that after she became a suspect. It was never proven. They never found the suspect."

"That's right. She never had any kind of closure. One day, she had a child. The next, she didn't. There's nothing more tragic than the grief of a mother. I think, in her twisted mind, Mrs. Olsen thought I was talking about her daughter in my books."

"Who knows?" he said. "But she's still out there and dangerous, Mary Kate, so you should continue to be careful. We found her husband."

"Not in Cleveland, I guess."

"No. In the freezer in the basement. Cut up in little pieces. The neighbors told us that he'd been threatening to have her committed."

Mary Kate shuddered. Then, after assuring him that they were safe for the night, she hung up distractedly. She couldn't help but picture what had transpired behind the soaped windows in the Olsen's basement. Her little kitty, Lestat, had shared freezer space with poor Mr. Olsen. "Ugh. Creepy."

She stood and stretched. It was about time for one of Anne Arundel's finest to come to the back door. She could put on a pot of coffee while she was up.

The knock came before she reached the bottom step. She went into the kitchen, smiling. Opening the door to the uniformed officer, she said, "Hello, again."

He returned her smile. "Everything okay?"

"We're fine. If you can hang around for a few minutes, I'll have fresh coffee."

"No, thank you, Mrs. Flaherty. I don't drink coffee, but I'll send Frank up on the next run. He's been saying he could use a cup."

"Great. Tell him I'll have it ready for him." She closed the door and turned to the counter with the coffee maker, her eyes passing over the basement door.

It was closed, but not all the way, not so completely that the latch had connected. She couldn't remember if it had been like that before.

The basement was the big, black appliance hole. The washer and dryer, the water heater and softener were kept down there with the spiders and silverfish. She only went in the basement to do laundry, and never used the door to the outside.

Until Friday night when she sneaked into her own house.

Did I lock it? The door is the last defense, Alissa had said. Somebody could be down there.

She pushed the door with her fingertips until it snicked shut and quickly turned the lock. She stood in front of it, bouncing on the balls of her feet, nervously twisting the hem of her shirt. *There. What do I do now?* She stepped up to the door and pressed her ear against it. *Nothing. Nobody's there.* She backed away again until she hit the counter behind her. Her nervous system was sending major squirts of adrenaline into her body.

Something was wrong. Very wrong.

Then it hit her like a blinding white flash from on high. Somebody could be up there.

Her feet began moving before her brain could process why. As she swung through the kitchen door, the words caught up. *My kids!* Flying through the foyer to the stairs, she caught her first whiff of Chanel No. 5. "Oh, my God!" she cried, grabbing the banister and vaulting up three steps at a time.

The sweet stench was stronger at the top. She uttered a brief prayer before leaning into her bedroom door. The boys lay still on the bed, very much as they had before. "Be sleeping, please, be sleeping," she whispered. She lifted her foot to take a step toward them, felt more than heard or smelled the presence behind her, and grabbed the knob, pulling the bedroom door closed.

The knife burned across her back.

Mary Kate cried out as she fell, rolling over to face her assailant. Towering above her, the hall light casting a glow to her back, Margaret Olsen stood, draped in executioner black, the red-tipped knife clutched in her gloved fist. Shaded by the cowl, her face was a pale ghostly orb hovering in its depths. Mary Kate slid closer to the top step, the rent in her back streaking fresh pangs. A thick, red puddle formed around her hand on the floor.

"Why?" Mary Kate cried.

A low chuckle emanated from the hooded figure. Mrs. Olsen extended her arm over her head, clutching the weapon as she drifted nearer. Her cape fell open as she stooped clumsily, almost arthritically, throwing out one arm for balance beside Mary Kate sprawled on the floor. She wore her baby pink sweat suit under the cape.

As the blade arched downward over her heart, Mary Kate grabbed Mrs. Olsen's heavy shoe with both hands and, heaving with all of her strength, threw her off balance and tumbling down the staircase. Exhalations of breath and thunderous thumps marked each impact with a tread. Seconds later, she lay still at the bottom, the cape thrown over her head, her broad pink butt stretching her pants like a pair of little girl's party balloons.

My children. Call police. Mary Kate dragged herself up on one knee, her wound stinging like an infected tooth, her blood-soaked clothes sticking to her skin. A wave of vertigo hit her as she looked down the stairs. She blinked her eyes.

I'm cold. Shock. She looked again. A tall, black shape floated up the stairs toward her. *Can't let her near the children.* Mary Kate forced herself to her feet and charged down the steps.

Doubling over and using her head as a ramrod, she plunged recklessly into Mrs. Olsen's thick middle, seeing stars as they fell together, colliding with the foyer floor. Mrs. Olsen grunted as she shoved Mary Kate off her chest.

Still feeling as if she were falling, Mary Kate flung her arms out, feeling for something to hang onto so she could pull herself up. Her fingers hit the newel post and she grabbed hold. As she hefted herself to her feet, she saw Mrs. Olsen, scrabbling around on the floor, a fat, black, twitchy spider.

She lost her knife! Mary Kate swung her foot back, and coming forward, kicked Mrs. Olsen in her pink butt. She lurched forward, her face smacking the oak floor. Hanging onto the newel post, Mary Kate kicked again and again. "Get out! Get out of my house!" she screamed.

Mrs. Olsen slowly turned and arose, her broad white face smeared with blood. "You," she breathed.

A lick of light reflected onto Mary Kate's face. Mrs. Olsen had found her knife. Mary Kate ducked below the arm holding it and hobbled to the kitchen door. She waited to be sure Mrs. Olsen followed.

Help was outside. Right across the street, an army of law enforcement officers stood ready to capture the Vampire Killer. And Mary Kate couldn't go. To Mrs. Olsen, gore and mayhem were all too real. The death of a child was a daily reality. The deaths of two more would be justice. If Mary Kate ran for help, her children would be murdered with a swift slice of the knife before she could reach the police. She had to stop the killer alone.

Mrs. Olsen's fingers locked into Mary Kate's hair halfway across the room. Mary Kate screamed from the pain of arching her back. She could see to the side the gloved hand rolling the hilt of the knife, finding a firm purchase. Mary Kate brought her arm up on the other side, fumbled with the rubbery face, and stuck her fingers in Mrs. Olsen's nostrils. She pinched her fingernails together until Mrs. Olsen shrieked and pushed her onto the floor.

Got to stay alive a little longer. Frank, the coffee-loving cop, would be making the rounds soon, though only minutes had passed since the last check-in. Mary Kate lay on the vinyl floor, panting, her vision blurring, then clearing as she blinked her eyes. *Hurts so bad.*

Mrs. Olsen's black hem swept across the floor, picking up stray dust and crumbs. She would have to bend to reach her, and bending had seemed difficult for her before. This might be the safest place.

Mrs. Olsen heeled back her clodhopper shoe and swung it full force into Mary Kate's ribs. Mary Kate gasped and curled up as the air was knocked out of her lungs. New pain erupted all over her body.

Through a fog of agony, she realized she had to get up. She opened her eyes and saw movement through wavering light. *Now!* She rolled, and as she blinked her eyes, she saw Mrs. Olsen wrenching the knife tip out of the floor where she had just been lying. Tears of pain trailed her cheeks. Mary Kate crawled to the cabinets beside the refrigerator and pulled herself up. A bag of flour and a box of macaroni from her big grocery shopping trip sat on the counter. Behind them was the wooden knife block, handles of many sizes protruding from the top invitingly.

Leaning on the counter for support, she touched the large handle of a knife with her fingers. As Mrs. Olsen fell on her from behind, the soft pads of her breasts pressing against her back, her arm coming around her throat, Mary Kate spun around and belted her in the face with a five-pound bag of all-purpose flour. Powder filled the air as Mrs. Olsen reeled backwards, more surprised than injured.

Muttering, "God help me," and praying she hadn't prepared this particular dish in her cooking spree last week, Mary Kate threw open the freezer, grabbed the plastic handle on the twelve-pound frozen turkey and swung it over her head for momentum. Mrs. Olsen's eyes bulged and her mouth flew open in realization and terror as Mary Kate swirled the rock-hard fowl into her face. It clunked into the hard surface of her skull, knocking her to the floor, teeth shooting across the room like popcorn.

Mary Kate grabbed the handle on the refrigerator door as she slid down, the last of her reserves gone. "Stay down, Mrs. Olsen," she said, though it was hardly necessary. The hood had fallen off her head, and a stream of blood ran from the thicket of fuzzy gray hair.

I'll close my eyes for a minute, Mary Kate thought.

An indeterminate time later, she heard the police kicking in the back door.

She squeezed her eyes tighter to clear them, then looked. "Oh, good. You're here."

The kitchen was packed with police officers. The one who did not like coffee stood over her. "The ambulance is on the way, Mrs. Flaherty. Hang on."

"My children," she said, feeling herself slip away now that she was no longer needed. "Upstairs." She wanted to go herself, but her muscles didn't respond as she tried to move. She turned her head to noises outside the door.

"Mary Kate! Get out of my way! Mary Kate!"

"Conner." It was no more than a squeak. She tried and squeaked a little louder. "Conner!"

He pushed his way through, his face stricken with fear and disbelief as he surveyed the carnage. He knelt beside her.

"My babies, Conner. I need my babies."

The police officer came back. "They're okay, Mrs. Flaherty. The older boy woke up and took the little one out the front door. They're sitting in a cruiser. Let's leave them there for now. You don't want them to see this."

Everyone turned to a groan across the room. Mary Kate saw Mrs. Olsen raise up on one elbow, holding her head. She turned to Mary Kate. "You," she moaned.

Mary Kate dug her fingers into Conner's shirt. "Hit her again! Quick!"

Conner wrapped his arms around her. "Shh, baby, you're okay. She can't hurt you anymore." He held her, kissing her hair until the ambulance attendants arrived.

Chapter 27

The carnations in the vase beside the computer were lovely. Too bad they were from Chuck. He didn't even get out of the car when he dropped off the boys. Mary Kate looked at the flowers a moment longer, then went back to her writing.

Dimitri gasped, his face speckled with the spray of blood from the wound in his chest. "How could you, Ursula?" he cried. His skin sizzled and popped from the killing rays of the morning sun. As he writhed and screamed, Ursula covered her ears to his torment, waiting for her own agony to begin.

The man who had been her lover, her murderer, her persecutor, burst into flame. "Oh, Dimitri! If you had only loved me as much as I loved you!" Ursula wailed. "It is better that I die, than live to be deceived like this again!"

But the only heat she felt was that from the torch of his body. She peered at the sun, perplexed by the warm comfort it gave her. "What is this?" It was then she realized the truth of Dimitri's worst lie. She had not completely joined the dark army of vampires. He had led her to believe she was one of the undead to control her. If she had not fought back, it would have been true in time. Ursula wiped the tears from her eyes and strode off toward the town to rejoin the living.

"The end," Mary Kate said. She shrugged. *So, I'll fix it up in the revisions.* There wouldn't be as much time for that as usual. Donna Brooks had called that morning to tell her that

Freeman Publishing wanted to get this book out lickety-split. Theodora Zed novels had been selling like crazy after the news broadcasts of Mary Kate's hand-to-hand combat with the Vampire Killer. Even Walter Truesdale had forgiven her and left a message on her machine. He must smell money.

She saved the file with the final chapter to disk and turned off the computer. Her recuperation had been quicker than the doctors expected, but she still tired easily. She got up from the chair slowly, her taped ribs aching.

Conner had stayed with her most of the three days she had spent at the hospital. He had wanted to come home with her. The boys had been so hostile toward him during visiting hours, she felt it was better to just take a taxi home and try to get things back to normal. She couldn't cook or clean, or sit up to write for more than an hour at a time, but she had been able to send the kids safely off to school yesterday and today. She approached the spot at the top of the stairs, still black and crusty with her blood. "Ugh."

Downstairs, there were more reminders. Everywhere she looked, it seemed. The violence on the evening news each day never mentioned who cleaned up the mess. Her stomach turned over just thinking about it. She tottered into the kitchen. Flour and blood. David had made an attempt to mop it up and left a thin pink paste on the floor. "That's just plain nasty."

The turkey was gone. She figured the police had taken it as evidence. With mashed potatoes and gravy on the side. She knew her disposition had been sour since she'd been home, but she felt so bad. The constant pain grated on her nerves. Would the hurting ever stop?

She poured a cup of coffee and took a couple of Darvon with the first sip, hoping it would kick in while she watched 'The Price Is Right' from the sofa. As she started on the long trek to the living room, she heard a knock on the back door. She sighed and headed back across the room to answer it.

"What are you doing up?" Conner asked.

"Answering the damn door."

Conner laughed. "Not such a good idea taking care of yourself, is it?" He took her cup of coffee and held her arm as they walked into the living room. She knew how pathetic she looked scuffling along, her hair uncombed, wearing her nightie in the middle of the day. She winced and grit her teeth as she stretched out on the sofa, careful not to put her weight on the stitches in her back.

Conner put her cup on the table and covered her legs with an afghan. "Is there somebody you can call to come stay with you?"

"My mother-in-law, but I'm all out of frozen turkeys."

He shook his head as he sat in the armchair. "You've proven that you're tough, Mary Kate. The toughest of them all. Now, let me take care of you. No strings attached, I promise. As soon as you're able to get around, I'll be gone. Unless you want me to stay."

She sighed. *It would be nice to be taken care of.* And complicated. That comfortable place where she could relax and rely on someone else no longer existed. Sure, Conner looked like a good guy, but she had learned her lesson well. Appearances are deceptive. She hardly knew him. She thought she had known everything about Chuck, nobody could have known him better, but he torpedoed her whole life with no advance warning. Conner was still a mystery man. Very desirable, but still a mystery.

She tried to sit up and was rewarded with a fresh barrage of pain. She leaned on her elbow instead. "I'm fine. Getting better every day. The boys cook soup or call out for pizza for dinner, and I lay back on the sofa and live the life of Reilly.

Give me a few days, and I'll be dancing on tabletops again."

"Okay, Mary Kate, if that's the way you want it." His acquiescence lacked sincerity.

"Yeah, sure," she said. His wide-eyed innocence act needed work. She smiled. *I'll never get rid of this guy.* He smiled back, and she knew they were on the same wavelength. She wondered how persistent he really was. "School's going to be out in a couple of weeks," she said. "I'm taking the boys to visit my parents in Florida."

"For how long?"

"As long as it takes. I don't know. I've got a lot to think about. Chuck's not too keen on the idea of a divorce, and I want to talk him into selling this house. I never liked it."

"Where would you go?"

She shrugged. "Doesn't matter. Anywhere. I've never had a choice before. I'm looking forward to finding my own home."

Conner leaned toward her, interested. "What's your dream house, Mary Kate?"

She smiled, warming to the subject. "I want the house no one else wants. It's too big or too small. Or someone put a hideous addition on it. Or, even better, one with stories about it, a scandalous history. There are pirate houses on the eastern shore, you know. I could spend the rest of my life digging for hidden treasure."

Conner nodded as if he were filing the information away for future reference. "You'll find treasure, Mary Kate."

Her head swam for a second as the medication began to take the edge off the pain. A nap would be in order soon. She shuddered as the image of a hooded, blood-smeared face, mouthing the word, "You," flashed into her mind. Sleep had been peppered with such images the last few nights. "What's the latest on Mrs. Olsen? I stopped watching the news because they kept showing that really crappy picture of me from the back of *Death's Delight*. Besides, I couldn't stand hearing their warped, sensationalized version one more time."

"She had a fork in her pocket, Mary Kate," Conner said, "with the center tines removed, tying her directly to the murders of Valentine and Alissa."

She grimaced. There was something about the fork. She remembered. "This might sound silly, but I wondered about the killer breaking up a set of silverware. Even if you disposed of the weapon, you could always be implicated by the set with the missing fork. Mrs. Olsen must have thought of that, too. I didn't think anything of it at the time, but I saw her putting her silverware out for Goodwill a couple of weeks ago." *And I tried to help her pick it up when she dropped the box. Duh.* "I heard they took her to the state mental hospital in Sykesville. What's next?"

"She'll be held there until they've completed a competency evaluation. She'll be charged with the assaults on you and me here, then they'll look at the murders in Atlanta and New York, and her attacks on you and George in Cleveland, but it'll all come down to the same thing. She's insane. She's looking at a long stretch in a rubber room."

"Until she convinces some shrink she's cured," Mary Kate said. "Has she said anything?"

"Not publicly. At a news conference, the police said that she thought you knew all about her daughter's murder, and you were writing about it to provoke her."

"Then why kill Randall Valentine and Alissa?" Mary Kate thought a moment. *Is it real yet?* "To show me what it's like when it's real. Is that right? Is that what she said?"

Conner nodded. "It could have been any one of us who set her off, Mary Kate. You just happened to live across the street from her. We can't be responsible for every person who might read what we write. There's no way of knowing how a work of fiction is going to affect a sick mind."

Mary Kate was unsure and confused about her level of culpability. As a gut reaction, she felt as if she had contributed to Mrs. Olsen's rampage, but the censorship required to keep all of the arts from sparking controversy and emotion was just as scary. Mrs. Olsen had asked her, "What does it mean?" Maybe that was the keystone. What had her novels said about violence in relationships? Was it "just for fun"?

Conner moved over to the sofa and knelt beside her. "It's not your fault," he said, taking her hand.

"Do you really believe we're not responsible for what we write?"

"No, that's not what I said. You have to know why you write what you do. You write fantasy that no one in her right mind would interpret as fact. The deaths in your books bore no more resemblance to reality than . . . your sex scenes." He held back a smile.

"What? I thought they were pretty hot."

He laughed. "I thought somebody was going to sprain something." He leaned his face close to hers. "Reality, Mary Kate, is much less athletic," he whispered. "It's much slower and gentler." He kissed her lightly on the lips.

"Hmmm. I'll remember that," she said, slightly breathless.

"I'll remind you any time you like." He kissed her again, soft and warm.

Kissing him, Mary Kate eased back onto the pillow, relishing his hand in her hair. She touched his throat and felt as if she were floating. Turning her head, she covered a yawn with her hand. "Sorry. The pain pills make me sleepy."

Conner straightened the afghan over her and stood. "Get

your rest, Mary Kate."

It sounded like a good idea. As her eyes fluttered shut, she saw him pick up a magazine and open it as he sat in Chuck's chair.

"You feeling better, Mom?" David stood beside the sofa, Ben behind him.

"Yeah, I guess so." She sat up slowly, but not as painfully as earlier. The nap was just what she needed, though she hadn't intended on sleeping this long. She rubbed her eyes. "Are you guys up to pizza again tonight? We can get it with green pepper so you get a vegetable." They gave her their "Weird Mom" look. "What?"

"I want to eat the spaghetti," Ben said.

"The spaghetti," she said dumbly.

"In the kitchen," David said.

She followed them back into the kitchen and was immediately struck by how clean it was. Not only were the blood and flour gone, but the floor was cleaner than before. David opened the refrigerator and showed her the spaghetti in the microwavable pot, a loaf of Italian bread, and a plastic-wrapped bowl of salad. She smiled. *A man who's a good kisser, and cooks and cleans, too. I think I'm in love.*

"There's a note," Ben said, pointing to the table.

White business-size envelope, no address? She turned and saw a folded over scrap of yellow legal pad with "Mary Kate" scrawled across the front. She opened it and read:

Wishing you sweet dreams. See you tomorrow.

Love, Conner.
P.S. Cook the spaghetti in the microwave on high for five minutes, stirring after three.

About the Author

Barbara J. Ferrenz is a writer of suspense, mystery, and horror, living in an old farmhouse in Maryland near the Chesapeake Bay. She and her husband of thirty years have two children and one grandchild. She is also a school psychologist, specializing in children with emotional and behavioral problems. Her short stories have appeared in magazines and anthologies for over a decade. She is currently writing more stories and working on another novel. Barbara enjoys attending horror conventions several times a year. To learn more about her and what she is up to, visit her web site at www.BarbaraJFerrenz.com.

The employees of Five Star hope you have enjoyed this book. All our books are made to last. Other Five Star books are available at your library, through selected bookstores, or directly from us.

For more information about titles, please call:

(800) 223-1244

or visit our Web site at:

www.gale.com/fivestar

To share your comments, please write:

Publisher
Five Star
295 Kennedy Memorial Drive
Waterville, ME 04901